A Garden of Marvels

A Garden of Marvels

TALES OF WONDER FROM EARLY MEDIEVAL CHINA

Robert Ford Campany

UNIVERSITY OF HAWAI'I PRESS
HONOLULU

© 2015 University of Hawai'i Press
All rights reserved
Printed in the United States of America

20 19 18 17 16 15   6 5 4 3 2 1

Library of Congress Cataloging-in-Publication Data

Campany, Robert Ford.
    A garden of marvels : tales of wonder from early medieval China / Robert Ford Campany.
        pages   cm
    Includes bibliographical references and index.
    ISBN 978-0-8248-5349-5 (cloth : alk. paper)—ISBN 978-0-8248-5350-1 (pbk. : alk. paper)
        1. Fantasy fiction, Chinese—Translations into English.   2. Chinese fiction—220–589—
    Translations into English.   3. Short stories, Chinese—Translations into English.   I. Title.
    PL2629.F35C358   2015
    895.13'0876609024—dc23   2014050180

University of Hawai'i Press books are printed on acid-free paper and meet the guidelines for permanence and durability of the Council on Library Resources.

Designed by Milenda Nan Ok Lee

For my mother, Linda

CONTENTS

CHRONOLOGICAL TABLE

Shang	ca. 1600–1027 BCE
Western Zhou	1027–771 BCE
Eastern Zhou	770–256 BCE
Spring and Autumn period	722–403 BCE
Warring States period	403–221 BCE
Qin	221–206 BCE
Western (Former) Han	206 BCE–8 CE
Xin	9–23 CE
Eastern (Later) Han	27–220
Three Kingdoms (Wei, Sui, Wu)	220–280
Western Jin	265–317
Sack of Luoyang; Jin court flees east to Chang'an and south	311
Sack of Chang'an	316
Eastern Jin	317–420
Northern and Southern dynasties	317–589
Wang Dun leads rebellion against Jin	322
Fu Jian completes reunification of north	381
Northern Wei capital established at Pingcheng	398
Liu Yu founds [Liu] Song dynasty in south	420
Northern Wei suppresses Buddhism	446
Qi dynasty supplants Song in south	479
Liang dynasty supplants Qi in south	502
Sui	581–618
Tang	618–907
Five Dynasties	907–960

Northern Song	960–1126
Southern Song	1126–1279
Yuan	1279–1368
Ming	1368–1644
Qing	1644–1912

CONVENTIONS

By "early medieval" I mean roughly the period from a few decades before the fall of the Eastern Han dynasty in 220 CE to the establishment of the Tang dynasty in 618 CE.

In designations of dates, CE stands for Common Era (the same time period as that designated by AD), and BCE stands for before the Common Era (the same as BC). All dates are CE unless otherwise specified.

In giving equivalents of official titles, I generally follow Hucker, *A Dictionary of Official Titles in Imperial China*, although his renditions are not translations of the meanings of the titles but are instead descriptions of the functions of offices.

"Monk" always means Buddhist monk and translates *shamen* 沙門, *seng* 僧, or *daoren* 道人. "Temple" consistently translates *miao* 廟, and "shrine," *ci* 祠, except where noted. "Haunt" (as a verb) usually translates *sui* 祟, and "possess" (as a verb describing something a spirit does to a person or other living creature) translates *ping* 憑.

Rendering weights and measures in smooth translation is always a challenge, particularly since the values of some of these units changed in China from one period to the next and since many instances of such terms in the stories translated here were not intended as exact measurements anyhow. I have left the term *li* 里, the basic measure of geographic distance, untranslated; one *li* was roughly equal to a third of a mile or half a kilometer (I find "third-mile" jarring as a translation) and was reckoned to comprise 360 *bu* 步 or paces. In regard to units of capacity, one *sheng* 升 or pint in most parts of China during the period in question equaled 200 ml; ten *sheng* equaled one *dou* 斗 or peck, and ten pecks equaled one *shi* 石 or bushel. (I also render *hu* 斛 as bushel.) As for units of length, one *chi* 尺 or foot was equivalent to between 23 and 25 cm, depending on the period and region (although in the north during the late period of division one *chi* was equivalent to 30 cm); one *chi* contained ten *cun* 寸 or inches, and one inch contained ten *fen* 分. Ten feet made a *zhang* 丈 or pole. I have chosen to translate these units rather than converting them to either English or metric quantities. Readers should therefore bear in mind that a figure said to be "a pole tall" was about 7.5 English feet in height, an object described as "eight feet long" was around 6 English feet in length, and so on. In all these cases I have based the English translations and equivalents on the discussion in Wilkinson, *Chinese History: A New Manual,* 552–556.

Occasionally stories mention a character's age. "From the Warring States to the twentieth century an individual was reckoned to have already entered his or her first year at birth and, following the same logic, to enter the second year at the start of the next (lunisolar) calendar year . . . , not at the birthday";* in other words, in traditional China, as in much of the premodern world, age was reckoned inclusively, not consecutively, as we now do. As a rule of thumb, then, in the early medieval period a person's age as given in *sui* 歲 was, in advance of his or her birthday, two years greater than what we would now consider that person's actual age at the time; after his or her birthday it was one year greater. This creates a dilemma for the translator, because in almost no early medieval tale is a character's birthday mentioned (and for good reason, since birthdays began to be celebrated only at the very end of the period†). In translating, I have generally subtracted one year from the age as given in *sui,* particularly when the characters involved are children, as they usually are. The reader should be aware that such indications of age are approximate.

Reference is occasionally made in the texts to someone's "byname" (*zi* 字). People in early medieval China, especially those of the official classes, had more than one name, each used in different social and textual contexts. The byname (often rendered "courtesy name") was chosen for them at their capping ceremony, the time when they reached majority and joined adult society. See the thorough discussion in Wilkinson, *Chinese History: A New Manual,* 136–138.

Each item is assigned a unique number for ease of reference. In each case the sources used for my translation are listed so that readers wishing to con-

*Wilkinson, *Chinese History,* 160–161.
†Ibid., 165.

sult the Chinese texts may do so. Generally the first source listed is the main basis of my translation except where indicated. In a few cases Lu Xun cites additional sources that I have not consulted. Usually they provide only partial quotations of the item in question. I do not list them all.

In giving information on texts, I sometimes supply an alternate title, based on how the work was referred to in medieval bibliographies and anthologies. The titles and contents of texts were more fluid in medieval times than we are now accustomed to.

In addition to a bibliography of sources cited, I append a list of further suggested readings. I intend this not as a comprehensive listing of relevant works but merely as a starting point for readers new to this literature.

Contrary to standard Sinological custom, the translations have not been annotated to the nth degree. In most footnotes I content myself with briefly explaining potentially mystifying things mentioned in the texts. In some but not all cases I provide information on historical figures. I do not give modern equivalents for most place names. In the endnotes I sometimes indicate variant readings in the source texts, but not exhaustively; the endnotes are intended primarily for specialists. I omit most Chinese characters, especially persons' names, except when terms of special interest or authors' names and titles of texts are mentioned or where seeing the characters is important for understanding puns or wordplay. In citing other relevant works I have emphasized ones in Western languages, primarily English. I made all these decisions bearing in mind the primary audience I have in mind here.

ACKNOWLEDGMENTS

I would like to thank Carrie Wiebe and an anonymous reviewer for their many helpful comments and suggestions, the National Endowment for the Humanities for enabling some of the research that went into this book, and Pat Crosby of the University of Hawai'i Press for her encouragement.

ABBREVIATIONS

BTSC   *Beitang shuchao* 北堂書鈔. Comp. Yu Shinan 虞世南. Facsimile reprint in 2 vols. of 1888 ed. Taipei: Wenhai chubanshe, 1962.

CCT   Kao, Karl S. Y., ed. *Classical Chinese Tales of the Supernatural and the Fantastic: Selections from the Third to the Tenth Century.* Bloomington: Indiana University Press, 1985.

CL   Knechtges, David R., and Taiping Chang, eds. *Ancient and Early Medieval Chinese Literature: A Reference Guide.* 4 vols. continuously paginated. Leiden: Brill, 2010–2014.

CXJ   *Chuxue ji* 初學記 by Xu Jian 徐堅 et al. 3 vols., continuously paginated. Beijing: Zhonghua shuju, 1962.

FYZL   *Fayuan zhulin* 法苑珠林 by Daoshi 道世. *T* 2122.

HWCS   *Han Wei congshu* 漢魏叢書. Comp. Cheng Rong 程榮. Printed in 1592. Place of publication and print house unknown; copy held at Joseph Regenstein Library (East Asia Collection), University of Chicago.

LX   Lu Xun 魯迅. *Gu xiaoshuo gouchen* 古小說鉤沈. Beijing: Renmin wenxue chubanshe, 1954.

LZG   Li Jianguo 李劍國. *Tang qian zhiguai xiaoshuo shi* 唐前志怪小說史. Tianjin: Nankai Daxue chubanshe, 1984.

SSHY   Mather, Richard B. *Shih-shuo Hsin-yü: A New Account of Tales of the World.* Minneapolis: University of Minnesota Press, 1976.

SW   Campany, Robert Ford. *Strange Writing: Anomaly Accounts in Early Medieval China.* Albany: State University of New York Press, 1996.

T   *Taishō shinshū daizōkyō* 大正新脩大藏經. Ed. Takakusu Junjirō 高楠順次郎, Watanabe Kaigyōku 渡辺海旭, and Ono Gemmyō 小野玄妙. 100 vols. Tokyo: Taishō Issaikyō Kankōkai, 1924–1935;

reprint, Taipei: Xinwen feng, 1983. In citing texts from this canon, I give the number assigned to them in it.

TPGJ *Taiping guangji* 太平廣記. Comp. Li Fang 李昉 et al. 4 vols. Shanghai: Shanghai guji chubanshe, 1990. Cited by scroll and serial position of the cited item in the scroll (e.g., "387.1" indicates the first passage anthologized in scroll 387).

TPYL *Taiping yulan* 太平御覽. Comp. Li Fang 李昉 et al. Facsimile reprint of Shangwu yinshuguan 1935 printing from a Song copy. 4 vols. Beijing: Zhonghua shuju, 1992.

WXS Wang Guoliang 王國良. *Wei Jin nanbeichao zhiguai xiaoshuo yanjiu* 魏晉南北朝志怪小說研究. Taipei: Wenshizhe chubanshe, 1984.

XJS Li Jianguo 李劍國. *Xinji Soushen ji, xinji Soushen houji* 新輯搜神記, 新輯搜神後記. 2 vols., continuously paginated. Beijing: Zhonghua shuju, 2007.

XJTY *Xuejin taoyuan* 學津討原. Comp. Zhang Pengyi 張鵬一. Facsimile reprint in *Baibu congshu jicheng* 百部叢書集成, ed. Yan Yiping 嚴一萍. Taipei: Yiwen yinshuguan, 1966.

YWLJ *Yiwen leiju* 藝文類聚. Comp. Ouyang Xun 歐陽詢 et al. Modern ed. by Wang Shaoying 王紹楹. 2 vols., continuously paginated. Beijing: Zhonghua shuju, 1965.

INTRODUCTION

We still do not have nearly enough translations of texts from ancient and medieval China—one of the great world civilizations—that might be recommended to students or friends. This book is a modest contribution toward filling that gap. It is intended primarily for undergraduate students and other curious nonspecialist readers. Everything about it is designed accordingly. It is short, so as to be affordable and usable in college classes. I have not added commentary on the translated material but have left readers to form their own interpretations. The few annotations are meant to explain details that might otherwise mystify and to point toward basic sources of further information. In this introduction I want to explain what the texts are, when and why they were written, and why they are worth reading today.

Starting by the third century BCE, and apparently in much greater numbers from the second century CE on, Chinese literati compiled reports of things deemed in some way anomalous. Some of these works took the form of catalogs of strange spirits, customs, flora, and fauna of outlying zones, organized geographically or topically. Some focused on oddities peculiar to one or another region of China, especially the exotic southern areas, which had assumed new importance with the third-century-CE collapse of the Han dynasty and the early fourth-century fall of the northern capitals to non-Chinese invaders.* Some were biographical, featuring anecdotes about individuals of unusual spiritual or moral attainments. But most were

---

*For works on the tumultuous history of the early medieval period, see Further Readings. On the interest (positive or negative) in distinctive regional customs and products in the period, see Chittick, "Pride of Place"; Chittick, "The Development of Local Writing"; Farmer, *The Talent of Shu*, 121–143; and Lewis, *The Construction of Space*, 189–244.

collections of stories of ordinary people's encounters with spirits, temporary sojourns in the land of the dead, eerily significant dreams, uncannily accurate premonitions, or other extraordinary experiences.

Although categories of literary genres remained fluid throughout early medieval times,* two terms had already begun to be associated with anecdotes of marvels. One was *xiaoshuo* 小說, which only a century ago came to mean "fiction" and to designate the novel as represented in such early modern masterpieces as *Dream of the Red Chamber, Journey to the West,* and *The Plum in the Golden Vase.* But in the Han and early medieval periods (i.e., from the last two centuries BCE until around 600 CE), *xiaoshuo* connoted not fiction—and certainly not the novel, a literary long form not yet invented—but local sayings, popularly derived anecdotes, or street talk.† The other quasi-generic term was *zhiguai* 志怪, "accounts of anomalies." *Zhiguai* figures in the titles of two of the works sampled in this book, and *Xiao shuo* is the title of one of them. Both terms had earlier been used in passages of the *Zhuangzi* 莊子 (ca. 320 BCE) associating them with reports of unusual phenomena.‡

Perhaps 80 percent or more of the contents of these works written before the Tang dynasty (618–907)—the temporal limit of this book—have been lost, but several thousand discrete anecdotes and other textual items survive, distributed over more than sixty titles.§ ("Item" is an important technical term used throughout this book. It designates a discrete unit of text, whether narrative or descriptive in form. All the works dealt with here are collections of such units, each ranging in length from a single line to several pages.) These numbers testify to the once-gargantuan quantity of

---

*On book collecting and schemes of bibliographic and genre classification in the period, see Knechtes, "Culling the Weeds and Selecting Prime Blossoms"; Tian, "Book Collecting and Cataloging in the Age of Manuscript Culture"; Swartz, "Classifying the Literary Tradition"; and Drège, *Les bibliothèques en Chine.*

†See Zhao, "*Xiaoshuo* as a Cataloging Term in Traditional Chinese Bibliography"; Wu, "From *Xiaoshuo* to Fiction"; DeWoskin, "The Six Dynasties *Chih-kuai* and the Birth of Fiction"; Nienhauser, *The Indiana Companion to Traditional Chinese Literature,* 423–426; and *SW,* 129–133. The "small" or "lesser" (*xiao* 小) in the phrase may have originally indicated not (or not only) the content of such works but instead (or also) their verbal and even physical format; see *SW,* 34, 131. For a good example of the arbitrariness with which particular works were slotted into this and similar generic categories by successive generations of Chinese bibliographers, see Reed, "Motivation and Meaning of a 'Hodge-Podge.'"

‡For further discussion, see *SW,* 129–133, 151–152.

§For an overview, see *SW,* 32–100.

writings about things deemed strange and the fascination their contents held for many.

Yet this fascination contrasts with the disdain expressed for such writings compared with texts treating canonical subjects or written in higher, more elegant literary forms. Repeatedly, in the few prefaces and other metatexts* that survive, we find compilers of anomalies taking a defensive stance, granting that their subject matter is of low status but still justifying their labor.† It seems, then, that these texts were a guilty pleasure for many. This ambivalence is deliciously captured in an anecdote, itself from a compilation of anomalies, about an important official and man of learning named Zhang Hua 張華 (232–300), his enormous compendium of oddities, and an emperor's reaction to it:

[Zhang Hua] liked to read books dealing with secret and marvelous matters and with charts and prognostications. He selected various remnant writings from all over the empire, examined records dealing with strange and divine things dating from the beginning of writing, and collected matters told of in the lanes and hamlets in recent times, and thus created *A Treatise on Curiosities* [*Bowu zhi* 博物志] totalling four hundred scrolls. He presented the work to Emperor Wu [of the Jin period; r. 265–289]. The ruler summoned him to question him, and said: "Sir, ... your broad-ranging learning is without equal.... But your recording of affairs and your choice of words are unsubstantial and exagerrated in many places.... In olden times, when Confucius edited the *Classic of Odes* and the *Classic of Documents*, he did not include obscure matters of ghosts and gods. He did not deign to speak of 'prodigies, feats of abnormal strength, disorders, or spirits.'‡ But in your case, when people read your *Treatise on Curiosities*, they will be startled by what they have never heard before and will marvel at what they have never seen. It will only frighten and confuse later generations, disturbing the eye and ear. You should there-

*By "metatexts" I mean texts about other texts. In early medieval China these included prefaces, bibliographic treatises incorporated into official histories, writings of a literary-critical nature, and anecdotes about the making or reception of texts.
†For more, see *SW*, 101–159; and Campany, "Two Religious Thinkers of the Early Eastern Jin," 200–202.
‡The ruler here alludes to a well-known passage in the *Analects* (7.21) attributing to Confucius a marked reticence to discuss these topics.

fore remove some of the more unsubstantiated, doubtful material and apportion the rest into only ten scrolls."*

Zhang Hua (who appears as a character in several stories translated in this book) was sent away with a gift of fine writing materials. The story ends by mentioning that the emperor henceforth "always kept the ten-scroll *Treatise on Curiosities* in his personal book chest and perused it on his days of leisure." Despite having chided the compiler about its weird and disturbing contents, the ruler simply could not put the book down.

One important reason these texts were made and circulated, then, was that people found them interesting, just as readers and listeners everywhere seem drawn to tales of the extraordinary. Such tales in oral form are surely as old as our species; meanwhile, entire theories of narrative and of religion have been built around the perceived power of the uncanny.† But to find this fascination with the uncanny in early medieval China might surprise some readers thanks to a persistent view of Chinese culture as inherently rationalistic, nonreligious, or this-worldly, focused on mundane practicalities and deaf to the call of the divine, the ghostly, or the mysterious.‡ After all, as we have just seen, Confucius was famously on record in the *Analects* (7.21) as having declined to speak of anomalies or prodigies (*guai* 怪) or of matters concerning spirits (*shen* 神).§ We too easily imagine that such pronouncements worked magically as prescriptions for a whole society for two and a half millennia, forgetting that the very presence of this

---

Shiyi ji 拾遺記 by Wang Jia 王嘉, 9.7a. On this late fourth-century text, see *SW*, 64–67, 306–318, and Foster, "The *Shih-i chi*." For more on Zhang Hua and his compendium of wonders, see Greatrex, *The Bowu zhi*, 8–26; *CL*, 50–52; *LZG*, 260–268; and *SW*, 49–52, 283–286.

†On the role of the uncanny and the fantastic in narrative, see Todorov, *The Fantastic*. The uncanny has played a key role in theories of religion for more than a century, the best-known example being Otto, *The Idea of the Holy*. A review of theories of this sort up to the mid-twentieth century may be found in Campany, "Chinese Accounts of the Strange," 6–76. For a recent theory of religion with the uncanny or "special" as its linchpin, see Taves, *Religious Experience Reconsidered*. On the power and uses of anomaly generally in cultures, see Douglas, *Purity and Danger*; and *SW*, 2–17.

‡For a trenchant diagnosis of the reasons for this, see Lagerwey, *China: A Religious State*, 1–17. For a representative statement of the stereotype, see Bodde, "Dominant Ideas," 293–294.

§The passage was so well known and so often linked in readers' minds to the contents of accounts of anomalies that the eighteenth-century compiler Yuan Mei titled his compilation of such accounts *Zibuyu* 子不語 or *What the Master Did Not Discuss*. For a study and translation of this text, see Santangelo and Yan, *Zibuyu*.

line in the *Analects* was surely due to the master's unusualness in remaining silent on such matters when almost everyone else was chatting about them incessantly. To see China—even contemporary China in the wake of one of the most far-reaching experiments ever conducted in purging a society of religion—as somehow essentially nonreligious is, quite simply, to ignore a mountain of evidence to the contrary. That evidence includes texts such as those translated here.*

Early medieval authors voiced reasons for compiling strange anecdotes other than the intrinsic pleasures they held. As legitimating precedents they cited old traditions that saw cataloging the wonders of outlying lands and reporting folklore as essential to governance. The ruler, in theory residing serenely in the capital city—the symbolic and ritual center of the cosmos—was thus apprised of conditions on the periphery. Institutional and mythical precedents cited by *zhiguai* compilers included the culture hero Yu's ancient ordering of the waters and lands of the realm, an activity that included a recording of strange creatures in outlying zones;† the legend of the nine tripods, royal palladia in which images of various sorts of strange creatures were cast; the tour of inspection, in which rulers would survey their domains and be presented with goods and cultural performances distinctive to locales; the travels of King Mu of Zhou, including the record of wonders he saw in distant realms; the system of tribute, in which emissaries presented exotic local products to the throne; the collection of reports of anomalies thought to portend the fate of the dynasty; and the gathering of popular songs and customs by the ancient Music Bureau.‡ Some of these justifications seem to protest too much, masking a fascination with the strange under a veneer of high moral and social purpose. But they also suggest that some *zhiguai* compilers seriously saw themselves as contributing to the ordering of the world by reporting the deviant so that it might be

*For two very different but equally impassioned arguments on the basically religious nature of Chinese society and of the Chinese state since its inception, see Yu, *State and Religion in China;* and Lagerwey, *China: A Religious State.*

†See Lewis, *The Flood Myths of Early China;* and Birrell, *Chinese Myth and Culture,* 47–78.

‡For more on these traditions and *zhiguai* authors' allusions to them, see *SW,* 101–159. Because anything unusual was potentially a portent with grave significance for the ruling dynasty's fortune, reports of strange phenomena possessed a gravity hard for us to overestimate. On the politics of omen interpretation in the period, see Lippiello, *Auspicious Omens and Miracles in Ancient China;* Lu Zongli, *Power of the Words;* Goodman, *Ts'ao P'i Transcendent;* and Campany, "Two Religious Thinkers of the Early Eastern Jin," 189–192.

rectified* or, in some instances, by showing that the realm of spirits, for all its apparent unruliness, was actually structured by an implicit order made visible through massed case reports.[†]

Some modern historians of Chinese literature, searching for the origins of self-consciously fictional writing, have pegged early medieval accounts of anomalies as a likely suspect.[‡] But this is massively anachronistic. It is one thing to focus on texts' narratological dimensions, that is, on how they work as stories; as Natalie Zemon Davis has shown, even archival records of first-person juridical testimony have such storytelling features, and they repay close study.[§] It is another thing to project a modern notion of fiction onto the ancient past without pausing to consider whether earlier authors and readers shared the accompanying assumptions about—for starters—the nature of the writing in question, the purposes of reading it, and the ontology of beings populating it. Early medieval *zhiguai* compilers saw their enterprise as a branch of history, albeit of a relatively undistinguished sort. Both these works' narrative forms and the generic suffixes incorporated into their titles (*ji* 記, "records"; *zhuan* 傳, "traditions";[‖] *zhi* 志, "accounts") were drawn from classical historical writings. The language of the texts (unmetered prose) is likewise comparable to that of histories, though a bit less formal: it is neither hyperliterary nor religiously technical or priestly, nor is it colloquial. The verbs used in metatexts to name *zhiguai* authors' activity

*This agenda of rectifying the anomalous was particularly strong in the writings of Confucian classicists such as Ying Shao 應劭 (140–206 CE), three chapters of whose *Fengsu tongyi* 風俗通義 or *Comprehensive Discussion of Customs* are devoted to recording and correcting what Ying saw as deviant regional customs and aberrant narratives. He helped create a classicist hermeneutics of the strange. See Lewis, *The Construction of Space*, 189–244; Campany, "'Survival' as an Interpretive Strategy"; *SW*, 335–340; Sterckx, *The Animal and the Daemon in Early China*, 222–225; and Nylan, "Ying Shao's *Feng su t'ung yi*."

†For an argument that one such text was designed to perform the latter task, see Campany, "Two Religious Thinkers of the Early Eastern Jin." See also Liu Yuanru, "Xingjian yu mingbao."

‡The most important early proponent of this view was Lu Xun 魯迅, whose history of "fiction"—to designate which he redefined the ancient term *xiaoshuo*—based on his lectures on literature at Beijing University in the 1920s has been hugely influential. See Lu Xun, *A Brief History of Chinese Fiction*, which isolates "fiction" as an obvious, discrete thing whose history can be unproblematically narrated from its rude beginnings in ancient times to its more sophisticated recent flourishing. See also Dudbridge, *Books, Tales and Vernacular Culture*, 11; and *SW*, 156–159.

§See Davis, *Fiction in the Archives*; and Campany, *Making Transcendents*, 17–18.

‖This term, when it functions as a noun, is often translated as "biographies," but the verbal and root meaning of the word has nothing specifically to do with biographies. As a verb, the word means "to transmit," and I believe that when Chinese authors wrote of *zhuan*, they envisioned collections of transmitted material on a figure, a type of figure, or a topic. Hence, contrary to much common practice, I translate it as "traditions"—that is, "things transmitted."

connote "collect" or "stitch together," not "fabricate."* Their compilers were not aiming at what we think of as fiction writing, and they did not consider themselves free to invent stories from whole cloth. They saw themselves as inheritors of a tradition in which to submit reports of oddities was to assist in governance. Their collecting and writing were attempts to understand the subtle workings of the actual unseen world, not to invent a new fictional world from their own imagination. And their notions of what was possible or likely in the world did not overlap completely with our own, so the scope of their historical case gathering ran wider than ours does.† It is tempting to compare these reports of oddities with accounts of UFO sightings, miraculous appearances of the Virgin, and near-death experiences in modern Western societies, but to do so is to risk understating their true function and their seriousness in early medieval China. And the Chinese reports were in many cases collected by some of the most learned men of the era, not by socially marginal figures, and were later incorporated into imperially commissioned digests representing the sum of knowledge at the time.

Three things clearly follow, each with implications for how we should read these texts if we want to understand them as products of their time. First, the events depicted in them were presented as having really occurred, and contemporary readers would have read them that way, although, of course, any particular reader might discredit the veracity of this or that account. Second, the total set of things that might happen or that existed in the world was clearly larger than is suggested by the stereotype of China as an inherently secular, this-worldly culture. Indeed, it seems that the whole point of the genre was to remind readers of the existence of this booming, buzzing world of spirits and oddities—things largely ignored in more canonical genres—and to explore its workings. Third, the making of these accounts was clearly the work of many more people than the few whose names are now attached to the titles of compilations. This means that in regard to what is recorded in these texts as having been the case,

---

*For examples, see the anecdote cited earlier concerning Zhang Hua's compilation of *Bowu zhi* and also Campany, *Signs from the Unseen Realm*, 19, 65; and *SW*, 131, 133, 145, 147–149, 155.

†For further discussion of this point, see *SW*, 156–159; Campany, *To Live as Long as Heaven and Earth*, 102–108; Dudbridge, *Religious Experience and Lay Society in T'ang China*, 16–17; and Dudbridge, "Tang Sources for the Study of Religious Culture," 148. This point has been made repeatedly (already, for example, in Bodde, "Some Chinese Tales of the Supernatural," 341), but many scholars have failed to grasp it.

we are dealing with a sort of crystallization of collective or social memory—
though a selective one, to be sure.* The texts record the sorts of things
that many people at the time believed possible.

Compilers' Sources, Motives, and Aims

Early medieval accounts of anomalies were compilations of previously circulating material—another reason that the term "'fiction,' with its conno-
tation of originality and authorial inventiveness,"[†] is misleading. The
source material included historical records of various sorts, both official and
private; personal and family memoirs; oral transmission; exchanges of
letters; local temple inscriptions and tomb epitaphs; and, in a small number of documented cases, narratives embedded in Daoist or Buddhist scriptures.[‡] Not a few anecdotes mention details of how they were transmitted—
previous texts, specific informants, or the folklore of a particular locale.[§]
Such passages suggest the sorts of social networks along which stories came
to the attention of our compilers. Compilers and others routinely character-
ized the making of anomaly accounts as a process of gathering, arranging,
and transmitting already-existing accounts from two basic types of sources:
past writings and "things heard and seen," that is, second- or thirdhand
hearsay regarding more recent events or the compiler's own experience.[‖]

---

*For elaboration of this point, see Campany, *Making Transcendents*, 15–22.

[†]Allen, "Tales Retold," 109.

[‡]On the sources of *zhiguai* and biographical works, see *SW*, 179–199; Campany, *To Live as Long as Heaven and Earth*, 102–108; Campany, *Signs from the Unseen Realm*, 19–28; Shinohara, "Two Sources of Chinese Buddhist Biographies"; Bokenkamp, "The Peach Flower Font and the Grotto Passage"; Reed, "Parallel Worlds, Stretched Time, and Illusory Reality"; Reed, "The Lecherous Holy Man and the Maiden in the Box"; Allen, "Tales Retold," 108; Woolley, "The Many Boats to Yangzhou"; and Wang Qing, *Xiyu wenhua yingxiang xia de zhonggu xiaoshuo*.

[§]On this point, see Campany, *Signs from the Unseen Realm*, 19–25; *SW*, 186–187; and Dudbridge, "Tang Sources for the Study of Religious Culture," 148–153. Dudbridge, *A Portrait of Five Dynasties China from the Memoirs of Wang Renyu*, 200–253, lists instances in which an informant is named in Wang Renyu's tales. As Allen ("Tales Retold," 136–137) notes, some scholars have "argued that the storytelling contexts described in some stories are themselves fictional constructs designed to 'bolster the veracity' of stories that were, in actuality, invented by their writers. But the most straightforward explanation for the existence of multiple versions of the same story is to take at face value the writers' claims to have heard the stories first in oral form. What we are unable to do is determine when the variations in the preserved versions were introduced, that is, to what extent each writer recorded a story as he had heard it and to what extent he made changes."

[‖]For examples, see Campany, "Two Religious Thinkers of the Early Eastern Jin," 201–202; Campany, *Signs from the Unseen Realm*, 66–67; and *SW*, 129–145.

Not coincidentally, at least fifteen men known to have compiled wonder tales in early medieval times served as official historians, librarians, or archivists—positions that provided access to a wide range of writings from which they might, and clearly did, cull material.*

So if these texts represent compilations from already-circulating materials by many hands, on what basis did our authors select them? Other than entertaining themselves and their readers, why did our authors go to the trouble of compiling them? There are two ways to answer this question. One points to surviving indications of personal motives—autobiographical or biographical comments about experiences that spurred authors to compile anecdotes of the kinds they did. The other either combs prefaces for explicit statements of authors' goals in writing or, more commonly (since only a few prefaces survive), works backward from the implied "points" or messages of any given text to reconstruct what the author's persuasive goals must have been for compiling it—what he must have been trying to convince readers of, given the material he chose to include. For convenience I will refer to the first as (personal) motive and the second as (rhetorical) aim.

About most authors we lack information that might allow us to reconstruct what motivated them. Indeed, the authorship of some texts is simply unknown. But there are exceptions. Regarding Gan Bao 干寶 (d. 336), chief historian at the early Eastern Jin court and compiler of (among other works) *Records of an Inquest into the Spirit Realm (Soushen ji* 搜神記), one of the largest and best-known early medieval collections of anomalies, we read in his official biography:

Bao's father had previously had a favorite female servant, of whom Bao's mother was extremely jealous. When the father came to die, the mother pushed the maidservant alive into the grave. Bao and his siblings were still young at the time and did not know of this. More than ten years later their mother died. When the grave was opened, the female servant was found lying over the coffin as though still alive. So she was taken back, and after several days she revived. She said that their father always brought her food and drink, and had shown affection for her just as when he was alive, and had told her of auspicious and unfortunate events in

*See *SW,* 177–179.

the household that when checked all proved accurate; and she said she had not found it unpleasant to be underground. They arranged for her marriage, and she bore sons.*

In addition, Bao's older brother once stopped breathing because of illness. For several days he did not grow cold. Then he regained consciousness and spoke of seeing the affairs of the ghosts and spirits of heaven and earth. He said it felt as though he were in a dream and did not know he was dead.

Because of these events, Bao compiled and collected [cases of] gods and spirits, numinous anomalies of humans and other creatures, and extraordinary transformations from past and present times, calling [the work] *Records of an Inquest into the Spirit Realm,* thirty rolls in all.†

Significantly, these events involving members of Gan Bao's family exemplify two story types common in early medieval *zhiguai:* survival in the tomb and the return from death.

Another author who left a record of his motives is Wang Yan 王琰, compiler of *Records of Signs from the Unseen Realm* (*Mingxiang ji* 冥祥記, ca. 490), a collection of anecdotes about the power of Buddhist devotion. In his preface to this work he narrates his lifelong relationship with a votive image of the bodhisattva Guanshiyin 觀世音 or Sound Observer,‡ an intimate relationship marked by a series of paranormal phenomena: the image mysteriously emitting light, urgently appearing to Wang in a dream to warn of impending danger, and later, after he had consigned it to a temple for safekeeping and lost track of its whereabouts, appearing in another dream to reveal its location so he could retrieve it. "Turning over in my mind these incidents involving the image, I was deeply moved, and so I tracked down more such signs and visions and stitched them together to make this rec-

---

*A version of this story appears in another compilation of anomalies; see item 9.

†*Jin shu* 82.2150. Two other incidents are recounted in *Soushen ji* concerning Gan's relatives' encounters with *gu* 蠱 or black magic (items 12.17 and 12.18), suggesting further personal motives for his interest in matters unusual.

‡Devotion to this bodhisattva was hugely popular in China from the third century on, probably thanks in large part to the chapter of the equally popular *Lotus Sutra* devoted to him. For more, see Campany, *Signs from the Unseen Realm,* 49–51; Campany, "The Real Presence"; and Campany, "The Earliest Tales of the Bodhisattva Guanshiyin."

ord," Wang writes.* Once more these unusual personal experiences of a compiler of tales are of a type with some of the tales he ended up including in his text. These passages by Gan Bao and Wang Yan strongly suggest that, having experienced strange phenomena of these sorts, they both went in search of similar cases involving other people, found and recorded them (and stories of similar phenomena), and circulated the resulting collection.

As for these texts' rhetorical aims, in only a few instances do compilers discuss them explicitly. Several prefaces to Buddhist tale collections unsurprisingly mention the goal of inciting more fervent devotion.† Gan Bao's statement regarding his *Soushen ji* requires a bit more parsing:

> As for what I have here collected, when it sets forth what has been received from earlier accounts, any fault that might be found is not my own; if there are vacuous or erroneous places in what has been garnered from inquiries into more recent events, then I would wish to share the ridicule and criticism with former worthies and scholars. Even so, when it comes to what is set down here, it should still suffice to make clear that the way of spirits is not a fabrication. The words of the hundred schools are too many to be read in their entirety, and what one receives through one's own ears and eyes is too much to be set down completely. But what I have roughly chosen here will at least satisfy my aim of developing an "eighth category" even if I make only an obscure explanation of it. I will be fortunate if future curious gentlemen take note of its basic substance and if there is that in it which sets their minds wandering and captures their attention, and if I am not reproached for this.‡

Gan's tone is defensive—typically so for such documents.§ The gist of the first sentence is that Gan cannot be reproached if his sources are inaccurate; he is, after all, not inventing his stories but culling them from past accounts, just as he is also following the example of texts such as *Suoyu* 瑣語,

*See the translation and discussion of this document in Campany, *Signs from the Unseen Realm*, 63–68.

†For examples, see Campany, "The Real Presence," 266–268; and Campany, *Signs from the Unseen Realm*, 27–28, 65–67, 82.

‡*Jin shu* 82.2150–2151.

§The rest of this paragraph paraphrases a passage in Campany, "Two Religious Thinkers of the Early Eastern Jin," 201–202.

one of the earliest anomaly compilations known to us, which had been re-covered from an early fourth-century-BCE tomb in 281 CE—an event that no doubt stimulated interest in *zhiguai* collections during the Jin period.*

By the phrase "to make clear that the way of spirits is not a fabrication," I believe that Gan means that he has compiled evidence that, despite con-trary appearances, the world's many spirits follow a *dao*—that their activi-ties are not capricious but instead display a discernable pattern. As for "de-veloping an 'eighth category' even if I make only an obscure explanation of it," a phrase likely more obscure to us than to his contemporaries, Gan means, I think, that he is adding a new category to the canonical seven-part taxonomy of books established in Liu Xin's Han-era *Qi lue* 七略.† The passage suggests that he saw himself as bringing narratives illustrating the "way of spirits" into the circle of legitimate subjects for inquiry.

But such statements are rare in the surviving record. In most cases the only evidence we have for what compilers were trying to convey is what-ever of their texts now remains for us to read. Plausibly reconstructing their aims from their texts is possible in some cases but is a complex enterprise. There are several reasons for this.

First, enough items must survive from a text that we feel confident about taking them as adequately representative of the whole. Often this is not the case. Second, each story can be seen as an argument of sorts. These stories are not idle exercises; most of them reveal, argue, or assume something sig-nificant about the world, about spirits, about relations between humans and other beings, or about the afterlife and the dead. These significant things implied or suggested are surely one reason that the stories were told and transmitted in the first place, but they were often not matters of complete consensus in society at the time. There would have been little point in trans-mitting the stories in that case, since people do not generally tell tales illus-trating the obvious. (In no culture would we expect to find stories making a point of noting that water runs downhill or that fire consumes objects.) The stories assert things to be the case that, on the one hand, many at the time believed to be the case (since these stories were the work of many hands, not just of their end-stage compilers) but that, on the other hand, some doubted.

---

*See Unger, "Die Fragmente des *So-Yü*"; *SW*, 33–34, 37; *LZG*, 86–97; *CL*, 413–414; and Shaugh-nessy, *Rewriting Early Chinese Texts*, 166–171.

†The best Western-language treatment of which I am aware is Drège, *Les bibliothèques en Chine*, 95–102.

They push against opposed viewpoints that are usually only implied but that occasionally surface in the texts. The more we know about alternative viewpoints in early medieval times, the more likely we are to see what a story's argument is. But discerning it is always a work of interpretation.

Third, a story's argument might in some cases have to do simply with what exists, but usually it is more complex. For example, a story in which a dead person appears in spirit form to a living person argues or assumes, at a minimum, that ghosts exist. (Some members of the elite were on record as arguing that no component of the human person survives physical death.) But often there is more. If the ghost requests some form of assistance from the living protagonist and the protagonist complies, and then later the ghost returns to repay him with a countergift, then we have to deal with a more interesting and specific argument concerning the nature of the relationship between living and dead persons. And if the ghost and the living protagonist in the story are unrelated by kinship, then the argument gains further complexity against a cultural background in which living families were normally obliged to care only for their own deceased kin.*

Fourth, the rhetorical aims of a text are best evidenced not in stories taken singly but in the whole ensemble of extant tales. The best way to see what arguments a whole text is making is to index its motifs or story types. These are not mere literary devices but are key patterns of action in the wider culture that produced the stories. And when one constructs such an index not just for a single compilation but for the entire body of pre-Tang tales, one finds something surprising: it turns out that, in a genre devoted to the unusual, the unusual comes in a limited number of forms. With few exceptions, there are only so many types of stories with only so many types of characters. Spirits, for example, might in theory have manifested themselves to people unexpectedly and in any number of ways, but from reading the extant accounts we get the impression that when they appeared, it was often in one of a small number of patterns of action. Furthermore, the spirits themselves fall into a small number of standard sorts (god, ghost, ancestor, demon of one or another sort). The stories come in recognizable types, and the beings that populate them come in recognizable roles. Once one has got a fix on the entire repertoire of story types and ensemble of roles, one is then in a position to step back and ask what is being affirmed

---

*As argued in *SW*, 377–384.

or argued through this whole genre of texts about the world and people's place in it.

In sum, it is not as if these texts are systematic. They build cases inductively for the way the world is; they wage arguments item by item. And that they largely use narrative to make their arguments allows for a degree of ambiguity or indeterminacy in the messages likely to be inferred by readers. So arriving at a view of what they were meant to argue is inescapably a work of interpretation and inference. But it is impossible to read the entire corpus of extant works of this genre in this era—or the entire corpus of items surviving from any particular work, in cases where a larger number of them survive—and not be impressed by a patterning in the story types and thus in the sorts of things being asserted about the cosmos and people's role in it. Of course, there is variation, but it occurs within a surprisingly limited range of story types, motifs, and character roles. Anomalousness was not random; it flowed in channels.

Rather than spelling out here what the story types and standard roles are, I prefer to leave it to readers to track these for themselves (although the index is intended to help readers locate stories dealing with similar topics and themes), as well as to ponder what their makers and compilers were asserting through them to be the case. What worldviews, attitudes, and behaviors did these stories recommend to contemporary readers? We do well to read the texts with this question in mind.

Sources for the Texts

Early medieval accounts of anomalies were compiled, then, from many sources. But what about our sources for them? Only very few of these works have come down to us in integral versions from medieval times.* In most cases we have to deal with piecemeal quotations in other works—primarily *leishu* 類書 or "category books," anthologies containing quotations organized by topic or keyword—dating to the Tang and Song periods. The late Ming (sixteenth and early seventeenth centuries) saw a boom in printed editions

---

*Some scholars think that Liu Jingshu's *Yi yuan* was not a late recompilation but instead was transmitted continuously through medieval into modern times; see *SW,* 78–79. A probably early twelfth-century manuscript of a collection of miracle tales concerning the bodhisattva Guanshiyin dating to the late fifth or early sixth century was found in a temple in Kyoto in 1943; see ibid., 68–69; and Makita, *Rikuchō kōitsu Kanzeon ōkenki no kenkyū.*

of *zhiguai* texts made by recompiling quotations found in these category books. Early in the twentieth century the writer and scholar Lu Xun 魯迅 (1881–1936) prepared a monumental collection of quotations of many *zhiguai* works in *leishu*, titled *Gu xiaoshuo gouchen* 古小說鈎沈. Since then other modern scholars have published print editions of particular *zhiguai* works. Some are also now available in electronic editions online. I have used all these resources in preparing the translations presented in this book.

Given this situation, we must bear in mind that what we now possess of any particular *zhiguai* work is only a portion of the original—although in saying this I must hasten to add that the very idea of "the original" in regard to early medieval books is something of a chimera anyhow. Before the invention of printing, texts were much more fluid than we are accustomed to, even during their authors' lifetimes.* Each time a copy of a text was made—by its author or compiler or by someone else—it was changed in the process, and contemporaries saw nothing unusual in this. This was true not only of the compilations made by *zhiguai* authors but also of the texts they used as sources. To some extent, then, the fact that most anomaly accounts survive only because of the selective interest taken in them by Tang and Song *leishu* compilers is simply an intensification of what was true of all texts, even the most canonical, before the widespread use of printing, which probably did not occur until the late sixteenth century: they were transmitted only to the extent that they drew the interest of copyists and editors; only those portions of them that related to the topics compilers were working on (or bibliophiles were fascinated by) were transmitted; and, in being transmitted, they were often altered.†

What are the consequences of all this for how we read those portions of anomaly accounts that did manage to survive? For one thing, we must be

---

*For more, see Tian, *Tao Yuanming and Manuscript Culture*; Nugent, *Manifest in Words, Written on Paper*; Shaughnessy, *Rewriting Early Chinese Texts*; Allen, *Shifting Stories*; and Campany, *Signs from the Unseen Realm*, 25–27. The best single book on Chinese paleography remains Tsien, *Written on Bamboo and Silk*. Manuscript texts were—and still are—more fluid but not necessarily, as one might imagine, more expensive or laborious to prepare than printed editions (on this point, see McDermott, *A Social History of the Chinese Book*, 73).

†On the origins of printing in China—a development inextricably bound up with religion and, more specifically, religious ritual (as were the origins of writing in China, for that matter—see Kern, "Introduction: The Ritual Texture of Early China")—see Twitchett, *Printing and Publishing in Medieval China*; and Barrett, *The Woman Who Discovered Printing*. On the surprisingly late date by which printed texts became more common than handwritten ones, see McDermott, *A Social History of the Chinese Book*, 43–78.

alert to the possibility that the extant passages of any given text do not adequately represent whatever versions of it circulated at or near the time of its initial compilation. We are on surer ground in this regard the larger the number of items and when, as sometimes happens, we also have a preface characterizing the compiler's intention, allowing us to match that characterization with surviving passages. Of course, this caveat gains force the smaller the number of extant items. Regarding a text such as *Collected Records of Numinous Phenomena* (*Jiling ji* 集靈記) compiled by Yan Zhitui 顏之推 (531–591), for example—listed in Sui and Tang records as comprising twenty or ten scrolls, respectively, but of which only a single item now survives—it would obviously be hazardous to assert very much. Another consideration is that, except in those rare cases where there is good reason to think that the text we now have preserves some early version from the preprinting era, it is impossible to deduce anything of importance from the ordering of items in a text. In almost all cases their sequence is simply an artifact of the recompilation done by late Ming editors.* Finally, arguments from silence are especially risky: to base an interpretation on the fact that a given text nowhere mentions this or that topic is fallacious.

Literary Form and Implied Worldview

At the level of poetics, how do most of the individual tales collected into *zhiguai* texts work? I want to point out some of the stories' typical rhetorical features and to argue that these are not content neutral: they imply or perform a certain view of the world and people's experience of it.†

Consider the following typical example, drawn from Ren Fang's 任昉 (460–508) *Shuyi ji* 述異記 or *Records of Strange Things:*

Beside the river in western Yudu district in the Nankang region there is a certain stone chamber called Mengkou Cave [literally "Cave of the Portal of Dreams"]. Once a boatman [nearby] encountered a man com-

---

*Even professional scholars who should know better occasionally make this mistake. For an example, see the otherwise fine study by Mathieu, *Démons et merveilles dans la littérature chinoise des Six Dynasties.*

†In this section I work exclusively at the level of the individual tale. I do not deal with non-narrative, descriptive items, but readers may find an introductory discussion of the poetics of these in *SW,* 213–222.

pletely dressed in yellow and carrying two baskets of yellow melons. The man asked him for a ride. When the boat had crossed the river and reached the other shore, the man spat onto the fare tray, disembarked, and headed directly into this cave. At first the boatman was angered by this, but when he saw the man enter the cave, he began to suspect that something strange was afoot. Looking then at the spittle on the tray, he saw that it had turned completely into gold.*

The item begins by laying a baseline of the ordinary: an unremarkable geographic area, a river, a cave. The narrative proper begins with the word "once" and the introduction of an ordinary protagonist, the unnamed boatman. A hint is then dropped that something strange is about to occur—a hint we are expected to pick up on, although the protagonist in the story does not: that the passenger is dressed entirely in yellow and carries melons of the same color. Even a reader unfamiliar with the history of Chinese clothing might surmise that the man's attire was odd from the fact that the story mentions it. Next is entrained a culturally familiar process, governed by standard expectations: that of hiring a ride on a boat. That the passenger spits onto the tray instead of laying down a coin violates these expectations. Both reader and protagonist wonder what this strange behavior can possibly mean. A further anomaly—the passenger's disappearance into the cave (boat passengers did not typically live in caves)—triggers the boatman's "suspicion that something strange was afoot." The climax then comes with the revelation of the saliva's contranatural transformation into gold. Exactly who the passenger was or how he had acquired this strange power is not explained—that is not the focus of this tale. Contemporary readers would have known of a body of lore about mysterious masters of esoteric skills who performed magical feats without explaining how the skills worked or had been acquired.†

Elsewhere I have discussed several of the rhetorical elements of such stories.‡ Here I wish to focus on the one that is fundamental to the genre: the way the text plays between the ordinary and the unexpected. For the sake of argument, imagine two narratological poles. One would be analogous to

---

*Shuyi ji 1.60 (HWCS ed. 1.10b).

†For more, see Campany, "Long-Distance Specialists"; and Campany, *Making Transcendents*, 88–150.

‡See SW, 222–233.

a children's tale set in a marvelous land in which anything, however surprising, can and does happen—a land invented by the author to delight young readers by virtue of its strong contrast with their familiar world. The other pole would be a sort of storytelling that confined itself to the quotidian, an everyday world in which nothing unexpected ever happens—perhaps a bare chronicle of unremarkable, known events laid end to end. The stories translated here operate in a narrative space between these two poles. The strange events of which they tell unfold on a canvas of the commonplace and the expected. Each story begins by establishing a backdrop of ordinariness. We find ourselves in a familiar world, a world about whose workings we, too, have some expectations even though we do not live in early medieval China. (For us, too, one often pays for a service rendered, but one does not normally do so by spitting saliva onto a plate, and saliva does not normally turn into gold.) But then against this backdrop something weird occurs. At a certain moment the narrative pivots from the expected into the strange. How will the protagonist respond, and what will the consequences be? All of this, furthermore, is narrated from the point of view of an ordinary human subject (albeit in the third person). In other words, all sorts of odd things happen in these stories, but they happen to people more or less like the implied reader. It is in the context of expectations shared by protagonist and reader that anomalousness is recognized and experienced as such.

This narrative form, basic to the *zhiguai* genre, is not, I suggest, content neutral: baked into it is a certain view of the order of things and people's place in that order. On the one hand, the world we enter through these texts is one in which spirits are everywhere; people may encounter them at almost any time and place. Such encounters were certainly possible, and everyone had heard of cases of them; many people probably knew of relatives or acquaintances who had had some such experience and had told of it. On the other hand, it is not as though such encounters were so commonplace as to be unworthy of note. Encounters with spirits or wonder-working mystery men were startling, and that is why they were the stuff of socially exchanged narratives and why they interested many parties. The point is that these facets of the cultural world of early medieval China can be discerned not just in the content of *zhiguai* texts but also in their rhetorical form: the rhythms of routine life might at any point be interrupted by an incursion from the "unseen world" alluded to in the titles of many compilations. Without the background of the ordinary, the strange would not appear as such.

This, incidentally, is why I eschew the designation "supernatural" often applied to these tales. *The Oxford English Dictionary* gives the basic sense of this term—apparently coined by Thomas Aquinas—as "belonging to a higher realm or system than that of nature"; *super* means "above," and, for the high medieval Latin doctors, *natura* was a realm distinct from and subordinate to that of the divine. It is precisely this metaphysically dichotomous view of the world that *zhiguai* narratives show to have been absent in medieval China. There, the gap between the "unseen world" and our everyday world was one not of being but simply of perception. Normally its denizens and workings, although all around us all the time, were imperceptible to us; but once in a while they suddenly became perceptible to someone, and these texts record such moments and invite readers to consider what they might entail.

On the Nomenclature of Spirits

The Chinese nomenclature for various sorts of spirit beings does not map neatly onto English. My initial plan was to provide the Chinese term in parentheses in each instance, but this proved unwieldy. For readers new to this theological terminology, a brief explanation is therefore in order.

Perhaps the most ubiquitous such term in these texts is *gui* 鬼. I have rendered it as "ghost" or "demon" depending on context. The English "ghost" implies a deceased human being still active somehow in the world of the living, so I have translated *gui* as "ghost" when it seems likely or certain that the being so denoted is a dead person who has returned or lingered in spirit form. Otherwise I have rendered it as "demon." The reader should be aware of this unexpectedly broad semantic range of *gui*—and also that the "demons" who populate these stories were not necessarily seen as malevolent, although they were certainly capable of maleficence (as were ghosts of the dead). Sometimes the choice of "ghost" or "demon" amounts to a toss-up, as in item 36, where the *gui* in question might or might not be a deceased human. Further complicating matters is that there were other terms also naming nonrevenant spirits of nature that usually trailed an air of mischief, among them *mei* 魅, which I have given as "sprite" or "demon" (including cases where it is used in compounds, such as *xiemei* 邪魅 in item 11), and the *xiao* 魈 of the compound *shanxiao* 山魈, "mountain sprite." Various other terms, such as the accusatory *yaoxie* 妖邪 of item 59, are also, unfortunately, rendered as "demon." The available English terminology appears sadly monochromatic when it is set beside the rich and colorful animistic palette of early China. Perhaps such vocabulary in any language is bound to remain fuzzy.

Also ubiquitous is the term *shen* 神, challenging in a different way. This word, along with the compound *guishen* 鬼神, was sometimes broadly used to denote "spirits" in general, and I have sometimes translated accordingly. But it also denoted the beings worshipped in shrines and temples, and when this sort of *shen* is in question, I have opted for "god" or "goddess." Some of the specific gods mentioned in our texts were furthermore assigned honorific titles drawn from the originally feudal vocabulary of officialdom. Among such titles appearing in the items, which may have sounded slightly archaic by early medieval times, are the "marquis" (*hou* 侯) assigned to Marquis Jiang 蔣侯 (as well as a few other deities) and the "earl" (*bo* 伯) used to honor the River Earl 河伯, god of the Yellow River, as well as the more broadly serviceable "lord" (*jun* 君) seen in item 14 and elsewhere.

Finally, the words *hun* 魂 and *po* 魄 were used to denote two groups of volatile spirits comprised in the human person, prone to wander out of the body during sleep—resulting in dreams—and to disaggregate at the moment of death, some remaining near the body, some installed in the tomb, some hauled off to a distant afterlife destination, and some perhaps left to roam about in the world at large. *Po* does not appear in any of the stories translated here; I have translated *hun* as "cloudsouls." Their usage was fluid, never dogmatically fixed. The previously mentioned word *shen* 神 was also used in this semantic area, where it designated whatever subtle, ethereal components of persons were thought to survive their physical death. In such contexts I have rendered it as "spirit" or "soul."

Why Read These Texts?

As seen earlier, stories such as the ones translated here have usually been treated as a chapter in the history of Chinese "literature" taken in isolation from most everything else, an early developmental stage culminating in modern fiction. For those interested in the history of Chinese narrative, these stories certainly constitute important evidence, however anachronistically such studies are usually structured. But are there any other reasons for us to read early medieval *zhiguai* texts—other than that they are for us, as they were for so many earlier readers, entertaining? I argue that there are.

First, these texts offer unparalleled material for the history of Chinese religion, as well as evidence that there was religion beyond the great traditions and their specialists. They do so in two basic ways. On the one hand, there is the enormous amount of religious terrain we can glimpse through these texts. We see represented a large variety of gods, with their temples and spirit mediums; the human dead, their lingering presence in their tombs, their more distant afterlife destinies, and their frequent spectral appearances to the living; demons and spirits of many kinds; views of sacred, mysterious places on the landscape; and special religious achievers and their spiritual powers. And we see all of these from lay viewpoints: although *zhiguai* texts treat almost exclusively what we would call "religious" matters, none of them in this period were compiled by someone we could call a religious professional, a priest or monk. Even more interestingly, we see how ordinary people responded to all these beings and phenomena and the attendant consequences. And, since the makers and compilers of these stories were telling and writing them for audiences who knew the culture being narrated, we can be confident that, on the whole, these depictions capture actual belief and practice at the time rather than being fanciful inventions by isolated authors.*

On the other hand, the texts are not mere neutral windows onto what they represent. They were important platforms for religious reflection, argumentation, and persuasion. They preserve claims some people were making about the way the world actually is, in constrast to how it might appear to be or how others maintained it was. The fact that all these people found it worthwhile to exchange and record all these stories and descriptions on these subjects is itself a religious and not merely an isolatedly literary phenomenon. As in any other sort of social exchange, each telling, hearing, writing, and reading of a *zhiguai* item depended on participants' interest in offering or receiving the narrative.† That interest, to judge from what the texts contain, is one we recognize as what we nowadays characterize as religious, although people in early medieval China did not think

*For more on this point, see Campany, *Making Transcendents*, 19–22.

†Here I draw on B. H. Smith, "Narrative Versions, Narrative Theories," 232–233; see also Campany, *Making Transcendents*, 10–11.

of what we term "the religious" as a sharply distinct domain.* Literature scholars have largely ignored this central facet of the early *zhiguai* genre. But religion scholars have often scanted these texts as well, habituated as they are to taking scriptural genres as centrally important.

Second, these texts—especially the ones that take narrative form—provide many glimpses of aspects of ordinary social life and material culture that can be hard to discern from other surviving evidence. They mention a great many details concerning domestic life, hospitality, foodstuffs, festivals, local customs and legends, games, medical practice, travel, architecture, furniture, clothing, and relations between genders that are otherwise scarcely accessible in the written record. They are also a repository for the history of the written language and have begun to be studied from that point of view.† One could perhaps write a partial and episodic but nonetheless unprecedented sort of sociocultural history on their basis.

Third, *zhiguai* texts preserve anecdotes about individuals and events known from more formal histories and often throw new light on them.‡ My point is not that these anecdotes preserve information about "what really happened" behind the scenes, but that they testify to the fact that some people were exchanging such representations as if they were true, or might be—and that is important for a good historian to know, since all we really have from the past is a riot of conflicting memories of what occurred.§ The best a historian can do is to compare accounts, and accounts of anomalies, when they involve politically or culturally important individuals or moments, can be used in this way much more than they have been.

Finally, I believe that these texts are worth reading precisely because they were not the inventions of a few individuals but were instead artifacts of many people's exchange of stories and representations. Most of the people involved in this exchange will always remain unknown to us by name, but in the thousands of textual items that survive we have a record of matters they considered important enough to write down and transmit to others—a large and stunningly rich body of social memory. This alone makes them

---

*On this point, see Campany, "On the Very Idea of Religions"; and Campany, "Chinese History and Writing about 'Religion(s).'"

†See Zhou Junxun, *Wei Jin nanbeichao zhiguai xiaoshuo cihui yanjiu.*

‡As remarked in Allen, *Shifting Stories,* 90–100.

§For more, see Campany, *Making Transcendents,* 263–265.

eminently worth studying. My only regret is that I was unable to include more of them in this modest-sized volume.

What Is Included in This Book, and Why

Several pre-Tang *zhiguai* compilations have been translated in their entirety into English. Even in cases where these publications are out of print or otherwise hard to obtain, I have not included items from these texts here. In chronological order by date of the Chinese text, they include the following:*

1. *Itinerary of Mountains and Waterways* (*Shanhai jing* 山海經, often rendered *Classic of Mountains and Seas*). This early,† large (837 items), geographically arranged compendium of wonders is a father text of the genre. It has been translated in its entirety into English, French, Italian, and other languages.‡ Its entries do not assume the shape of narratives involving human pro-

---

*Here I do not include hagiographic and biographical texts. Of those, the perhaps second-or third-century *Traditions of Exemplary Transcendents* (*Liexian zhuan* 列仙傳) has been translated in its entirety into French, with annotations (see Kaltenmark, *Le Lie-sien tchouan*), and Ge Hong's *Traditions of Divine Transcendents* (*Shenxian zhuan* 神仙傳, ca. 317 CE) has been translated in its entirety, with annotations and notes on sources and variant versions, into English (see Campany, *To Live as Long as Heaven and Earth*). Both of those works contain stories about the lives of purported Daoist immortals or transcendents (*xian* 仙). Quite a few stories from the early medieval period about the lives of recluses have also been translated into English; see Berkowitz, "Biographies of Recluses"; Berkowitz, *Patterns of Disengagement*; and Vervoorn, *Men of the Cliffs and Caves*. No reader should approach this material without also consulting Ashmore, *The Transport of Reading*, 56–101. Biographies of healers, diviners, and specialists in other esoteric arts are translated in DeWoskin, *Doctors, Diviners, and Magicians of Ancient China*. On early medieval biographies of Buddhist monks, of which hundreds survive, see, as entrées into the literature, Kieschnick, *The Eminent Monk*; Shih, *Biographies des moines éminents*; Li Jung-shi, *Biographies of Buddhist Nuns*; Tsai, *Lives of the Nuns*; Benn, *Burning for the Buddha*; and Shinohara, "Two Sources of Chinese Buddhist Biographies."

†Just how early is a matter of scholarly dispute. For an overview of the opinions, see Loewe, *Early Chinese Texts*, 357–367.

‡English translation in Birrell, *The Classic of Mountains and Seas*; French translation in Mathieu, *Étude sur la mythologie et l'ethnologie de la Chine ancienne*; Italian translation in Fracasso, *Libro dei monti e dei mari* (*Shanhai jing*). For a comparative review of these translations, see Campany, review of Fracasso and Birrell. Good interpretive studies in Western languages are few, but see Birrell, *Chinese Myth and Culture*, 146–177; Dorofeeva-Lichtmann, "Conception of Terrestrial Organization in the *Shan hai jing*"; Dorofeeva-Lichtmann, "Mapping a 'Spiritual' Landscape"; Dorofeeva-Lichtmann, "Topographical Accuracy or Conceptual Organization of Space?"; Lewis, *The Construction of Space*, 284–303; and Schiffler, "Chinese Folk Medicine." Strassberg, *A Chinese Bestiary*, offers translations of selected passages paired with illustrations drawn from a rare set of woodblock prints executed in 1597 (see Campany, "Review of *A Chinese Bestiary*").

tagonists; instead, they are descriptions of the strange, numinous phenomena associated with successive zones of the earth. One of the most suggestive characterizations of this text in English says that it "records a sequence of environmental spheres extending in a given direction each of which usually consists of mountains, bodies of water, or foreign lands. Each sphere is a kind of ecosystem whose strange creatures denote its level of spiritual power. Distinctive topographical features, resident gods and strange creatures, and valuable objects are catalogued in repetitive, formulaic language that may have facilitated memorization and that also conveys a sense of cultural order common to cosmographies."* Another says that it "forged diverse myths and local lore into a systematic account by assigning every creature, divine being, or ancient story to a place. These places were then compiled to form a world picture" that was structured according to a system of concentric zones of a sort familiar from other early Chinese cosmographic schemes.†

2. *Treatise on Curiosities* (*Bowu zhi* 博物志) by the polymath Zhang Hua, mentioned earlier. This once-enormous third-century compendium contains mostly nonnarrative descriptions of various sorts of strange things (over three hundred of them) organized into topical categories.‡ There is a copiously annotated English translation.§

3. *Records of an Inquest into the Spirit Realm* (*Soushen ji* 搜神記) by the court historian Gan Bao 干寶 (d. 336 CE). This work, probably the most celebrated of early medieval *zhiguai* compilations, today contains over 460 items distributed across twenty topically organized chapters. Like most other early medieval *zhiguai* texts, it was once much larger. Some of its contents are of the descriptive form, but most of the work is taken up with narratives of encounters of one or another anomalous sort.‖ There are complete translations into English and French.**

---

*Strassberg, *A Chinese Bestiary*, 29.
†Lewis, *The Construction of Space*, 285.
‡For a list of these categories, see *SW*, 51–52.
§See Greatrex, *The Bowu zhi*. For a list of studies and editions of the text, see *CL*, 50–52.
‖For listings of the topics treated in each of the twenty chapters, see Campany, "Two Religious Thinkers of the Early Eastern Jin," 192–193. For an overall interpretive reading of the implicit purpose and argument of *Soushen ji*, see ibid., 192–202; and for a study of several of its dominant themes and topics, see Mathieu, *Démons et merveilles dans la littérature chinoise des Six Dynasties*. For a recent critical edition of the text, see *XJS*, vol. 1.
**See DeWoskin and Crump, *In Search of the Supernatural* (on which, see Campany, "Review of *In Search of the Supernatural*"), which is only very lightly annotated; and Mathieu, *À la recherche des esprits*, which offers more thorough notes.

4. *Records of Signs from the Unseen Realm* (*Mingxiang ji* 冥祥記) by the scholar-official Wang Yan 王琰. Completed around 490, this is a collection of narratives of events in China argued to demonstrate the efficacy of Buddhist piety. Over 130 narratives plus the compiler's preface survive. The work has been translated into English with annotation and a running commentary.[*]

5. *Accounts of Vengeful Souls* (*Yuanhun zhi* 冤魂志) by the scholar-official Yan Zhitui 顏之推 (531–after 591). In its extant form this work gathers over sixty stories in which someone who has wrongfully died files a brief with Heaven or the Celestial Thearch (*tiandi* 天帝) seeking divine justice or else takes retribution into his or her own hands by directly confronting the perpetrator. There is a critical English translation incorporating multiple printed editions as well as a manuscript dated 882 found at Dunhuang.[†]

In addition to these entire texts, many *zhiguai* items have been translated piecemeal into English and other languages.[‡] With very few exceptions (always noted) I have here avoided retranslating any items that have, insofar as I am aware, been translated in published form before. I have operated

[*]Campany, *Signs from the Unseen Realm*. Further interpretation of some of the stories may be found in Campany, "Religious Repertoires and Contestation." On this work, see also Wang Guoliang, "*Mingxiang ji* xiao kao"; Wang Guoliang, *Mingxiang ji yanjiu*; and Liu Yuanru, *Chaoxiang shenghuo shijie de wenxue quanshi.*

[†]Cohen, *Tales of Vengeful Souls*. On this work, see also Dien, "The *Yuan-hun chih* (Accounts of Ghosts with Grievances)"; and Wang Guoliang, *Yan Zhitui Yuanhun zhi yanjiu.*

[‡]In *CCT*, five stories are translated from *Lieyi zhuan*, two from *Qi Xie ji*, three from Zu Chongzhi's *Shuyi ji*, three from *Soushen houji*, two from *Xu Qi Xie ji*, eight from *Youming lu*, two from *Luyi zhuan*, two from *Linggui zhi*, and two from *Zhenyi zhuan*. In addition, this volume includes renditions of tales from texts that have been translated before or since in their entirety elsewhere (to wit, *Soushen ji*, *Yuanhun zhi*, *Shenxian zhuan*, and *Mingxiang ji*). The main criterion for choosing items to be translated in this volume appears to have been their length: only atypically long stories are included. Groot's *The Religious System of China* pioneered in using generous translations of early *zhiguai* items as evidence of beliefs concerning ghosts, gods, and demons; I have not compiled a list of items translated in his work, and so a few of them may be duplicated here. Twelve stories from *Youming lu* are translated in Campany, "Tales of Strange Events." Simmons, "The *Soushen houji* Attributed to Tao Yuanming (365–427)," translates all 117 stories in the traditional ten-*juan* arrangement of that text, but scholarship has since shown that a nontrivial number of those tales are likely misattributed. A number of items are translated from *Youming lu* in Zhang, *Buddhism and Tales of the Supernatural in Early Medieval China* and from this and other texts in Lin Fu-Shih, "Chinese Shamans and Shamanism in the Chiang-nan Area," and Miyakawa, "Local Cults around Mount Lu." A variety of Buddhist tales are translated in Gjertson, *Gods, Ghosts, and Retribution*; Campany, "Buddhist Revelation and Taoist Translation"; Campany, "The Earliest Tales of the Bodhisattva Guanshiyin"; Campany, "Notes on the Devotional Uses and Symbolic Functions of Sutra Texts"; and Campany, "The Real Presence." A few tales relating to spectral appearances are translated in Campany, "Ghosts Matter," and a few return-from-death accounts are translated and discussed in Campany, "Return-from-Death Narratives."

with a few other loose principles of selection as well: (1) I have tended to choose items that survived at enough length to allow us to get a good sense of the story they have to tell. Many *zhiguai* items exist only in partial quotations, brief excerpts from what were clearly originally much longer stories, or summaries. I have avoided what appear to be the most severely truncated. (2) I have not included certain texts that have been relatively often written about, even when they have not yet been fully translated—for example, the dozens of narratives of cases in which the bodhisattva Guanshiyin rescued devotees from distress. These texts in any case exhibit only a very limited range of story types and no real variance in the arguments they make. (3) I have largely avoided texts that would not be well represented in piecemeal fashion—texts that are more tightly integrated than most of those translated here. An example is the group of texts containing legends surrounding the Han emperor Wu (r. 141–87 BCE), which in any case are somewhat marginal to the *zhiguai* genre. Another is *Shiyi ji* 拾遺記 or *Uncollected Records* attributed to Wang Jia 王嘉 (fourth century), another text with a tenuous relation to the *zhiguai* genre. Both these sets of texts have also been extensively studied and translated, although not in published form.* (4) I have mostly chosen narrative over descriptive items, feeling that stories are more accessible to readers. (5) I have given some preference to texts that, despite their large size, have been relatively neglected in published scholarship.† (6) But, countervailingly, I have also tried to impart a sense of the range of the texts. Rather than attempting to capture the bulk of any one work, that is, I have preferred to represent titles not already translated elsewhere, even when only very few items from them survive. (7) Finally, in the interest of affordability and convenience for readers, I kept a close eye on the total number of items so as not to exceed a predetermined word limit for the entire volume. The resulting selection is far from perfect and even has elements of randomness, but at least it considerably widens the range of texts accessible to readers of English.

Shiyi ji has been studied and translated in its entirety in Foster, "The *Shih-i chi*." On it, see also *SW*, 64–67, 306–318. T. E. Smith, "Ritual and the Shaping of Narrative," translates copiously from the material on the Han emperor Wu in several texts. The one English translation of a text from this batch that has been published is of *Shizhou ji* 十洲記, a Daoist cosmography; see T. E. Smith, "Record of the Ten Continents." On this material, see also Schipper, *L'empereur Wou des Han dans la légende taoïste*; and Li Fengmao, *Liuchao Sui Tang xiandaolei xiaoshuo yanjiu*.

†These primarily include *Youming lu* attributed to Liu Yiqing, *Shuyi ji* by Zu Chongzhi, and *Yi yuan* by Liu Jingshu, all fifth-century texts.

TRANSLATIONS

Jiling ji 集靈記
COLLECTED RECORDS OF NUMINOUS PHENOMENA
Compiled by Yan Zhitui 顏之推 (531–591)*

1 extant item

[1]

Wang Xu was a native of Langye. He served during the Liang as a record keeper on the staff of the prince of Nankang. Several years after his death, his wife and children had difficulty finding clothes to wear and food to eat. At the end of the year his form appeared. He said to his widow, "Are you lacking for clothes and food?" His wife set out wine for him; then they said farewell. Departing, Xu said to her, "If I can get anything of value, I will leave it for you."

The following month, their young daughter was searching about and found a pair of gold finger rings.

Jingyi ji 旌異記 (alternate title: Jingyi zhuan 旌異傳)
CITATIONS OF MARVELS†
Compiled by Hou Bo 侯白 (fl. during the Sui [581–618])

12 extant items

[2]

During the Wu regime [220–280], when ground was being leveled in Jianye for the palace harem, a metal image was unearthed. When its origins were

---

*For studies of Yan Zhitui's life and writings, see the following works by Dien: "Custom and Society"; *Pei Ch'i shu 45*; "The *Yuan-hun chih* (Accounts of Ghosts with Grievances)"; and "Yen Chih-t'ui (531–591+)." On *Jiling ji* and *Yuanhun zhi*, see also *LZG*, 442–450; and *SW*, 91.

†On this work, see *LZG*, 434–436; *WXS*, 331; and *SW*, 90. Item 8 (that is, the eighth item of the twelve extant items of this collection) is translated and discussed in Campany, "Buddhist Revelation and Taoist Translation," 11–12, and Campany, "The Real Presence," 249–250.

investigated, it turned out to have been fashioned early in the Zhou period by King Aśoka and installed there in the precincts of the Jiang River.* How was this ascertained to be so? Since the Dharma of Buddha did not reach the south [of China] during the Qin, Han, and Wei dynasties, how else could a [Buddhist] image have come to be buried there?

Sun Hao [242–284]† then got possession of it. Never having believed in Buddha and irreverent by nature, he had the image placed in the latrine area and ordered that it remain there. On the eighth day of the fourth month, Sun said in jest, "It's now the eighth day—time to bathe the Buddha!"‡ He proceded to urinate on the image's head. Very soon afterward he suffered acute pain throughout his body, and it felt as if his genitals were being pierced. He screamed in unbearable agony. The grand astrologer divined and concluded, "This has been brought on by your having offended some great deity." Offerings were then made to all the gods in the [official] pantheon, but to no avail. A woman of the palace harem who had long believed in Buddha said, "The Buddha is a great deity. Your Highness recently defiled him. Since your difficulty is now so urgent, perhaps you might try inviting him."

Sun Hao concurred. He prostrated himself, took [the triple] refuge, and confessed and repented with great feeling.§ In a little while he felt somewhat better. So he sent a horse and carriage to invite the monk [Kang] Senghui to the palace.‖ He bathed the image with perfumed water and again expressed his remorse. He undertook an enlargement of Jian'an Monastery to accrue merit. The affliction in his genitals gradually disappeared.

*The text here alludes to the notion that this early, Buddhist-inclined Indian ruler had long ago included parts of China in his widespread distribution of stupas, images, and relics of the Buddha. See Zürcher, *The Buddhist Conquest of China*, 277–280.

†Last ruler of the Wu kingdom (r. 264–280); surrendered to the Jin in 280.

‡This was the date on which the Buddha's birthday was most commonly celebrated in China. Part of the ritual involved bathing an icon, replicating the hagiographic moment just after the young prince's emergence from his mother's armpit when the gods cleansed him with pure rainwater. See Boucher, "Sutra on the Merit of Bathing the Buddha"; and Hureau, "Buddhist Rituals," 1235–1237.

§All were standard ritual gestures upon first becoming a Buddhist layperson. To take the triple refuge was to declare reliance on the Buddha, on his teachings, and on the Buddhist community.

‖Kang Senghui, a famous monk from Sogdia who arrived at the Wu capital Jianye from the southern outpost of Jiaozhi (modern Hanoi in northern Vietnam) in 247 and was among the earliest wave of translators of Buddhist scriptures into Chinese. See Zürcher, *The Buddhist Conquest of China*, 51–54.

During the Jin era there was a shrine* beside the river in Yangzhou, where the god of the lake was excessively severe and wicked. At that time a monk named Fazang visited there. He was skilled at using mantras and always achieved good results in avoiding evil influences. There was also a younger monk who was learning from him how to chant spells and sutras. Over the years he had made considerable progress, so he, too, was able to subdue all sorts of evil beings. So the disciple† spent the night in the temple inn, planning to recite sutras and mantras in order to subdue the god. That night the god appeared, and when he did so, the disciple died. When the master heard that his student had recited sutras unto death, he himself came to the temple the next night, full of anger. He recited sutras with all his powers of concentration, but when the god appeared, the master, too, died.

There was another monk of the same monastery who constantly maintained himself in a state of meditative absorption. When he heard that the master and his disciple had both died, he went to the god's abode. At nightfall he began reciting the *Diamond Sutra*‡ in the temple. Come midnight there was heard an extremely loud rushing of wind, and then in a flash a creature appeared: its form was huge and frightening, truly strange and awful. It had long, sharp fangs, the light from its eyes was like lightning, and it was capable of many divine transformations, too many to describe. The sutra master sat erect and composed, concentrating on reciting the sutra, not surrendering to fear in the slightest. When the god saw him sitting there, it took on all sorts of fearsome shapes. But then it came directly before the master, bent its right knee to the ground, joined its palms, and listened reverently until the recitation was complete. The master then asked the god: "What god are you, honored layman? At first you were fierce and severe, but now you are calm and subdued." The god replied: "Because

---

*The structure is designated a *ting* 亭, a term that, standing alone, would normally suggest a small inn for travelers, but the ensuing lines make clear that a temple is intended. Stories from this period sometimes depict travelers staying overnight in temples, and *tingmiao* 亭廟 was occasionally, though not often, used as a compound term during the period to refer to temples (an example occurs at *FYZL* 31.525a21).

†Here it is not yet clear from the wording whether one or both of the monks spent the night in the temple, but the next lines imply that the disciple did so alone.

‡One of the most popular Mahāyāna sutras in East Asia, and one about which many miracle stories were recorded.

of bad karma, your disciple was requited in this way. I am the god of this lake, but I deeply revere the faith." The sutra master asked, "If you revere the faith, why did you beat the first two masters to death?" "The deaths of the first two masters were due to their own inability to maintain faith in the sutras of the Greater Vehicle," the god replied. "At first they concentrated on their recitation [of sutras], but as soon as they saw your disciple approaching, they stopped [reciting sutras] and instead began uttering imprecations and chanting only hateful words, intending to subdue me. But I did not submit. When they saw how hideous my form is, they simply died of fright. It was not that I killed them intentionally."

Now laymen and monks nearby, having seen how the first two monks had been killed, expected this sutra master to be dead as well. But when they rushed in to look, they found him sitting there, serene and composed. Shocked, they clamored to ask him how this was possible, and he told them what had happened. It must [they concluded] have been due to the majestic power of meditation; the holy teaching must be genuine! They all therefore began to develop the thought of enlightenment, and many of them came to sustain meditative absorption themselves.

[4]

During the Wucheng period of the Qi,* someone was digging in the ground near Mount Dongkan in Bingzhou when he came upon a patch of earth that was yellowish-white, different from the surrounding soil. Investigating, he saw an object in the shape of a pair of human lips. Within was a tongue, fresh and bright red. A memorial was sent up about the incident, and various monks were asked about it, but none recognized what it was. Then the monk Datong sent up a memorial that read: "This was an upholder of the *Lotus Sutra.*† This caused [one of] his six sense organs [i.e., the tongue] not to decay. Because he recited the sutra thousands of times, this sign was produced in response." The emperor then ordered the Secretariat drafter Gao Zhen

---

*Both early source texts, as well as LX, have 齊武成世. The Qi, a short-lived southern dynasty (479–502), had no such reign period, but the Northern Zhou dynasty did (559–561).

†Arguably the single most influential Buddhist sutra in East Asia, at least in its impact on devotional practice and pious narrative, and one about which many miracle stories were transmitted. See Campany, "Notes on the Devotional Uses and Symbolic Functions of Sutra Texts"; and Stevenson, "Tales of the Lotus Sutra."

as follows: "You are a man of piety. If you go personally and see it, there must be some numinous anomaly. Set up a pure ritual space and perform an abstinence ceremony and offerings there."*

Gao Zhen carried out the order and traveled to the spot. He assembled monks who upheld the *Lotus Sutra*. Each of them had ritually purified himself, and each held an incense burner as they circumambulated and prayed: "Bodhisattva, your nirvana occurred long ago. But the semblance Dharma† has been passed down without error and we have received it. We ask that you manifest a numinous response."‡ The moment they had spoken these words, the lips and tongue began to move. Although there was no audible sound, the lips appeared to be reciting [the sutra]. All who were present and saw this felt their hair stand on end.

Gao Zhen reported this [to the ruler], who ordered that [the remains] be interred in a stone casket and moved into a cave on the mountain.

---

*In the standard Buddhist abstinence ceremony (*zhai* 齋) in China, participating laymen and laywomen for one day and night six times per month (and for longer periods three times per year) observed more precepts than the five normally required of them and thus behaved more like monks and nuns. These merit-making services also featured confession of sins and the invitation of monastics to lay households to chant sutras, impart a Dharma message, and receive a ceremonial meal. For more, see Hureau, "Buddhist Rituals," 1213–1230; and Campany, *Signs from the Unseen Realm*, 51–55, 107n213.

†Referred to here is an old Buddhist conception of the projected future vicissitudes of Buddhist teaching (i.e., of Dharma [*fa* 法]) that divided it into three eras of varying lengths depending on the text: the period of the True Dharma (*zhengfa* 正法) immediately following the death of the Buddha, during which it was still possible to attain enlightenment following his teachings; that of the Semblance Dharma (*xiangfa* 像法), in which some might still attain enlightenment, but the religion had begun to be degraded and misunderstood; and that of the Final Dharma (*mofa* 末法), during which traditional Buddhist practice lost all efficacy and the ancient teachings were obliterated. See Nattier, *Once upon a Future Time*, 65–132; and Tokuno, "The Book of Resolving Doubts."

‡That is, offer a striking, palpable responsive gesture—a "miracle" (in the sense of an unexpected but not necessarily a contranatural event) or "numinous response" (*linggan* 靈感)—to the prayers of those assembled. For more on this notion, see Campany, *Signs from the Unseen Realm*, 49; and Campany, "The Real Presence."

Jiyi ji 集異記 (alternate title: *Jiyi zhuan* 集異傳)
COLLECTED RECORDS OF ANOMALIES*
Compiled by Guo Jichan 郭季產 (fl. during the Song, 420–479)
11 extant items

[5]

Song Jin[1] of Yangping was skilled at interpreting dreams. A certain man named Sun was seeking an official appointment. He had a dream in which a pair of *fenghuang* birds[†] perched on his two fists. He inquired of Jin about it. Jin said, "If it's not a paulownia tree,[‡] the *fenghuang* won't nest in it, and if it's not bamboo fruit, it won't eat it.[§] You will experience something greatly inauspicious. It indicates someone will have a funeral."[2] Soon thereafter Sun indeed was bereaved of his mother.

[6]

During the Song, Liu Xuan of Zhongshan lived in the city of Yue. One day at sunset he suddenly saw a figure wearing a black gown coming toward him. When Xuan shone lamplight on it, he saw that the figure's head had none of the seven apertures, and its face was a shapeless mass. He had a divination master divine it by stalks. The diviner said, "This is an object from a former generation of your family. Over a long period of time it has become a demon that can kill people. You should expel it soon while it still lacks eyes!"

So Liu caught the creature, tied it up, and stabbed it several times. It transformed into a pillow. It turned out to be a pillow used in former times by his ancestors.

---

*On this work, see *LZG,* 386–387; *WXS,* 326; and *SW,* 81.

†The *fenghuang* 鳳凰 was a mythical bird with many symbolic associations, usually auspicious. See Diény, "Le *Fenghuang* et le phénix."

‡On the symbolic and poetic associations of the *wutong* 梧桐 tree in medieval literature, see McCraw, "Along the Wutong Trail."

§Bamboo typically flowers and fruits only very rarely (sometimes just once in decades).

You Xianqi[3] of Guangping, shortly after burying his wife, saw a personage wearing a red gown. Recognizing it as a demon, he stabbed it with a knife and killed it. After a long while it transformed into a pair of his own frequently worn shoes.

Kongshi zhiguai 孔氏志怪
ACCOUNTS OF ANOMALIES BY MR. KONG*
Probably compiled by Kong Yue 孔約 (late fourth to early fifth century)†
10 extant items

[8]

Lu Chong was a native of Fanyang. Thirty *li* west of his home was the tomb of a certain Cui, chamberlain of the wardrobe. Chong first went there when he was out hunting one day to the west of his home. Spotting a musk deer, he raised his bow, shot, and hit it. The animal fell, then got up again. Chong chased after it, mindless of how far he was going.

Suddenly he saw the gate to a hamlet, like that of a government office. In the middle of it was a bell, and beneath that was a watchman. Chong asked, "What office is this?" The reply: "The office of the chamberlain of palace revenues." Chong said, "I am not appropriately dressed. How can I have an audience with an honorable personage?" At once someone brought new clothes for him and welcomed him. Chong put them on, and they fit perfectly. The watchman then led him in for an audience with the chamberlain, announcing his name. Wine was warmed, and several rounds were served. Then Cui said, "I have recently received a letter from your late father, agreeing to your marriage with my young daughter. I've only been waiting for you to arrive here." He then held up the letter to show to Chong. Although Chong had still been quite young when his father died, he recognized his father's handwriting. He heaved a sigh and was speechless.

---

*On this work, see *LZG*, 332–333; *WXS*, 333; and *SW*, 94.
†A work titled *Kong Yue zhiguai* 孔約志怪 is cited in *TPGJ* 276.25.

Cui then gave an order to the inner chambers for his daughter to adorn herself [for the wedding], and he had Chong proceed to the east apartment. When Chong arrived, the daughter had already disembarked from her carriage and was standing there at the head of the mat. They bowed to each other.

After three days Chong returned to see Cui. Cui told him, "You may go back, sir. My daughter shows the signs of pregnancy. If she gives birth to a boy, we will return him to you; if a girl, we will keep her here and raise her." He then gave an order to those outside to prepare a carriage and see the guest off. Cui personally escorted him to the gate, took his hands, and wept. The feelings at saying farewell were no different than those of living persons. Cui sent with him another suit of clothes and a set of bedding fabrics. Chong then mounted the carriage to depart.

The carriage traveled as quickly as lightning, and in a moment he was back at home, his family members both saddened and delighted upon seeing him.* Upon making inquiries, he realized that Cui was a dead man and that what he had entered was his tomb. He was overcome with depression.

Four years later, on the third day of the third lunar month, he was enjoying himself by the river† when he suddenly saw two calf-drawn carriages coming across the water, alternately floating and sinking. They then came ashore. Chong went to open the back door of one of them and saw Cui's daughter inside, holding a three-year-old boy. On seeing her, Chong was happy; he wanted to take her hand, but the daughter raised her hand, pointed to the rear carriage, and said, "The chamberlain is here to see you." Then he looked and saw Cui and went over to ask after his health. The daughter handed their son over to Chong. She also presented him with a golden bowl as a gift of parting, along with a poem that read:

Brilliantly shining, the numinous excrescence!‡
Radiant and fair, how flourishing it grows!
The flower's beauty, soon to be revealed,
By goodly portents showed a divine wonder.

---

*This phrase, common in reunion scenes, refers to the mixed emotions often felt on reuniting with someone given up for lost.

†The third day of the third month was the date of the Lustration Festival, which, like spring festivals in other cultures, was associated with revelry and sex, along with (in this case) floating wine cups on winding streams. See Bodde, *Festivals in Classical China*, 273–288.

‡On these, see Campany, *To Live as Long as Heaven and Earth*, 27–29.

Harboring her splendor, not yet in full bloom,
In midsummer she suffered the frosty blast.
Her glory, now forever dark and quenched,
Her path on earth eternally undone.

Oblivious of yin and yang's succession,*
Till the wise one's sudden-coming rite.
The meeting superficial; the parting all too swift!
Both wrought through spirits of heaven and earth.

With what can I endow my dearest love?
This golden bowl may wean our son.
With love and kindness, from henceforth we part,
Severed and cut, my liver and my spleen!

Chong took the child, the bowl, and the poem, and then the two carriages suddenly vanished.

When he took the child back home, everyone in his family said that it was a demon. They tried poking and shaking him and spitting on him, but his form remained just as before. When they asked the child, "Who is your papa?" he went directly to Chong and hugged him. Everyone at first thought the whole thing strange and inauspicious, but when they read the poem, they could only sigh at the mysteriousness of the connections between the living and the dead.

Chong took the bowl to the market to sell. He asked a high price for it because he was not willing to part with it quickly, and he also hoped that someone would recognize it. Suddenly an old slave woman asked him how he had come by the bowl, saying she wanted to report what he said back to the great family she served. This great family, it seemed, might be that of the aunt of the woman [he had married]. When someone was sent to see, this was confirmed.

[The aunt] told Chong, "My niece was Chamberlain Cui's daughter. She died before she was married. In their grief for her, her bereaved family gave her a golden bowl, placing it in the coffin. This bowl of yours is very similar to it. Might we hear the details of how you acquired it?" Chong told her

---

*I.e., still a virgin.

everything. She went right away to visit Chong's home and greeted the child. The boy had certain features of the Cui clan, but his face also resembled Chong's. The aunt said, "My niece was born late in the third month. Her father said, 'Spring is a time of warmth and mildness [*wen* 溫]. May she grow up happy [*xiu* 休] and strong.' So they gave her the byname Wenxiu 溫休." *Wenxiu* must indicate "posthumous marriage" [*youhun* 幽婚].* Her future fortune was thus prefigured in her name.

The boy grew up to have the mettle of an official. He served in a succession of commandery posts at a salary of two thousand bushels and was decorated in all of them. Among his descendants was Lu Zhi,[†] who served as a chief steward for writing under the Han. Zhi's son Yu served as minister of works under the Wei. This heritage of official achievement has been passed down [in the family] to present times.

[9]

Gan Bao's[‡] father had a favorite servant girl, of whom Bao's mother was extremely jealous. When Bao's father was being buried, his mother pushed the girl into the grave and buried her. Ten years later the mother died. When the tomb was opened,[§] the servant was lying on top of the coffin. When they examined her, they found that she was still warm, and gradually she began breathing again. They carried her back home, and at the end of the day she regained consciousness. She said: "Bao's father always brought me food and drink and slept close to me. His kindness toward me was like that while he was alive." She proceeded to relate to them all the fortunate and unfortunate events that had befallen the family, and they all corresponded with what had happened.[‖]

She lived normally for several years before dying herself. It was because of this that Gan Bao wrote his *Records of an Inquest into the Spirit Realm*

---

*In other words, if the syllables of the woman's name are reversed, the name Wenxiu and the term *youhun* as pronounced at the time would have sounded very similar.

†He appears as a character in an anecdote in *Shishuo xinyu;* this *Kongshi zhiguai* story is cited in a commentary to the passage. See *SSHY,* 158.

‡Historian and court official responsible for omen interpretation. His *Records of an Inquest into the Spirit Realm* is one of the largest early medieval *zhiguai* collections.

§Multiple burials in the same family tomb were common.

‖Gan Bao's father presumably would have shared these with her as they were reported to him by the family.

(*Soushen ji* 搜神記), and what he mentions in [the preface to] that work as having stimulated him to write it was this event.

[10]

Sheng Yi, a native of Guiji,* one day rose at dawn before anyone was out in the streets. Atop a willow tree inside the gateway he saw a personage a little over two feet tall dressed in a crimson gown and a hat, looking down and licking the dew off the tops of the leaves. After a long while the personage finally noticed Yi. The spirit appeared startled. It quickly hid itself and was no longer to be seen.

[11]

A subofficial functionary in Guiji, Xie Zong, once traveled through Wu on a leave from duty. He was alone on a boat when a bewitchingly fetching young woman suddenly came aboard. She asked, "Do you have any fine silk? I'd like to sell it in the market." So Zong flirted with her, and the woman gradually warmed to him. She spent the night on board, and they ate and amused themselves together. When dawn came, she asked if she could ride with him on the boat, and Zong consented. From then on, people on [other nearby] boats would hear talking and laughter every night [from Zong's boat], and there was always a powerful aroma.

A year passed, with the woman coming and going, often spending the night. But one night [others who were nearby]⁴ secretly observed her and saw no human there. Only then did they realize she was a demon. So together they set a trap. After a while they caught a creature the size of a pillow; soon they caught two more, each the size of a fist. When they examined them closely in the firelight, the creatures turned out to be three turtles.

Zong was in a melancholy daze for several days before finally coming to his senses. He said, "In one year this young woman gave birth to two sons, the elder named Daomin, the younger Daoxing." Since they were turtles, he let them go in the river.

*On this, the name of an important region in the southeast, often read as Kuaiji, see Hargett, "Guaiji? Guiji? Huiji? Kuaiji?"

Lieyi zhuan 列異傳 (alternate title: Lieyi ji 列異記)
ARRAYED ACCOUNTS OF MARVELS*
Attributed to Cao Pi 曹丕
(187–226; reigned as Emperor Wen 文 of the Wei dynasty 220–226)
50 extant items

[12]

During the Ganlu reign period,† Gongsun Da of Rencheng, while serving in Chen commandery, died in office. When it was time to dress him for burial and place him in the coffin, and his sons and some functionaries from the commandery, several dozen people in all, were gathering for the funeral, his four-year-old son suddenly began speaking as one possessed in a voice like that of his father. He cried aloud to everyone present, "Cease weeping! I have something to say!" He then summoned the other sons and gave them instructions one by one. The sons could not contain their sorrow, but he consoled them by saying, "In the cycling of the seasons, everything must end. Human life is brief and fragile; how could it go on without end?" He went on this vein for several thousand words, all of his speech in good literary form. His sons then asked, "Is it the case that normal people, after they die, have no awareness, but that you alone, with your superior intelligence, are special and therefore have a spirit?" The father replied, "In these matters of the living and the dead there is nothing that is easy to explain. As for matters of ghosts and spirits, they are not knowable by living persons."

---

*The *lie* 列 in such titles can also have the sense of "noteworthy"; thus the title might be translated *Accounts of Noteworthy Marvels*. On this work, see *LZG*, 245–246; Wang Guoliang, *Liuchao zhiguai xiaoshuo kaolun*, 45–70; and *SW*, 46–47. Cao Pi's authorship has been questioned. On his life and works, see *CL*, 75–85. Items 14, 23, 28, 41, and 45 have been translated in *CCT*, 56–63; items 23 and 41 have also been translated in Gjertson, *Miraculous Retribution*, 5–7; and item 28 in Bodde, "Some Chinese Tales of the Supernatural," 351, and Yu, "'Rest, Rest, Perturbed Spirit,'" 406.

†This is probably the Ganlu period of the Wei dynasty, which lasted from 256 to 260. The Former Han dynasty and the Wu kingdom (during the Three Kingdoms period) also had reign periods so named; the latter lasted only one year starting in February 265.

He asked for paper to make a declaration and wrote out a letter, filling the whole sheet. He then threw it on the floor and said, "This is a letter to Wei Junzai. This evening a letter from him will arrive. Send this as a reply." That evening a letter from Junzai did indeed arrive.

[13]

Shou Guanghou lived in the time of the Han emperor Zhang [r. 57–75]. He could exorcize all manner of demons and sprites. There was a woman who was sickened by a sprite; Shou exorcized it and obtained a large serpent. On another occasion there was a large tree. If anyone stopped under it, he would perish. Shou performed an exorcism on the tree. It withered, and from it was found suspended a huge serpent, seventy or eighty feet long, dead.

[14]

In the time of Yuan Benchu,* a god appeared in Hedong; he was called Lord Dusuo. The people established a temple for him. A sick woman of the Su clan in Yanzhou went there to pray. She saw a man wearing a white singlet† and a tall cap that resembled a fish head. This man said to [the temple icon of?] Lord Dusuo,⁵ "Once, on a visit to Mount Lu, we ate white plums together beneath the mountain. That was three thousand years ago already! The passage of time surely can make one depressed." After this man had left, Lord Dusuo remarked, "That was the Lord of the South Sea."

[15]

In Wei commandery there lived Zhang Fen, whose family was very wealthy. When his fortunes suddenly declined, he sold his house to the Cheng family from Liyang. After the Chengs moved in, there was a series of deaths and illnesses, so they in turn sold the place to He Wen from Ye. At sundown, Wen took a knife and went up to a ceiling beam in the northern hall and

---

*This is Yuan Shao, a famous general who died in 202 CE. See *SSHY*, 611; and Lewis, *China between Empires*, 33–34.
†A one-piece, single-layer gown.

sat down on it. At the second watch,* he suddenly saw a man over eight feet tall wearing a tall hat and a yellow gown. Entering the hall, he called out, "Slimwaist! How is it that there is the *qi*† of a living human in the hall?" The answer came: "There isn't!" In a moment, a man clad in black with a tall hat entered, and after him, yet another man in a tall hat wearing a white gown also entered. Each time they asked the same question and received the same reply.

At first light, Wen descended from the beam into the hall and called out in the same fashion as the others had, "Who is the one in yellow?" The answer was, "Gold! He's under the west wall of the hall." "Who is the one in black?" "Coin! He's five steps to the side of the well in front of the hall." "Who is the one in white?" "Silver! He's under the pillar in the northeast corner." "And who are you?" Wen asked. The answer was, "I'm the pestle! I'm underneath the stove."

When it was fully light, Wen dug in each place by turns. He found five hundred catties each of gold and silver and over ten million coins. He took the pestle and burned it. From then on the home was peaceful.

[16]

In Yingling in Beihai there was a monk who could cause people to have meetings with the dead. In that same commandery there was a man whose wife had been dead for several years. Hearing of the monk, he went to see him, saying, "I wish for you to enable me to see her. Even if it's only for one short meeting, I will not resent it." So the monk arranged the meeting. The man was able to see his wife. They conversed and were happy and sad by turns; their feelings of kindness toward each other were no different

*Sometime in the early evening. For a thorough explanation of the medieval system of night watches, see Wilkinson, *Chinese History*, 535–537.

†This is the first occurrence in this volume of a ubiquitous Chinese term and concept, that of *qi* 氣, sometimes translated as "pneuma," "vital energy," or "breath"; no English word begins to capture the range of Chinese meanings, so I leave the term untranslated. *Qi* was that by which all things—both things physical and things we would call "spiritual" in English—lived and moved and had their being. To respire and circulate *qi* was to live; to lose *qi* was to die. When it was sufficiently refined, *qi* could become *jing* 精 or "vital essence"—a process in which some of the "demonic" beings encountered in these pages were understood as being engaged. Many texts were written in early medieval times imparting instructions for cultivating, purifying, and storing *qi* as a form of self-cultivation; for an introductory discussion, see Campany, *To Live as Long as Heaven and Earth*, 18–47.

than while she had been alive. After a long while the man heard an urgent drumming sound.* At first he was unable to leave through the door, but then he pushed it open and fled. His sleeve was caught in the door as it closed behind him, but he ripped it loose and left.

A year or so later, this man died. When his family went to bury him, opening the tomb, they saw his sleeve trapped underneath the lid of her coffin.

[17]

Shi Jun of Chenliu, byname Weiming, contracted an illness. When he was near death, he told his mother, "I will come back to life. When you bury me, bury a staff vertically over my grave. If the staff is pushed out, excavate the grave." He died, and the staff was buried as he had instructed. When [his mother] went out to the tomb after seven days and looked, the staff was indeed pushed out. So they dug up the grave and extracted Jun. He reverted to exactly the way he had been before.

[18]

A woman of the Dai clan in Yuning who had long been ill once went outdoors and, noticing a small stone, said to it, "If you have divinity and can cure my illness, I will worship you." That night she dreamed of a personage who said, "I am about to bestow blessings on you." Afterward she gradually recovered. So she established a shrine for the deity, calling it the Shrine of the Stone Marquis.

[19]

Tan Sheng, at forty, had no wife. He often drew inspiration from studying his books.[6] Suddenly one night a young woman of fifteen or sixteen appeared; her looks and attire had no equal in the world. She had come to be Sheng's wife. She then warned, "I am different from other people. Do not shine a light on me. Only after three years have passed may you do so." And so they married and had a son. After two years Sheng could wait no

---

*The *Soushen ji* version specifies that this was the monk's signal for the man to return.

longer. After bedtime he snuck in, shone a light on his wife, and looked at her. From her waist up she had flesh like a normal person, but from the waist down there were only bones. His wife awoke and told him, "You have betrayed me.* I was in the process of coming to life. Why could you not have waited one more year before shining a light on me?" Sheng apologized and wept incessantly. His wife then said, "Although our relationship is forever severed, I am thinking of our son. If you are poor, you will not be able to support him. Follow me. I will give you something." Sheng followed her out. They entered a floriated chamber appointed with unusual items. She gave Sheng a pearl-stitched gown, saying, "You can use this to provide for yourselves." She then tore off Sheng's clothes and made him leave them behind as he left.

Later, Sheng took the gown to the market. Someone from the household of the prince of Weiyang gave him ten million in cash for it. The prince recognized the gown, saying, "This was my daughter's. The man must have robbed her tomb."† So Sheng was brought in and interrogated. He answered all questions truthfully. But the prince still did not believe him, so he had his daughter's tomb opened. It appeared to be intact. When they opened it, they indeed found Sheng's clothing underneath the coffin lid.‡ The child was then summoned, and he closely resembled the prince's daughter. Only then was the prince convinced. He summoned Tan Sheng, returned the gown to him, and declared him to be his head son-in-law. He also announced that Sheng's son was to be made a palace attendant.

[20]

A local inspector in northern Runan, Liu Boyi of Xiping, was very capable and clever. Once while he was on an inspection mission, he stopped for the night at Fearful-of-Troops Inn. Someone in his party said, "This inn is not to be stayed at," but Boyi spent the night there alone. After dousing the light, he recited the *Odes, Documents,* and others of the five classics and then lay down. In a little while he turned so that his head was toward the east. He

---

*The verb *fu* 負 may also mean "to support," so it is possible to read this sentence as beginning, "During the time you have supported me."

†A very common worry in this period.

‡In other words, the tomb's occupant had given Sheng her own burial gown and had retained his clothes so that she would have something to wear in the coffin.

tied a kerchief around both his feet, put his cap over them, grasped his sword, and loosened his sash.

In the darkness a strange creature made its way stealthily toward him, then suddenly leaped on top of him. Boyi jumped up. He used his sleeves to trap the sprite and his sash to tie it up. Calling for a torch, he shone light on the creature and saw that he had captured an old fox. It was red and had no fur. He took the torch and burned the fox to death with it.

The next day he opened up the upstairs room and looked inside. He saw several hundred heads of hair from victims the sprite had killed. From then on the inn was calm and peaceful.

There is an old saying: If a fox shaves the heads of a thousand people, it can become a spirit.*

[21]

During the [Wei] Zhengshi era [240–249 CE], the prince of Zhongshan, Zhou Nan, served as chief magistrate of the city of Xiang. There was a rat dressed in a gown and cap that emerged from a hole in his office [wall] and said, "Zhou Nan, you are due to die on such-and-such a day of such-and-such a month." Zhou Nan made no reply. The rat returned to the hole.

Later, when the announced day had arrived, the rat reemerged, having replaced its cap with a headcloth and wearing a red gown, and said, "Zhou Nan, you will die at noon today." Again Zhou Nan made no reply, and again the rat returned to the hole. In a little while the rat emerged to announce, "It will be today precisely at noon." The rat returned to the hole, came out again, entered again, and reappeared again several times, each time saying the same thing.

When noon arrived, the rat said, "Zhou Nan, if you make no reply, what recourse do I have?" When it had spoken these words, it fell down and died, and its gown and headdress vanished. Zhou Nan had an attendant pick it up and examine it. It was in every respect like an ordinary rat.

---

*In the background here is the prevalent belief, reflected in several other stories translated here, that fox spirits (or, perhaps more accurately, spirit foxes), so as to further their self-cultivation and empowerment, took on the forms of attractive young men or women in order to coax unsuspecting humans into having sexual relations. See Kang, *The Cult of the Fox;* and Huntington, *Alien Kind.* Foxes were not the only sorts of animals thought capable of this sort of transformation and trickery, as other stories demonstrate; see *SW,* 254–255, for further discussion. For a clearly related tale, see item 98.

Lushi yilin 陸氏異林
MR. LU'S GROVE OF MARVELS*
Apparently compiled by one of Lu Ji's 陸機 (261–303) two sons
1 extant item

[22]

Zhong Yao once failed to appear at court for several months running and did not seem himself. When someone asked him the reason, he said that an unusually comely woman had been visiting him. The inquirer said that the woman must really be a demonic creature and that Yao should kill it.

Next time the woman called on him, she stopped outside the door and would not proceed inside. Yao asked why, and she said, "You intend to kill me." Yao said "No I don't" and repeatedly coaxed her until she finally entered. He was filled with reluctance and could not bear to kill the woman, but he nevertheless stabbed her once in the thigh.[7] She fled, wiping the blood from the wound with a fresh piece of cotton cloth as she made her way along the road.

The next day Yao had someone track her. The trail led to a large grave mound. Inside it[8] was the comely woman. Her body was like that of a living person. She wore an unlined gown of white cotton, vermilion embroidered trousers, and a waistcoat. She had a wound on one of her thighs, and a cotton cloth had been inserted underneath the trousers to wipe up the blood.

My paternal uncle, the governor of Qinghe, told of this. (This refers to Lu Yun.)[†]

---

*On this work, see *LZG*, 256–257. Lu Ji was an important political and literary figure; see *CL*, 611–628.

†This final line appears as an added comment in *Sanguo zhi;* it is not quoted in *TPYL* or LX. Lu Yun (byname Shilong, 262–303) was the younger brother of Lu Ji and was appointed governor of Qinghe in 302; see *CL*, 638–644.

Luyi zhuan 錄異傳
A RECORD OF ANOMALIES*
Compiler unknown
28 extant items

[23]

During the Jian'an period [of the Eastern Han, 196–220],[†] Liu Zhao served as governor of Hejian. While he held office there, his wife died. He buried her coffin in the garden of the headquarters building. When the Yellow Turban rebellion broke out [in 184], Zhao abandoned his office and fled.

Later, after the new governor had arrived, he dreamed one night that a lady came to see him. Later she [came again and] left a pair of bracelets as a gift. The governor did not know what this sort of bracelet was called. The woman said, "These are Solomon's seal bracelets.[‡] They are linked together with gold threads so that they bend and stretch on the wearer. They are truly rare! I must soon depart, so I bid you farewell with these. Tell no one of this!"

Twenty days afterward, the son whom Liu Zhao had sent to retrieve his mother's coffin for reburial arrived. The current governor then realized the whole situation.[§] When the son saw the bracelets, he was overcome with grief.

*On this work, see *WXS*, 336; and *SW*, 94. Items 17 and 20 are translated in *CCT*, 151–153. Item 19 is translated and discussed in *SW*, 231.

†This chronology is incorrect since the Yellow Turban rebellion mentioned a few lines later broke out in 184, before the start of the Jian'an period.

‡Presumably so named because the gold threads of the bracelets resembled the rhizomes of Solomon's seal, an herb that figured in medical recipes as well as herbal methods of longevity.

§The text here has *yun yun* 云云, an elliptical expression equivalent to our "and so on and so forth," indicating that the compiler (either of *Luyi zhuan* itself or of this entry into *Taiping yulan*) has skipped some lines in quoting the text. On this sort of ellipsis and what it tells us about the ways in which texts were assembled, see Campany, *Signs from the Unseen Realm*, 23.

24

He Yu, byname Yanju, a native of Shanyin in Guiji, once fell ill and unconscious. Only a place beneath his heart remained warm. After three days he revived. He said that a functionary had taken him up into the heavens to appear before a magistrate. The magistrate's official quarters were very imposing. He ordered Yu to be taken into a secret chamber with several shelves. On the shelves were a seal and a sword.* Yu was directed to take whichever of the items he liked. He was short and could not reach the top shelf, so he took the sword [from a lower shelf] and went out. He was asked, "Which did you choose?" Yu said, "I chose the sword." The functionary replied, "What a pity you didn't choose the seal. With it you might have commanded the hundred spirits.† With the sword you may command only local earth gods."‡

After he had recovered from his illness, whenever Yu traveled about, he saw earth gods along the roadside bowing to him as if to a superior.

25

Qiu You[9] of Wucheng once died of illness. The next day he revived. He said he was taken up into the heavens to a large official hall, where he saw a man, seated, wearing a purple headcloth.[10] Someone told him that this was his ancestor Qiu Xiaobo, who was now serving as master of records, and that You should not have died yet. An escort was dispatched to take You back home. As he went out through the gate, You caught sight of his grandfather and grandmother beside a tree, each with one leg shackled. He died the following month.

A certain Wang Gengsheng was governor of Hanzhong. In his jurisdiction there was a temple to Mr. Yuan that was noted for being efficacious. Pass-

---

*It is possible that multiple seals and swords are intended.

†"The hundred spirits" here is a way of saying "a great many spirits" and does not designate a specific set of one hundred gods.

‡Each hamlet had its "earth god" (*shegong* 社公), whose jurisdiction was strictly limited to the locale in question. Such gods, nowadays more commonly called *tudi gong* 土地公, still figure importantly in popular religion.

ing by the temple on one occasion, Gengsheng made a sacrifice but accidentally left his knife behind. He sent a clerk, Li Gao, back to retrieve it. [On entering,] Gao saw the knife on the temple altar, but when he went forward to take it, he looked up and saw a lordly personage on the seat,* dressed in a high cap and a gown, his hair half white. The lord said to Gao, "You may take it and go. If you say nothing of this,† I will bless you in times to come."

Gao returned and said nothing of the matter. Afterward he continued to serve at the commandery headquarters and was eventually promoted to a governorship in his own right. By now he was over sixty and had over one hundred descendants. So [one day] he said to someone, "Long ago, when I was serving as a minor functionary under Gengsheng and was sent back to the [Yuan] temple to retrieve a knife that had been left behind, I saw the god of the temple. He told me not to speak of it. Down to today I have never dared to mention it to anyone, but I have often felt ashamed of witholding [the incident] from my superior." The moment he had spoken these words, this same knife pierced him beneath the heart, and in moments he was dead.

[27]

The magistrate of Jiaxing, Wu Shiji, once was suffering from malaria. Passing the temple at Wuchang by boat, he sent someone to beg pardon on his behalf‡ and to pray for the expulsion of the malaria-causing demon in him.§ When he had traveled on to a point some twenty *li* past the temple, just as he was dozing off, he suddenly dreamed that he saw a horseman riding up on the water behind him, seemingly with great urgency. When the rider saw Shiji, he dismounted and boarded the boat along with a subofficial functionary. They bound up a young boy and took him away.

Shiji was soon cured of malaria.

---

*"On the temple altar" translates *zai miao chuang shang* 在廟床上; in a household *chuang* would indicate a couch or bed, but I take it here to indicate a bench-like altar standing between the image of the god and approaching supplicants. "A lordly personage" translates *yi jun* 一君, and "on the seat" translates *zuo shang* 座上.

†From the ensuing text it seems that the god requested that Gao not only not mention having glimpsed him but also that he not return the knife to Wang Gengsheng.

‡Probably for not appearing in person at the temple to present offerings.

§Diseases were often attributed to the work of demons and gods; this tale is not unusual in that respect.

Jiang Yan[11] often went into Wu to gather medicinal herbs. Upon reaching the south side of Mount Qingquan in Fuchun district, he saw from afar a beautiful woman, alone, dressed in a purple gown, squatting on a stone and singing. Her voice had the timbre of stone. Yan repeatedly took several dozen steps toward her, but each time she moved away. All he saw was the stone she had squatted on.

After several days of this, Yan struck the stone and broke it open. Inside the stone he found a purple jade a foot long.[12] Afterward he saw the woman no more.

Qi Xie ji 齊諧記
QI XIE'S RECORDS*
Compiled by Dongyang Wuyi 東陽无疑 (fl. ca. 435)
15 extant items

Dong Zhaozhi of Fuyang[13] in [the state of] Wu was once crossing the Qiantang River by boat when, in midstream, he saw an ant on a short twig floating on the current. It was scurrying to and fro and clearly in fear for its life.[14] So he used a length of rope to get the twig and bring it on board the boat.† That night he dreamed that a black-clad personage thanked him, saying, "I am king among ants. I am grateful to you for your kindness in saving me. If in the future you find yourself in difficulty, you must let me know."

More than ten years passed. There was rampant banditry at the time, and Zhaozhi was wrongly arrested for being a bandit leader and was jailed at Yuyao. Suddenly he remembered his dream of the ant king. As he thought

---

*On this work, see *LZG*, 388; *WXS*, 323; and *SW*, 80–81. Item 2 is translated in *CCT*, 134–136.

†In some versions, other passengers criticize Dong for bringing the ant on board and threaten to kill it.

it over, he asked his cellmates, "The ant said that I should let him know at any time. Where could I let him know now?" One of the others in the cell said, "Just take two or three ants, place them in your palm, and make your request to them." Zhaozhi followed his advice. He dreamed that the black-clad personage told him, "You should flee quickly into the Yuhang hills. The emperor will soon issue a pardon." Zhaozhi then awoke to find that ants had chewed through his fetters, allowing him to escape the prison. He crossed the river and headed into the Yuhang hills. A pardon soon arrived, and so Zhaozhi was spared.

[30]

In the fourth year of the Jin Yixi period [408–409] there lived one Wu Daozong, a native of Taiwei district in Dongyang commandery. His father had died while Daozong was still a boy. He lived alone with his mother and had not yet married or had children. One day Daozong was away from home on business when neighbors heard a clamor coming from their house. Peering in, they did not see Daozong's mother; all they saw was a black-striped tiger inside. Everyone in the village was alarmed, fearing that a tiger had entered the house to devour the mother, so they beat the drums and assembled a party to go and rescue her. The men encircled the house, then went in to look around. They saw no sign of the tiger. Only the mother was there, and she spoke to them as if everything were normal. They did not understand why.

When Daozong returned home, his mother said to him, "I am being punished for sins in a former life. I am about to be transformed."

About a month later his mother disappeared. At the same time, tiger attacks in the district suddenly spiked. People said the animal responsible was a black-striped tiger. Parties were sent out with weapons to find it, while it meanwhile killed several more people. Someone shot it in the chest; someone else managed to spear it in the abdomen; but they were unable to capture the animal.

Several days afterward, the tiger returned to the house and lay down on the mother's bed. It was unable to return to human form. It lay down on the bed and died. Daozong wailed and wept, just as he would in mourning his mother. Morning and evening he remained beside her, weeping.

31

The regional inspector of Guangzhou returned home to conduct a funeral for a family member. His eldest son, Anji, had died of illness in the third year of the [Song] Yuanjia period [426–427]. Then in the fourth year his second son also died of illness. Someone advised him to place a rooster in the coffin. Each morning when dawn was approaching, this rooster crowed three times from within the coffin, a very piercing and sorrowful sound; it crowed no differently than if it was still in the chicken coop. Finally, after more than a month had passed, its crowing was heard no more.

32

A man named Fan Guanglu fell ill. His abdomen and legs were swollen, and he could not eat or drink. Suddenly a man showed up one fine morning and, without announcing himself, came right into Guanglu's studio and sat down beside him. Guanglu said, "I have never met you, sir. How is it that you come in without announcing yourself?" The man replied, "The Buddha sent me to cure your ailment." Guanglu removed his gown and let the man look at him. The man took out a needle and rapidly pierced all the areas where there was swelling; in all, he made over a hundred holes. He expressed around three pints of yellow pus. Then he departed.

The next day the places where Guanglu had been pierced did not hurt. He gradually recovered from the illness.

33

In Yuhang district there lived a man named Shen Cong. His home was near the mountains. One night he and his father were on the mountain when, during the third watch, they suddenly saw a person wearing a muslin cap and a thin, crimson damask gown. The man said that he was the king of Mount Dou. (Mount Dou is in Yuhang district.)

Wang Yuanzhi,[15] a native of Guanghan, served as magistrate of Xin'an. One day when he was at the district headquarters, there suddenly appeared a ghost announcing itself as surnamed Cai and named Bojie. Sometimes it would engage in learned discussion or recite poems and passages from books; it was familiar with matters both ancient and modern, and there seemed to be nothing it did not know. Someone asked it, "Are you the Cai Yong of days past?"* The ghost replied, "No! It's just that I share his surname." Someone asked, "The former Bojie, where is he now?" The reply: "He is up in the heavens, playing the role of transcendent. He is very fortunate. There has not been another like him before or since."

[35]

In the middle of the first month, a spirit descended on the home of the Chen clan and announced: "I am the goddess of silkworms. If you make offerings to me, I will multiply your worms and mulberry trees a hundredfold." This is why people today make [and offer] cakes and gruel at the end of the first month.

[36]

A demon often visited the home of Zhu Zizhi in Dongyang commandery. Zizhi's son fell ill; there was pain near his heart. The demon said, "I will seek a cure for you. It's said that a bolus of still-warm tiger flesh, if consumed, will cure this ailment. If you find me a long lance, I will secure the bolus of flesh for you." The family brought the demon a lance; the demon took it and left. After a while it returned and placed the lance in the central courtyard, then dropped the tiger bolus on the ground. It was still warm.

[37]

On Mount Guobu there is a temple with a small inn attached. Lü Si and his young wife once spent the night there. The wife vanished. Si went looking for her and came across a great city with a court chamber and a man in a muslin cap leaning on a desk. The man's attendants moved forward to strike Si, so he drew his sword and fought them off. He killed over a

---

*Cai Yong (132–192), byname Bojie, was "a poet, calligrapher, and musician noted for his filial devotion to [his] ailing mother" (SSHY, 577–578). See also CL, 60–69.

hundred of them; the rest fled. He saw that all the men he had just killed had become foxes. What had earlier seemed to be a court chamber was actually a large, ancient tomb. The tomb was broken open at the top so that the interior was brightly lit. He saw a group of women in the tomb, and among them he saw his wife, looking as if she had lost her wits. Si grabbed her and went out through the opening in the tomb. He then re-entered the tomb and pulled out the other women. There were several dozen of them. Some among them had already grown hair all over their bodies; others had hairy legs and faces and had [partially?] become foxes.

In a little while it was dawn. He returned to the inn with his wife. The innkeeper asked what had happened; Si told him the whole story. There had been a string of cases of women and children gone missing in the area, leaving several dozen people abandoned and bereft. A local functionary arranged to have members of these bereft [families] brought to the mouth of the tomb to reclaim and welcome home their missing, no matter how far away they lived.

Within a year or two, the temple was no longer efficacious.*

Shen lu 神錄 (alternate title: Shenyi lu 神異錄)
RECORDS OF SPIRIT MATTERS†
Compiled by Liu Zhilin 劉之遴 (477–548)
3 extant items

[38]

During Qin times, what is now Youquan district was known as Changshui district. During the reign of the First Emperor of Qin, there was a children's song in the district that went:

When there is blood on the city gate
The city will sink to form a lake.

---

*The implication is that the temple to which the inn was attached had in fact been inhabited all along by these spirit foxes, not by a proper god.

†On this work and its compiler, see *LZG*, 424; *WXS*, 329; and *SW*, 88–89.

Now there was an old woman who, hearing this, became troubled and fearful. Every morning she would go to look at the city gate. The gatekeeper wanted to detain her, so the old woman explained the reason for her action. After she left, the gatekeeper slaughtered a dog and smeared its blood on the gate. The next time she went, she saw the blood and at once hurried away, not daring to look back. Suddenly there were floodwaters high enough to submerge the whole district. The assistant magistrate, whose name was Gan, went in to report this to the magistrate. When the magistrate saw Gan, he exclaimed, "Why are you suddenly acting like a fish?" Gan replied, "You are also acting like a fish, sir!"* And so the place sank down to become a lake.†

The old woman led her dog sixty *li* north until they arrived at Yilai Mountain, and so they escaped. On the southwest corner [of the mountain] there is today a cave known as Temple of the Divine Mother. On the stone in front of the temple there still exist dog tracks.

[39]

In Guangling district there lived a woman named Du Mei who possessed Daoist arts. The district magistrate, taking her to be a demon, had her placed in shackles. But suddenly she changed form, and no one knew where she had gone. So on that same spot they erected a temple for her, called Dongling. Worshippers referred to her as Divine Mother.‡

---

*This seems to mean that the people in the city were all transformed into fishes; these two local officers were the first signs of transformation.

†LX has "valley"; I have emended by reference to the *Soushen ji* version, which ends at this point. This was a recurrent story type in early medieval times; see Kaltenmark, "La légende de la ville immergée en Chine."

‡For more on this divine figure, see Campany, *To Live as Long as Heaven and Earth*, 146–147, 393–394.

Shenguai zhi 神怪志
(possible alternate title: *Shenguai lu* 神怪錄)
ACCOUNTS OF SPIRITS AND ANOMALIES*
Compiler unknown
2 extant items

[40]

General Wang Guo earlier [in his career] had served as governor of Yizhou. As he was passing through the Three Gorges,† he saw from the deck of his boat an object hanging halfway down a ten-thousand-foot rock cliff on one side of the river. It appeared to be a coffin. He ordered someone to scale the cliff, and on close inspection it turned out indeed to be a coffin. They opened it and found an intact skeleton inside. There was also a stone inscription inside that read:

> Three hundred years from now, water will set me adrift.
> I will course along the river, and I might fall.
> Whether I fall or do not fall depends on Wang Guo.

When Guo read the inscription, he was shocked, commenting, "If this person knew my name hundreds of years ago, how can I abandon him and leave?" So he stayed to supervise a funeral and burial and set out offerings. Only then did he continue his journey.

---

*On this work, see *LZG*, 469; and *SW*, 97.
†Three famous narrow points on the Jiang River, up which one had to travel to enter what is now Sichuan from points east.

Shengui zhuan 神鬼傳
RECORDS OF GODS AND GHOSTS*
Compiler and date unknown
8 extant items

[41]

Ziying Chun was a native of Shuxiang. He was a skilled diver. He once caught a red carp. Enamored of its color, he took it home and raised it in a pond, regularly feeding it rice and other grains. After a year it had grown to be over eight feet long. Then it grew horns and wings. At this, Ziying became frightened. He made obeisance and apologized to the creature. But the fish said, "I have come to welcome you. Climb on my back and we will ascend together." Each new year Ziying would return to visit his wife and children, and then the fish would once again come to take him back up. This is why people in the region of Wu make offerings to the divine fish and Ziying at the doorways of their homes.

[42]

Below the dam at Qu'e there is a temple. During the time of the Jin emperor Xiaowu [r. 373–397], there was a bandit fugitive who, pursued by ten officers, entered the temple, knelt, and prayed to be rescued, promising in that event to offer up a pig to the god. He thereupon suddenly found himself under the dais[†] without being aware of how he got there. When his pursuers arrived, they looked but could not see him, even though all had

---

*Eight stories are cited from a text of this title (which may possibly function there more as a generic label than as the title of a specific work) in *TPGJ*. Besides the two translated here, they are *TPGJ* 100.8, 142.3, 293.10 (another version of which is attributed in *TPYL* 710.11a–b to *Shenyi ji* 神異記 and translated as item 43), 382.3, 468.2, and 471.6. Li Jianguo (*LZG*, 437) suggests that *Shengui zhuan* may be an alternate title for *Guishen lu* 鬼神錄, a Sui-period collection by the pro-Buddhist polemicist Shi Yancong 釋彥琮. In *SW*, 92, I accepted this hypothesis, but I now think that this is unlikely. All dates and rulers mentioned in the eight extant items predate the Sui. LX does not collect items from this text.

†Translating *chuang xia* 牀下. I am assuming a raised platform holding the seat on which the image of the god rested.

seen him enter the temple and there was no other way out. So they, too, made a request, saying that if they caught the bandit, they would offer up a large bull. Soon the bandit's form became visible again. The officials bound him and started to lead him away. The bandit cried, "Your divine efficacy has been demonstrated in excess! How is it that there is any difference between a pig and a bull, that you would go against the blessing you first bestowed?" No sooner had the words left his mouth than he became aware that the color of the face* of the god's image had changed. When they went out the temple gate, a large tiger came toward them, its mouth wide open, and seized the bandit, carrying him off.

Shenyi ji 神異記
RECORDS OF SPIRIT ANOMALIES[†]
Compiled by Wang Fou 王浮 (fl. ca. 300)
7 extant items

[43]

Chen Min was appointed to serve as governor of Jiangxia during the time of Sun Hao [r. 264–280]. He set out from Jianye to take up his post. Having heard that the temple at Lake Gongting was especially efficacious, he went there, praying that everything be calm and settled during his tenure in office and promising that if it was, he would offer the god a silver ingot. When his term was completed, he had an ingot made, planning to return to the temple with it. He had a piece of iron worked into the shape of an ingot, then added a silver coating. Seeking appointment as senior recorder,[‡] he presented the ingot in the temple, made his prayer request, and continued on his way.

Toward day's end, the god proclaimed through a spirit medium: "Chen Min promised me a silver ingot. Today I received from him an ingot that

---

*This phrase (*shenxiang mianse* 神像面色) can also be interpreted as meaning that the expression on the image's face changed.

[†]On this work, see *WXS*, 317; and *SW*, 53. Wang Fou, a Daoist priest, is remembered primarily for having written the anti-Buddhist *Huahu jing* 化胡經 or *Scripture on the Conversion of the Barbarians*.

[‡]An alternate interpretation of this title is cavalier attendant-in-ordinary.

was merely plated with silver. I will throw it into the water to return it to him. This sin of cheating and slighting cannot be tolerated." With this, [the medium] picked up the ingot, inspected it, and broke it open to reveal the iron within. He then threw it into the water. It floated along the surface as swiftly as if it were flying. When it reached Min's boat, the boat capsized.

[44]

Yu Hong of Yuyao went into the mountains to pick tea leaves. He encountered a Daoist master leading three black goats to drink from a pool under a waterfall.[16] The master said, "I am Master Cinnabar Mound. I hear you are a connoisseur of tea and cherish it as a gift from above. On this mountain there is a superb variety of tea to be found. I will give it to you. I only ask that, whenever you have even a single bowlful of it left over, you leave it out for me."

So Yu Hong built a tea shrine. Afterward he often went with others into this mountain to pick the superb tea there.

Shenyi jing 神異經
CLASSIC OF DIVINE MARVELS
Traditionally attributed to Dongfang Shuo 東方朔 (fl. 100–73 BCE),
with a commentary attributed to Zhang Hua 張華 (232–300)*
57 extant items plus 10 or so fragments

[45]

To the southeast there is a personage who travels everywhere under heaven. His body is seven poles tall, and he is as big around as he is tall. On his head he wears a rooster-shaped exorcist head. He wears a crimson gown

---

*The commentary, whoever authored it, has become intermixed in many places with the text—a common occurrence in texts from this period. Passages I have placed in parentheses are commentarial additions reflected in some sources. On this text, see *WXS*, 307; *LZG*, 151–152; Zhou Ciji, *Shenyi jing yanjiu*; Wang Guoliang, *Liuchao zhiguai xiaoshuo kaolun*, 71–112; and *SW*, 43–45, 280–282. A fragment from it is translated in *SW*, 282.

with a white sash. Vermilion-colored snakes encircle his neck, their heads and tails joined. He neither drinks nor eats [ordinary comestibles]; rather, each morning he swallows three thousand noxious demons and each evening three hundred of them. He takes demons as his food and dew as his drink. One name for him is Chiguo; another is Demon-Eater (Daoist masters say that this is because he devours noxious demons); another is Vermilion-and-Yellow Father. Today there is a Yellow Father demon.

[46]

Beyond the sea to the northwest is a personage two thousand *li* tall, his feet a thousand *li* apart, his torso 1,600 *li* around. Each sunrise he drinks five pecks of celestial wine ("celestial wine" being sweet dew). He eats neither the five grains nor fish nor meat but only drinks celestial wine. Whenever he develops a sudden hunger, he simply lifts his head heavenward and drinks. He is fond of roaming about the mountains and seas. He does not harm people, nor does he interfere with the ten thousand creatures. He was born together with heaven and earth. He is named No-Roads Man (he is called No-Roads because he is too tall and wide for any road to accommodate him). Another of his names is the Benevolent (the *Rites* speaks of "the benevolent man"); another is the Dependable (the *Rites* speaks of "the dependable man"[17]); another is the Numinous.

Shuyi ji 述異記
RECORDS OF STRANGE THINGS*
Compiled by Zu Chongzhi 祖沖之 (429–500)
90 extant items

[47]

In southern Nankang commandery there is Mount Dongwang. Three en-camped[†] men once climbed it. At its summit they saw that there was a clear and deep lake, as well as a grove of fruit trees about four *li* in circumference. The trees had clearly all been planted there, for there were no other varieties of trees among them and they were lined up in rows as if by human labor. The fruits were at their perfect point of ripeness, so the three men all ate some. When they had eaten their fill, they packed up two more to take away, as they wanted to show them to others. Then they set out for home.

The men looked for the path they had taken, but they went in circles for half a day, became lost, and could not find the way back. At that moment they heard a voice in midair say, "Put down the two fruits, and I will let you go." The men were terrified and dropped the fruits on the ground. Looking around, they then saw the path home, and so they returned.

[48]

In Yudu district in Nankang, a river emerges and flows westward.[‡] Three *li* from the district [there is a place] called Mengkou. There is a cave there,

---

*On this work, see *LZG*, 390–396; *WXS*, 327–328; and *SW*, 83–84. Items 37, 38, and 82 are trans-lated in *CCT*, 154–158; items 49 and 56 in Campany, "Return-from-Death Narratives," 97–99; and item 81 in Campany, "Ghosts Matter," 30.

[†]Here and in item 83, this expression translates *yingmin* 營民 or *yinghu* 營戶. These terms refer to dispossessed families or individuals, often refugees from defeated states, who were detained to work on the lands of their captors. It was a status only slightly above that of slave. See *Hanyu daci-dian* 7.266a, 267a.

[‡]The versions vary about the direction in which the river flows; some name the river and some do not.

shaped like a stone room, and it is called Mengkou Cave. A legend has been passed down that there was once a divine chicken the color of fine gold that would emerge from the cave, flap its wings, and emit a long cry. Whenever people heard the sound and went looking, the chicken would always fly back into the cave. So the rock there came to be called Golden Chicken Rock.

Once there was a man plowing beside this mountain. From a distance he saw the chicken emerge from the cave and begin to amuse itself. Then a tall man appeared and shot at it with a crossbow. The chicken, seeing this from a distance, flew back into the cave. The crossbow bolt went into the cave and traveled around six feet;* after that the cave continued downward through a crack, but it was not wide enough to permit a person to pass through.

On another occasion there was a man traveling the river by boat. When he was still several *li* from this place, he saw a figure standing on the bank, completely clad in yellow and carrying two baskets of yellow melons, asking him for a ride. So the boatman took him on board. The man in yellow asked for something to eat; the boatman gave him a plate of food and some wine. When the man had finished, they reached the shore beneath the cave. The boatman asked for one of the melons [as payment], but the man in yellow refused. He only spat onto the plate, went ashore, and disappeared straight into the cave. At first the boatman was incensed, but, upon seeing the man enter the cave, he began to suspect that something numinous and strange was afoot. When he picked up the plate, he saw that the spittle on it had all turned to gold.

[49]

In western Zhang'an district there is Red Wall Mountain. It is thirty *li* around. One of its peaks is especially tall, perhaps over three hundred poles high. During the Taiyuan period of the Jin [376–397], a foreign monk[18] named Bai Daoyou lived on this mountain. The mountain god repeatedly sent wolves, strange forms, and odd noises against him to try to frighten him, but Daoyou remained unmoved. Thereupon the mountain god went to call on him, saying, "The Dharma master's† virtue is imposing indeed!

---

*One surmises that the bolt was attached to a line for retrieval—a common practice.
†A respectful way of addressing a Buddhist monk.

I now cede this mountain to you. Your disciple will divine another place to go and live." Daoyou said, "What god are you? How long have you resided here? If you must go now, where will you go?" The god replied, "Your disciple was the son of a prince of the Xia royal house. I have resided here for over a thousand years. I have a relative who dwells on Hanshi Mountain. I will go and stay there for a while. In the future I hope to be able to return to the temple at Guiji Mountain."

As he was about to depart, the god sent a letter and three cases of incense. He also came personally to say farewell, clasping his hands together as if in regret. With a cry and a crack of his whip he mounted upward into the air and departed.

[50]

When Huan Chong served as regional inspector in Jiangzhou, he dispatched a party of men to explore Mount Lu and observe its numinous wonders. They reached a lofty peak where they found a lake. Around the lake grew mulberry trees. There was a large flock of white geese there, and in the lake was the wreck of a skiff and a type of fish with vermilion scales. The envoys were extremely thirsty and wanted to drink from the lake, but when they approached it, the vermilion-scaled fish flared their dorsal fins toward them, so they did not dare to drink.

[51]

In the Jin Yixi period [405–418], there lived a certain Liu Dun in Jiangling. A ghost suddenly took up residence in his home. Dun was poor and had no stove in the home; he would cook food in a makeshift canister. Each time he did so, however, the canister would disappear. He would find it outside near the fence, emptied of food. So Dun secretly went to the market, bought some kudzu, cooked it down, and mixed it with some rice gruel. The ghost stole this too. Dun found the canister on the north side of his house. He could hear the sound of someone vomiting.*

Thereafter the disturbances stopped and things were quiet.

---

*At this writing I am not aware of any nausea-inducing effects attributed to kudzu (ge 葛), but the plant (probably specifically its root), perhaps in very concentrated form, clearly had a deleterious effect on this ghost. Perhaps it had apotropaic properties.

When he was young, Qin Zhoufang was once traveling up the Jiang River with merchants. They stopped for the night below the Gongting [Lake] temple. The men said to one another, "Which of us can enter the temple and spend the night there?" Zhoufang was bold by nature and so decided to do it. So he went into the temple and passed the night there. Nothing happened.

Next morning there appeared in the temple a white-haired old man. Zhoufang caught him, whereupon he metamorphosed into a male duck. Zhoufang returned to the boat clutching the creature and intending to cook it, but it flew off. Nothing else untoward happened.

Zhang Jun was ill. He dreamed that he went out on a sightseeing excursion to a place he did not recognize. A sweet spring came bubbling up from the ground, and he saw a dark-colored turtle. The turtle opened its mouth toward Jun and spoke, saying: "Nine days from now, you will receive some very good news." Then he suddenly awoke.

He wrote a record of the dream and sealed it inside a tube. No one else knew of it. From then on he was bedridden with his illness, and nine days afterward he died.

During the Song Yuanjia period [424–453], in Zhongdu village of Wu district there lived Shi Xuandu and his family. They had a yellow dog that gave birth to a white male puppy. The mother loved this puppy more than usual for dogs. She would carry food in her mouth to feed the youngster. The puppy grew up. Each time he would go out hunting, the mother dog would always wait outside the door, watching for him till he returned.

Now Xuandu had long had trouble breathing and had a bad cough. These conditions took a turn for the worse and became serious. His doctor advised him to make a broth that required the lungs of a white dog as an ingredient. He was unable to obtain this in the market, so he slaughtered the white dog they had raised so that he could make the broth. The mother dog jumped and bayed around the place where her son had been killed. For an entire day without stopping she threw herself on the ground there and then got up again, over and over. The family cooked the dog meat and served it to guests, who threw the bones on the floor. The mother dog gathered these and placed them in an urn. When they had finished eating, the mother dog went outside into the back courtyard, dug a hole beneath a large mulberry tree, and buried the urn there. Each day she would face the tree and whine, stopping only after more than a month had passed.

Xuandu's condition gradually worsened. When he was near death, he said repeatedly, "The broth didn't cure my illness. I regret having slaughtered that dog." His younger brother, Fadu, from then on ate no more dog meat for the rest of his life.

[55]

Early in the Yuanjia period of the Song [424–453], a man from Fuyang surnamed Wang set a crab trap in a mostly dried-up stream bed. When he went to check it in the morning, he found a piece of wood about two feet long in the trap. The trap was broken open, and all the crabs had escaped. So he repaired the trap and put the piece of wood up on the bank. When he went to look the next day, the piece of wood was back inside the trap, and the trap was broken open as before. Again Wang repaired the trap and removed the piece of wood. Next morning he found things the same way again. Wang suspected that the piece of wood must have something demonic and strange about it. So he picked up the crab pail, shouldered it, and started home, saying, "When I get home, I'm going to cut up [the piece of wood] and burn it." When he was still three *li* from home, he heard something stirring in the pail. When he looked, he saw that the piece of wood had morphed into a creature with a human head, a simian body, one arm, and one leg. It spoke to Wang, saying, "By nature I love to eat crabs. On these days all that happened was that I went into the water, entered your trap to eat crabs, and was captured. I hope you will forgive me and let me out of this pail. I am a mountain spirit and I will help you. I'll even see to it that you catch a lot of crabs in your trap." Wang replied, "The times when you have harmed people are many. By rights you ought to die for your crimes." The creature begged incessantly for its life. Wang turned his head away and made no response. The creature then asked, "What is your surname and given name? I'd like to know." It asked this repeatedly. Wang still made no reply. When they neared Wang's home, the creature said, "Since you won't let me go and won't tell me your names, what recourse do I have? I guess I'll just have to die." When Wang reached home, he lit a fire and burned the creature. Afterward things were quiet, with no further anomalies.

The common folk call these creatures mountain sprites.* It is said that if they know your names, they can do you harm. This is why it so persistently asked Wang his names, and it explains how he escaped harm.

[56]

During the Yuanjia period of the Song [424–453], Huang Miao, a native of Pinggu in Nankang, was serving as a subofficial functionary at the prefecture level. He was late returning from a leave of duty. Soon after he started on his way back to his post, he passed by Lake Gongting. He went into the temple there to pray that he might avoid punishment and return home safely. He promised that if his prayer was granted, he would offer up a pig and some wine. When Miao returned to his post, all went as he had hoped, so he returned home. Because his provisions were meager, he did not pass by the temple. He went only as far as the boundary of its precincts and then put down anchor and slept on the boat with his traveling companions.

In the middle of the night the boat started moving with the current as rapidly as the wind. By the fourth watch Miao had reached Gongting and was awakened. He saw three men on the boat, all dressed in black and holding ropes. They tied him up and while it was still night went into the main hall of the temple. Miao saw the god, who appeared to be about forty years of age, with a yellow face[19] and an open-collar brocade gown. From the ceiling beam overhead hung a pearl the size of a crossbow pellet; the light from it illuminated the room. One person reported from outside the door: "Huang Miao of Pinggu. He vowed to provide a pig and wine. He tried to escape back home. You ordered him apprehended. Here he is." He was found guilty and sentenced to serve three years and seize thirty persons.

A functionary was dispatched to escort Miao to a desolate area in a mountain forest, where he was shackled around the waist and tied to a tree. Each day he was fed raw meat. Gradually his thoughts grew depressed, and

---

*Mountain sprites or *shanxiao* 山魈, familiar denizens of the world of Chinese demonology, are discussed in the *Dinggui* 訂鬼 chapter of Wang Chong's *Lunheng* 論衡 and in a great many texts in the Daoist canon.

he was aware only of whether he was hot or cold or had any sores on his skin. His whole body started to grow striped fur, and after a week he was covered in it; he grew claws and fangs as well. His temperament grew more combative and ravenous, so the functionary undid the shackles and released him, following his movements. After three years he had seized twenty-nine persons. Next he was due to seize a girl from Xinyi. But this girl belonged to an aristocratic family. At first she never came outdoors. Then she came out the back gate with her female relatives to pay a call on another family member. Since the girl was following along last, he was able to seize her. Because this girl had been so hard to capture, he had now served five years. His quota of persons having been filled, the functionary took him back to the temple. The god ordered him released and sent back. He was now fed cooked food and rice. The fur on his body gradually fell out, and his own head and facial hair returned. The claws and fangs also fell out, and he grew new [nails and teeth]. After fifteen days he was back in human form. His thoughts returned to normal. He was taken out to a main road [and released].

The district magistrate called Miao in to relate the matter in detail. Note was made of every person he had seized, and when inquiries were made of those families, the information tallied perfectly.

[During his arrest] Miao had been injured on his buttocks by a spear. He still bore the scars from that.

Miao was back home for eight years before he died of illness at a ripe old age.

[57]

Yu Jisui was of sturdy build and had great physical strength. During the Song Yuanjia period [424–453], he contracted an illness and was lying down to rest one day when a white vapor like a cloud, perhaps five feet tall, appeared in his room. In a moment it metamorphosed into a rooster and alighted on another bed. Jisui chopped at it. There was a sound as his hand hit something; the form of the thing vanished, but blood was splattered on the floor. He then heard the sound of an old Man* woman wailing, calling out only "My son!" The sound came from far off and drew closer and closer

---

*The Man 蠻 people were an ethnic group in southern regions.

until it stopped at the bloody spot. Jisui again chopped with his hand. A creature resembling a monkey fled out the door, turned and glared angrily at him, and then disappeared.

Late that same afternoon two blue-clad youths came straight in through the gate and called out, "Yu Jisui has killed an official!" Soon over a hundred other people, some dressed in black, some in red, reached his door and called out in unison, "Yu Jisui has killed an official!" Jisui brandished his sword and yelled at them. All the demons ran outside and then vanished. As he walked backward,* Jisui suddenly found himself on the grounds of a Buddhist temple, and his son [who had followed him] suddenly lost track of where his father was. When the son reached the temple, he saw his father being pursued from behind by a demon. The demon caught his father's breath in a leather bag. Within several days Jisui was dead.

[58]

Deng Deming of Nankang was once in Yuzhang to study with Lei Cizong.[†] Lei's home was out beyond the eastern edge of the town, half a *li* past the tomb of the Scribe of Yuzhang.[‡] In Yuanjia 14 [437–438], Deming was strolling under the moonlight with a group of other students when they suddenly heard the sound of instrumental and vocal music. That same night they went to Lei to tell him of it, and he went out to hear it for himself, saying, "That place is far from any human habitation. The music must be that of ghosts or spirits." So he went together with them to seek the source of the sound. As they approached the tomb, they could hear sounds of wind and string instruments, singing girls, speaking, and chanting coming from beneath the grave mound. All of them sighed in wonder at it.

---

*Huanbu 還步 here seems to mean not simply that the man was "retracing his steps" but was also walking backward as he did so. Judging from scattered mentions of the term in the Daoist canon, it seems to have been an apotropaic practice.

†Lei Cizong was a noted Buddhist layman who was part of the circle of devotees who formed around the monk Huiyuan on Mount Lu in what is now Jiangxi province. See Zürcher, *The Buddhist Conquest of China*, 218.

‡*Shi* 史 can function as a surname, but Yuzhang is a place name and is indeed where this episode is set. Either this is a sobriquet for some locally well-known individual with a prominent tomb (but this name shows up nowhere else I am aware of), or some words have dropped out of the text here, and without other versions to compare to this one, it is hard to know which is the case.

During the twenty-fourth year of the Song Yuanjia era [447–448], Bo Shaozhi was serving as adjutant in charge of supplies and was temporarily lodging in the western guest quarters of the eastern administrative seat.[20] He was in the unit next to that of Zu Fakai. Fakai's mother, née Liu, had been bedridden with illness for several weeks and had then died on the first day of the fifth month of the twenty-second year [of Yuanjia]. Starting the next day, Shaozhi saw a group of rats, the largest of which were as big as piglets, shiny and five-colored, others of which were single-colored, or multicolored, or wearing pillbox hats* or dragon heads. There were over a hundred of them, and they were present every day and night. By dusk on the nineteenth day a white rat about two feet long appeared on the eaves of his inner room. It ran underneath the wall, and at the point where it had entered a fire broke out. Although Shaozhi doused it with water, the fire would not go out until finally, after a long time, it burned out on its own. That night he saw a strong man, red in color, his body glowing like fire-light, emerge from the burned wall, pass beneath his bed, and exit again through the wall. Although there was a wall there, the light at that time was so penetrating and bright that Shaozhi could perceive no division between his room and the next. At the fourth watch that same night, four other personages appeared. Some of them said that they were there to protect Shaozhi, while others glared and stuck out their tongues. They remained from dusk to dawn. The following night there was again a fire in the room, and then two men, each some nine feet tall, arrived on horseback bearing bows and arrows. They were attended by several dozen retainers who addressed them as "general." Shaozhi asked, "Where are you going?" The reply was, "We were sent to bring back the sick person to the east of you."

On the twenty-first day the whole crowd returned. The family† had a white dog. Ever since the spirit disturbances had begun, the dog would disappear every night at dusk and return home only at dawn. On this night

---

*Here and throughout, I render *pingshang ze* 平上幘 (or simply *ze* 幘) as pillbox hat or cap. These were tight-fitting caps, often lower in front and higher in the back. For a brief discussion and illustration, see Dien, *Six Dynasties Civilization*, 313. Item 65 contains a clue about why they are so often mentioned in these tales.

†It is not entirely clear from the wording whether the family mentioned here is that of Bo Shaozhi or that of Zu Fakai, his neighbor. I surmise that Zu's family is the one meant.

they tried tying the dog up. In a little while a young woman came and said, "Do not tie up this dog. We would like to ask for it." The family replied, "Then we hereby present it to you." They handed her the rope, not daring to untie the dog, and she led it away. The dog let out a yelp and lay down to die, unable to move for the rest of the day.

Then a man wearing a brocade cloak appeared; he was drawing his bow and pointing his arrow directly at Shaozhi. Shaozhi told him, "You are a demon. How dare you frighten people? I do not fear you. If you do not leave quickly, I will command gods of the great Dao to come at once and arrest you!" The demon unstrung his bow, quivered his arrow, whipped his horse, and galloped off.

[60]

Cao Zongzhi, a native of Gaoping, in the twenty-fifth year of the Yuanjia period [of the Song, 448–449] was in Pengcheng when he lay down to sleep one night and was dead by morning. By late in the afternoon of the same day he had started breathing again. He spoke of what he had seen: A man in a singlet and a pillbox cap, holding a tablet, announced himself as an envoy of the king of Beihai and informed him that he was being summoned to the palace. Zongzhi followed the envoy there. In the central hall there were airy clouds several dozen feet above the floor, billowing about. Among the curtains and screens a purple smoke wafted; whenever a breeze blew it toward them, an extraordinary fragrance could be detected. The envoy said, "Wait here. I will go in and announce you." In a little while he returned to transmit a directive that said: "Our apologies to you, Lord Cao. Your service and ability, sir, are estimable indeed, and we have long admired you. We would like to trouble you to serve as an assistant on our staff. How old are you, sir, and have you ever served as an escort carriage rider?" Zongzhi replied, "My capabilities are plain and feeble. I am unworthy of your sagely favor. This year I am thirty-one. I have never served as escort carriage rider." Another directive was issued: "Although your year counts are yet few, sir, you have a prior store of good fortune.* It is appro-

---

*This good fortune could be the result of his own karma from previous lives or of merit accumulated by his ancestors. "Year counts" translates *suan* 算. Each individual was thought to be destined by default to live a certain length of time, measured in "counts" and adding up to his or her *ming* 命 or allotted life span. The number of counts could be raised by certain means or lowered on

priate that you receive recognition for this, and you will serve as escort carriage rider. For now, we say farewell. You may return home for a while. We will speak again at a later time." The same envoy as before then escorted him back out through the palace gate. Suddenly he woke up.

Zongzhi later served in Guangzhou. He was forty-seven at that time. The following year he was returning to his post there after a leave of absence when he fell ill and died.

[61]

During the Song [420–479], Hu Bizhi,[21] a native of Yuzhang, once served as an aide in Wuchang commandery. As soon as he took up his post, in the twenty-sixth year of the Song Yuanjia period [449], there began to be ghostly disturbances. In the middle of the night on moonlit nights, if he left the door to his chamber open slightly, there would be a person resembling a little child standing there outside the door. If the door was closed, he would hear the sound of someone wearing wooden clogs walking; if he looked, he would see no one there. This happened many times. In the third month of the twenty-eight year [451] his entire household fell ill. Voices were heard in the air, and tiles and stones were thrown, or sometimes dirt. By midsummer those who were ill were all worse, and the voices and throwing of objects grew more severe. So they invited [Buddhist] monks to perform abstinence services there, chanting scriptures through the night.* The voices and thrown objects now came like rain, but they did not touch the monks or their rolls of scriptures. By fall and winter there gradually came [new] sounds. When the tiles or stones hit someone [in the household], they would leave a black mark on the flesh, but they did not cause much pain.

In his household Bizhi had an old nanny who loved to curse and swear. Whenever the ghost was beside her, it would grow very angry [at this]. Bizhi invited a [Daoist] libationer† to send up a petition and deploy talismans to

---

account of certain factors; also, certain esoteric techniques allowed practitioners to bypass this entire life-span-enforcement system. These ideas are referred to in several of the stories here; in 142, an unusual tale, the protagonist's life span is even pictured as a physical object. For details on how the system and the esoteric techniques worked, see Campany, *To Live as Long as Heaven and Earth*, 47–60; and Campany, "Living Off the Books."

*On this sort of abstinence service or *zhai* 齋, see the note to item 4.
†That is, an ordained Daoist priest in the Celestial Master hierarchy.

drive the ghost off.* The disturbances gradually tapered off. But in the twenty-ninth year the ghost returned, and the disturbances were worse than before. The following year [Bizhi] was [still] in office as aide when wild-fires broke out everywhere in the area, putting a strain on the water supply. Each time the ghost made a noise like that of a dog, family members would call it to come and eat; afterward it would suddenly speak in what sounded like Wu dialect.[22]

[One night] at the third watch there came a knock at the door. Bizhi asked who it was. The reply: "It's Cheng Shaoling." Bizhi stepped out with a candle but saw nothing. Several nights later there was knocking on the door at the second watch. Bizhi cursed at it, but there came a reply: "Do not curse me, sir. I am a spirit of goodness,[†] not the spirit who came previously. Censor Tao sent me to repay you." Bizhi said, "I do not know a Censor Tao." The ghost[‡] said, "Tao Jingxuan. You used to know him." Bizhi said, "I was with him in the capital and we served together in Hengyang. But he was never a censor." The ghost said, "Tao now dwells in a domain of the fortunate.[§] He is serving as censor in the heavens above. The attacks on your family were the doing of Sire Shen. This office was once Shen's residence. So he came back here to see the place. Then he began talking and throwing things simply to amuse himself. But you responded excessively, permitting your nanny to curse and behave rudely and having the libationer send up the petition to bring charges against him, so that the matter reached the celestial bureaus. Shen has now appealed to Heaven, saying that you are a Buddhist disciple who has taken the triple refuge; why then did you not ask for blessings on his behalf, as Buddhists do, but instead have a libationer file a petition? It is his wish that from now on you will focus solely on upholding the Dharma so that you do not become entangled in any difficulties with noxious ghosts."

Bizhi then invited nuns[23] to recite sutras, perform an abstinence cere-mony, and offer prayers. The next night he heard a voice outside his door again, saying, "The censor sends his greetings and wishes you to know that Shen has filed a serious grievance against you. According to what it says,

---

*These are typical Daoist responses to such a situation. The petition (*zhang* 章) was a written and visualized request to the gods on high, and the talismans (*fu* 符) were divinely authorized apotropaic commands.

†On these spirits, termed *shanshen* 善神, see Campany, *Signs from the Unseen Realm*, 54, 161–162, 187–188, 210, 220.

‡*Sic;* the being is here unexpectedly referred to as a *gui* 鬼.

§On the "domain of the fortunate" or *fudi* 福地, see Campany, *Signs from the Unseen Realm*, 182.

you were a bit out of bounds, sir. If you can take refuge in sincerity and right awakening, reciting sutras and keeping the precepts, then all these disturbances will cease. Thinking with affection of your past times together, he wishes to report this to you."

[62]

Suo Wanxing, a native of Dunhuang, was sitting during daylight hours one day in the eastern studio of his [government] office when one of his slaves suddenly saw a personage. He was wearing a pillbox cap and leading a black horse, and he entered directly through the gate. On the back of the horse was an object resembling a cushion covered in black skin. The person set the object on the brick floor and then led the horse back out through the gate. The cushion then began rolling and went straight into the studio. When it reached the base of the couch, it climbed up and stopped in front of Wanxing's knees. The skin covering then unfolded open on all sides, revealing that it was lined completely with eyes that moved and winked in a revolting way. After a long while the cushion folded itself back up and rolled down off the couch and back out onto the brick floor and then left toward the west. Wanxing ordered the slave to follow it, but when it reached the eastern end of the office, it vanished.

Wanxing found it revolting. He consequently fell ill and died.

[63]

Guo Xiuzhi resided in Hailing. In the twenty-ninth year of the Song Yuanjia period [452], he was seventy-two, ill, and confined to his home. On the north side of his residence there was a large date tree, about four poles tall.

One morning at daybreak a maid in the household rose, opened the doors, and was sweeping when she saw a man in the date tree. He was decked out in black, including a black turban and gown. In his hands he held a bow and arrow. He stood facing due south. The whole family went out to look at him; they could see him quite clearly. Xiuzhi then made his way out to look, supported by a cane. The man said to him: "I came to summon you, sir. Make haste to prepare yourself." By the time the sun had fully risen, he was no more to be seen.

This went on for fifty-three days. Once Xiuzhi died, the appearances stopped.

In the jurisdiction of Huangzhou there is the Yellow Father demon. Whenever it appears, it causes hauntings. The gowns and skirts it wears are all yellow. When it approaches people, opens its mouth wide, and laughs, they never fail to break out in sores, whether for longer or shorter periods. It appears in a body of varying height but usually no taller than a fencerow. It had not appeared for over a decade, but the people of the region were still terrified of it.

Guo Qingzhi of Luling had a slave girl named Caiwei born into his household. She was young and beautiful. During the Xiaojian period of the Song [454–457], there suddenly appeared a personage claiming to be a mountain spirit. His body was naked and over eight feet tall. His arms and chest[24] were yellow, his skin and face were clean, and his speech and voice were standard. The people of the region called him the Yellow Father demon. He had come in order to have relations with this slave girl. She said that his thoughts and conduct were like those of a human being. The demon came many times but often hid his body in doing so. But sometimes he would inadvertently let his form be seen, and it changed without apparent rhyme or reason: now large, now small; now resembling smoke, now stone; sometimes appearing as a small child, sometimes as a woman, sometimes as a bird or beast but with human-like feet around two feet long, sometimes leaving what looked like goose tracks. His hands were as big as plates. Whether coming in through a closed door or an open window, his entrance was like that of a spirit. But in his manner of enjoying himself with the girl he resembled a human.

During the Xiaojian period of the Song [454–457], Fei Qingbo was serving in provincial administration. He was on leave of duty and returning home when he suddenly saw three mounted escorts,* all in red pillbox caps, approach him and announce: "You are officially summoned." Qingbo replied, "I was only just now given leave to return home to visit. How is it that I'm

---

*A rather nonspecific term (*zou* 騶) that figured in the titles of several offices in the period in which the story was recorded.

being summoned now? Also, your sort generally wears black caps. Why are you wearing red ones?" They said, "We are not officers of this realm." Qingbo then realized that they were not living persons. He knocked his head on the ground and begged them [for his life]. The escorts talked among themselves and agreed to go back and exchange [names]. They told him, "Nevertheless, we will be back in four days to see you again. You might perhaps serve us some wine and food. Be sure to tell no one of this!" At the appointed time they arrived again, saying, "We were able to get it done." Qingbo happily prostrated himself and thanked them. He personally served the wine and food, observing as the ghosts ate and drank no differently from living persons. As they were about to leave, they said, "We did this out of pity for you. We ask that you keep it secret."

Qingbo's wife was by nature suspicious and jealous. She said to him, "This is surely a case of deception by demons." So he had no choice but to relate the whole situation to her in detail. A little while after doing so, he saw the three escorts standing angrily before him. They were in pain and bloodied from having been flogged. They said, "Why did you betray us?" and then immediately vanished. Qingbo was suddenly stricken with a malady and died the same night.

[66]

A man surnamed Yu (given name unknown) from Yingchuan died of illness during the Xiaojian period of the Song [454–457]. A place beneath his heart remained warm. After passing a night, not yet encoffined, he suddenly woke up. He said that when he first died, two men in black arrived, bound him, and took him away, driving him on ahead of them. He saw a city with gates and towers of imposing height, ringed with defenses. They led Yu into a great hall; a great crowd entered at the same time. At the head of the hall sat a noble person facing south. He was attended by several hundred subordinates who addressed him as "magistrate." The magistrate held a writing brush and consulted records on each person arriving. When it was Yu's turn, the magistrate said, "This man's counts have not yet expired. Quickly return him!" An attendant mounted the stairs and led Yu out. When they reached the city gate, the man leading him spoke to the functionary there about dispatching someone to escort him back. But the functionary said, "He needs a return permit. Only then will he be able to leave."

Just outside the gate was a beautiful girl of fifteen or sixteen who said to him, "You, sir, are very fortunate to be able to return. The reason you are being detained in this way is that the gatekeeper is seeking a bribe." Yu said, "Just now I was arrested and was brought here with no bags. I have nothing to offer him." The girl took three golden armlets off her left arm and handed them to Yu, saying, "Give these to him." Yu asked the girl her name, and she said, "I am surnamed Zhang. My home is in Maozhu. I died yesterday in a cholera epidemic." Yu replied, "When I was near death, I had set aside five thousand in cash, intending it to be used to purchase things at market.* If I revive, I will make a gift of this sum to repay you." The girl said, "I cannot bear to see you in difficulty. These are my own personal possessions. You need not trouble yourself to repay my family for them." So Yu took the armlets and gave them to the functionary. It turned out that there was not really any return permit needed; the functionary simply dispatched someone to escort him home. Yu and the girl said goodbye. She sighed and wept.

Yu then suddenly revived. When he later went to Maozhu to make inquiries, he did indeed find a Zhang family that had recently been bereaved of a young girl.

[67]

In the third year of the Song Daming period [459–460], Wang Yao died of illness in the capital. After he had died, there was a skinny, tall, black-colored ghost wearing short trousers that repeatedly came to his home, sometimes singing or whistling, sometimes imitating human speech. It often threw excrement or filth into people's food. Likewise, it often assaulted people in similar fashion in the neighboring Yu household just east of the Wangs.

Yu told the ghost, "We don't fear it if you throw dirt and stones at us. What would really bother us is if you were to throw money at us." The ghost then threw several dozen new coins, hitting Yu right in the forehead. Yu added, "New coins don't hurt. We're only afraid of coins that have been darkened [with use]." The ghost then threw darkened coins at Yu. In all, this happened five or six times, and Yu collected over a hundred pieces of cash in this way.

*Presumably provisions for his own funeral and burial.

Bi Zhongbao, a native of Dongping, lived in Pengcheng. He had a black horse that was very fast, and he often rode it; it was his pride and joy. In the sixth year of the Song Daming period [462–463], he saw in a dream his deceased older brother, Zhongqing, who said to him, "I've been drafted into military service and have been assigned to a very hazardous post. But I've been unable to find a fast horse. Perhaps you'd give me your black horse." Zhongbao assented. When he awoke, he called together all those who had been sleeping nearby and told them about the dream from start to finish. It was at that point that they heard the sound of the horse collapsing outside. He sent someone out to look. The horse was breathing with difficulty and seemed to have been struck by some ailment. In his mind Zhongbao knew why this was happening, but he nevertheless tried a remedy for the animal.

The next morning the horse died. Zhongbao returned to his quarters and lay down as if intending to sleep. He heard Zhongqing say to him, "I had requested the horse from you, but then your cure arrived. Without begrudging, I now return the horse to you and will seek elsewhere for another one." The next morning the horse had revived, and within only the space of a meal it was back to normal.

During the Daming period of the Song [457–465],[25] a man of the Xu clan of Wukang was ill with malaria. Repeated attempts at treatment failed to cure him. Someone told him: "You should lay down several circles of rice out beside a road, call out the surname and given name of someone who has been wrongly killed, and say, 'If you cure me of malaria, I will give these circles to you!' Throw the rice down and return directly, and do not look back."*

The sick man did as instructed. He called out the name of the former Jin general Shen Chong. In a little while, a man on horseback at the head of a train of attendants arrived and asked, "Who are you, that you dare to

---

*Making offerings and prayers to persons deemed to have been unjustly killed is an ancient and still-common pattern in Chinese popular religion. Their spirits were thought to be especially powerful to do good or ill.

call the name of an official?" They then tied the sick man up and led him away. His entire family went out looking for him for an entire day. They finally found him in the underbrush beside a tomb, still tied up as before. His malaria was subsequently cured.

[70]

During the Taishi period of the Song [465–472], there lived a certain Zhang Yi. He had been whipped, and the sores were unbearably painful. Someone told him to burn the tip of the bone of a deceased human and apply it to the wounds. He hired a lad from his household to climb a nearby hill, bring back a skull, burn it, and apply it to his wounds. That night a fire broke out, burning the boy's hands. There was also a creature in the air that pressed down on the boy's head and held it into the fire, scolding him: "Why did you burn my head? I'm paying you back with this fire here!" The lad cried, "It was Zhang Yi who burned you!" "If you hadn't taken [my skull] and given it to Zhang Yi," said the creature, "how would he have ended up burning it?" The creature pressed down on the boy's head for a long while, until all his hair had been burned off and the flesh had been melted away. Only then did he release him.

Zhang Yi was terrified. He took the remaining bones back to be reburied at the former spot on the hill, and he made offerings of wine and meat there. There were no further disturbances.

[71]

Zhu Daoxiu once served as magistrate of Canling, while Liu Kuo of Nanyang served as an adjutant in Jingzhou. Day and night they played chess with each other, almost without cease.* On the twenty-sixth day of the sixth month of the third year of the Song Yuanhui reign period [10 August 475], Daoxiu died. Come the ninth month, Kuo was sitting in his studio when he suddenly saw a man arrive and hand a letter to him, saying that it was "a letter from Zhu of Canling." Opening it, Kuo recognized Daoxiu's handwriting. The letter said: "Whenever I think of our meetings over chess,

---

*On the popularity of the game of *weiqi* 圍棋 or East Asian chess during this period, see Dien, *Six Dynasties Civilization*, 382–384.

I grow nostalgic. But I believe there is reason to hope we will soon see each other again." When Kuo had finished reading the letter, it vanished.

Afterward Kuo was bedridden with an illness and soon died.

[72]

Zhu Tai lived in Jiangling. During the Yuanhui period of the Song [473–477], he died of illness. He had not yet been encoffined when his form suddenly became visible. He returned and sat down beside his corpse. He sought to reassure and exhort his mother. Everyone present saw him as he gestured at the grave goods that had been assembled and urged that they be restricted and made more frugal. He told his mother, "Our family is rather poor. And now that I am dead, I will necessarily be lax in serving and nurturing you. Why must you spend so lavishly on my funeral?"*

[73]

Feng Taozhang lived in Jiangxia. Stricken with severe illness, he repeatedly sent up petitions. At night he saw a creature resembling a pig but red in color. It was followed by a dozen or so men corralling it and tying it up. They entered through the door, encircled the bed, and then departed.

He went to ask the Daoist master Zhang Xuanming about it, and the master told him: "What you saw was the creature that is haunting you being subdued and charged with offenses. The black-clad men who entered your residence were sent by the village earth god to inspect the premises and protect you, that's all. Your illness should clear up soon." From this point on, everything returned to normal.

[74]

Xun Xiang, byname Shuwei, served his mother filially. He was fond of literary composition and Daoist arts. He lived alone and shunned grains.

---

*In the background here are a great many early medieval discussions of the desirability of frugal burials, on which see Dien, "Instructions for the Grave," and Knapp, "Confucian Views of the Supernatural," 642, 647–649. Among the rationales for frugal burial were not only concern for the welfare of the living but also fear of violation of rich tombs by grave robbers—a fear reflected in several items in this volume (e.g., 153 and 156).

Once while traveling in the east he was resting at the Yellow Crane Tower in Jiangxia when, looking off into the southwestern distance, he saw a creature come wafting down from the empyrean. In a moment there arrived a guest riding on a crane. The crane came to rest beside the door, and the transcendent sat down near Xiang on a mat. He wore a feathered cloak and a rainbow skirt. Guest and host had a delightful conversation. When it was done, the transcendent said farewell, remounted the crane, and soared aloft into the air until, growing smaller and smaller in the distance, he finally vanished.*

[75]

After Zhuge Jingzhi had died, a voice was once[26] heard above his former residence. [Someone in the family] had just returned home from buying wine, but the household lacked a tripod vessel to warm it in. The ghost said, "How can anyone drink wine if you have no vessel to warm it in?" A bronze tripod then arrived from midair.

[76]

When Xiahou Zuxin[27] was serving as regional inspector in Yanzhou, he died in office. Shen Sengrong replaced him. Zuxin manifested his form† and paid a call on Sengrong. On the couch was a gem-ornamented woven sash. Xiaohou said, "This sash is rare and fine. How can I be presented with such a thing?" But Shen replied, "It is very appropriate." Xiahou said, "If you insist on presenting it, sir, could you perhaps have it burned?" Shen then burned the sash before him, and before he had even finished doing so, he saw the sash around Xiaohou's waist.‡

---

*Transcendents or immortals (*xian* 仙) were commonly depicted as feathered or wearing feathered garb and as able to fly; they were often associated with cranes. They also often were reputed to shun "grains," that is, ordinary, mainstream foods. See Campany, *Making Transcendents*, 49, 52, 62–87.

†This phrase, *xian xing* 見形, was often used to describe a ghost's or god's sudden appearance to living persons.

‡Burning an object was (and is) a common way to transmit it to the world of spirits.

A servant of the Chenliu Zhou clan named Xingjin once entered the hills to gather firewood. Tired, she lay down. She dreamed of a woman who told her: "I am not far from where your head now lies. There are thorns in my eyes. If I could trouble you to pull them out, I will richly reward you for it." The servant found a rotted coffin, its head end crumbled away, the skull fallen to the ground with brambles growing up through the eye sockets. She uprooted the weeds for the coffin's occupant, put her back in the coffin, and closed up the head end with tiles. Where the skull had been lying, she found a pair of golden rings.

When Chen Min was serving as governor of Jiangxia, he promised a silver ingot to the god of the temple at Lake Gongting. Later he had an ingot of iron plated with silver and sent it to the temple. One of the temple's spirit mediums declared: "Chen Min's offense cannot be overlooked." He then threw the ingot into the lake. It floated on the surface of the water. Chen's boat subsequently capsized in a crosswind.

Yu Miao and a young woman named Guo Ning were having an illicit relationship. Before the altar to the earth god he swore that he would take her as his concubine, and [they swore] that if either of them proved disloyal, that one should die. Miao remained unwilling to marry anyone else.[28]

Two years later, Miao heard that Ning had suddenly died. When he went out the door and looked off into the distance, he saw a person approaching. It was Ning. He joined his hands together and uttered a cry of lament over her. She told the young man, "I was returning from a village to the north when I encountered a bandit on the road. He drew a knife and forced himself on me. Fearing for my life, I submitted. Because I was not able to keep our oath, I was held responsible by the earth god. I felt a sudden pain in my heart and died the next day." Miao said, "Why don't you stay here a while?" But Ning answered, "People and ghosts follow different paths. You shouldn't trouble your thoughts with such ideas." She then wept till her collar was soaked with tears.

After Wang Zhaozong of Taiyuan had died of illness, his form suddenly appeared to his mother, née Liu, and his wife, née Han, and conversed with each of them. From his mother he requested wine. When she lifted the cup to give to him, he said, "Excellent wine!" To his wife he said, "We will be apart for only three years."

After her [three-year] mourning period was over, the wife fell ill. She said, "The rule of coburial* has ever been hard to avoid. If I were to go on living, would I not be in violation of my vow?" She refused medicine and died.

Zhou Yi of Runan took the daughter of Liu Dansun of Pei as his wife. Yi was the younger brother of the governor of Ai district in Yuzhang. While they were en route [together to the district], Yi fell ill. Yi said that he wouldn't last much longer, [so the older brother] proceeded on ahead with Yi to the district headquarters, leaving the other family members to follow behind. Yi died the following day.

When his wife arrived and approached his body, Yi lifted his hand to say farewell to her. As she combed his hair for him, he reached up and took her hairpin. When the burial preparations [29] had been finished and Yi's wife was keeping vigil in the room with him, Yi climbed onto the bed with her and said, "Although the life you and I shared was meager, our feelings were deep. Unfortunately it has come to this. My older brother was unkind to separate the members of our family, preventing me from ever having the chance to say farewell to you. That was regrettable! Earlier I raised my hand toward you and took hold of your hairpin, and then I intended to rise, but because there were many people nearby at the time and there was thus insufficient *qi*, I was unable to." From this time forward [throughout the period of vigil over the corpse], each night he would come to lie down beside his wife, no differently than when he had been alive.

*This "rule of coburial" (*tong xue zhi yi* 同穴之義) refers to the expectation that a widow be buried in the same tomb as her husband.

When Dong Yi of Chenliu was young, he had a girl named Liang Ying as a neighbor. She was young and very beautiful, and Yi was completely smitten. He gave her gifts, and Ying accepted them, but he had not obtained any results.

Once his neighbor Zheng Chong was spending the night at Yi's place. During the second watch there came the sound of a knock on the door. From where he was lying, Chong, who was also acquainted with Liang Ying, could see that it was she, and he said to Yi, "Liang Ying is here." Yi, startled, sprang up and went out to meet her, taking her by the arms and leading her inside so as to sleep with her that night.* She then tried to leave, but Yi detained her, begging her to stay till the morning. He promised to cook her a suckling pig for breakfast and said that she could leave after the meal. When he got up to close the door and draw the bedcurtain, Ying metamorphosed into a fox and escaped by running out atop the rafters.[†]

Wu Kaozhi, a member of an encamped family[‡] from Nankang, was cutting timber for building boats when he suddenly noticed a pregnant monkey in the tree of an earth-god shrine. He climbed up the tree in pursuit, scampering up nimbly as if flying. The tree was isolated, and there were other people on the ground below, so the monkey, realizing that there was no escape, held on to a tree branch with her left hand while with her right hand she rubbed her abdomen. Kaozhi caught her, took her down to the ground, and killed her. When he cut open her abdomen, there was a baby monkey inside that looked as if it had been about to be born.

That night Kaozhi dreamed that he saw a personage who called himself a god. The god reproached him for killing the monkey. Afterward Kaozhi was ill for a week. At first he seemed deranged. Then he gradually transformed into a tiger, growing fur, whiskers, talons, and teeth; even his voice changed. He ended up running off into the mountains. No trace of him was ever found.

---

*The language is ambiguous on whether they indeed slept together or Yi only tried to persuade the girl to do so.

[†]On the ideas underlying this tale, see the note to item 20.

[‡]On this term, see the note to item 47.

During the Southern Qi, Ma Daoyou served as scribe in the office of the director of the Secretariat. In the first year of the Yongming period [479–480], he was sitting in the palace when he suddenly saw a demon directly in front of him. Others beside him saw nothing. In a moment two demons entered his ears and pushed out [one of?] his cloudsouls.* It fell and landed on his shoes. He pointed at it and said to those beside him, "Do you all see this?" None of them did. They asked what shape it had, and Daoyou answered, "The cloudsoul looks exactly like a toad! It says† that there is no way I can survive since the demons are still in my ears!"

Upon inspection, his ears were both swollen. He died the next day.

Shuyi ji 述異記
RECORDS OF STRANGE THINGS‡
Compiled by Ren Fang 任昉 (460–508)
283 extant items

[85]

Formerly, upon the death of Pangu, his head became the four sacred mountains,§ his eyes the sun and moon, his fat and marrow the rivers and seas, and his hair the grasses and trees. During the Qin and Han it was commonly said that Pangu's head became the eastern marchmount, his belly the central marchmount, his left arm the southern marchmount, his right

---

*The wording is ambiguous about the number of *hun* 魂 involved; according to a widespread belief, people normally had three. For a study of related beliefs in the Han period, see Brashier, "Han Thanatology and the Division of 'Souls.'"

†It is not entirely clear whether the speaker of this line is the cloudsoul(s), Ma Daoyou, or the bystanders.

‡On Ren Fang, see *CL*, 751–758. In addition to the studies listed there, see Campany, "'Survival' as an Interpretive Strategy."

§The text refers here to the ancient idea of four or five sacred mountains situated roughly in the cardinal directions (and center) from the viewpoint of central China.

arm the northern marchmount, and his legs the western marchmount. Classicists* of former times said that Pangu's tears became the rivers, his breath the wind, his voice the thunder, and the pupils of his eyes the lightning. Anciently it was said that Pangu's joy became the light and his anger the darkness. In Wu and Chu it was said that Pangu was the progenitor of husband and wife, yin and yang. Today in Nanhai there is Pangu's tomb, more than three hundred square *li* in area. It is commonly said that in later times someone pursued and buried Pangu's cloudsouls. In Guilin there is a Pangu Temple where people today make offerings.

Beyond the Southern Sea there is Pangu Land, where today people take Pangu as their surname. In my opinion, Pangu is the progenitor of all things in heaven and earth. Living creatures therefore have their origin in Pangu.†

[86]

On Mount Lanling is a well in which strange birds nest. These birds have golden wings and black bodies. Whenever they are seen, there will be much water. The well cannot be peered into. All who have peered into it have died within the year.

[87]

Mollusk Inn is in Nankang commandery. Once there was an upright woman who harvested mollusks for her living. One time she spent the night at this inn. During the night she heard a sound of wind and rain in the air. She then saw a mass of mollusks, their mouths open, moving toward her. They fed in a frenzy on her flesh, and in the morning only her skeleton remained at the place. That is why this inn is called Mollusk Inn.

[88]

Near Xuancheng is Mount Gai. On it is the Spring of Maiden Shu. The folk there say that there was once a girl of the Shu clan who was cutting

---

*Classicists or *ru* 儒 were those scholars especially well versed in texts of the Confucian canon.

†On this and related cosmogonic myths relating to the figure Pangu 盤古, see Bodde, "Myths of Ancient China," 382–386.

wood with her father near this spring. The girl sat down beside it. She then became stuck there and despite being tugged and pulled could not be moved. The father rushed home to tell his family.

When they all returned, all they saw was the clear spring bubbling up. The girl's mother said, "Our daughter loves music." So they sang and played stringed instruments, whereupon the spring frothed forth.

[89]

Wu Kan[30] was a lesser subofficial functionary serving in Yangxian district. His home was in Xi'nan. One day, while crossing the stream in a skiff, he suddenly noticed in the water a floating five-colored stone. Kan fetched it and took it back home, placing it at the head of his bed. Come nightfall it metamorphosed into a young woman. She said that she was the daughter of the River Earl.[31]* When dawn came, she was a stone again. Later Kan threw the stone back into the stream.†

[90]

Wuling Spring is in the region of Wu. On the mountain there grow no trees other than peach and plum. People of the area call it the Peach Plum Spring. Above the spring is a stone cavern. In the cavern is milk water.‡ For generations it has been said that during the disorder at the end of the Qin dynasty, some people of Wu fled here to avoid danger, and that all who ate of the peaches and plums here became transcendents.§

*The River Earl (Hebo 河伯) was the chief god of the Yellow River, an important figure in the popular pantheon since ancient times.

†Thus ends Ren Fang's version. The *Shuyi ji* version attributed to Zu Chongzhi ends: "She was upright and proper, and she and Kan became husband and wife."

‡This term, *rushui* 乳水, which might also be translated as "water from the nipple," denotes mineral-rich water that drips from stalactites.

§Some readers may be reminded of the similar but much better known tale of the Peach Blossom Spring attributed to Tao Qian. In fact, as this item and item 121 show, that tale was but the best-known example of a story type quite common during the early medieval period.

Soushen houji 搜神後記 (alternate title: *Xu soushen ji* 續搜神記)
FURTHER RECORDS OF AN INQUEST INTO THE SPIRIT REALM*
Traditionally attributed to Tao Qian 陶潛 (365–427)
99 extant items

[91]

During the Jin there was a man named Hu Maohui of Huainan. He could see spirits. Although he disliked seeing them, he was unable to stop.

On one occasion he had traveled to Yangzhou and was returning to Liyang. East of the city wall there stood a shrine where people habitually employed spirit mediums to pray to the god on their behalf. A little while after arriving there, Maohui saw a group of spirits shouting to one another, "High officials are coming!" They all scattered and fled out of the shrine. He then looked and saw two monks enter the shrine. The demons huddled in twos and threes, standing outside the vegetation surrounding the shrine and peering in, quaking with fear as they watched the monks from a distance. Shortly after the monks departed, all the spirits reentered the shrine.

From that point on, Maohui began to venerate the Buddha somewhat.[32]

[92]

Liu Guang, a native of Yuzhang, was young and as yet unmarried when, arriving at a hut in the fields, he saw a girl who said to him, "I am the

*On this text, see *LZG*, 343–355; *WXS*, 320; Wang Guoliang, *Liuchao zhiguai xiaoshuo kaolun*, 113–156; Wang Guoliang, *Soushen houji yanjiu*; and *SW*, 69–75. Research on this text must now start with the new, critical edition of 99 items deemed correctly attributed to *Soushen houji* in *XJS*, vol. 2; Li Jianguo convincingly shows that 24 of the items included in traditional editions are probably incorrectly attributed. (He accepts without discussion the text's attribution to the famed poet Tao Qian.) I adopt Li's numbering of items. Simmons, "The *Soushen houji* Attributed to Tao Yuanming," provides an accurate translation of the traditional ten-chapter edition in its entirety. *CCT* translates three items, but one of them is in fact a *Soushen ji* story that found its way into some traditional editions of *Soushen houji*: this is the lovely tale of the Immaculate Maiden of Pure Waters 白水素女, translated in *CCT*, 132–133; see *XJS*, 116–119. The other two (see *CCT*, 129–131) correspond to items 1.3 and 4.1 in traditional ten-chapter editions and items 1 and 80 in Li Jianguo's numbering; see *XJS*, 467–468 and 563–567. Item 96 (*XJS*, 589–590) is translated and discussed in *SW*, 223–226.

daughter of Adjutant He. At the age of thirteen I died but was then raised by the Queen Mother of the West.* She sent me to pair with a human here below on earth." Liu Guang became intimate with her.

The next day he found under his mats a handkerchief, inside of which were bundled some cloves. His mother seized the handkerchief and put it in the fire, but it turned out to be asbestos.†

[93]

Zhu Bi, a native of Guiji, served as chamberlain for attendants in a princedom. He was constructing a mansion for himself but died before it was finished. Xie Zimu, of the same commandery, took his place. Zimu took advantage of Bi's having died, altering the ledgers and embezzling over a million in cash from public funds. He then falsely blamed the embezzlement on Bi when in fact the funds had gone to him.

Zimu was asleep one night when he suddenly heard someone announce Bi's surname and byname. In a moment Bi was standing in the main hall of Zimu's house. He said to him, "You imagine that dried bones and rotted flesh can simply be slandered. But I will use the fact that you altered the records on such and such a day as proof." When he had spoken these words, he suddenly vanished.

[94]

A gentleman of Qiantang, surnamed Du, was traveling by boat. It was dusk and a heavy snow was falling when a young woman in a white gown appeared. Du said, "Why don't you come aboard?" And so they enjoyed themselves together.

Du then closed up the boat and transported her as a passenger. Later she transformed into a white egret and flew away. Du was revolted. He then sickened and died.

---

*The Queen Mother of the West (Xi wang mu 西王母) was an important goddess thought to dwell on Mount Kunlun in the lands west of China and to bestow methods and elixirs of longevity on fortunate mortals.

†Asbestos—the Chinese term for which literally translates as "fabric that one washes in fire"—was known to the Chinese since at least the Han as an exotic import from the distant west. It is mentioned as a marvel elsewhere in *zhiguai* texts (for example, *Bowu zhi* 2.38; *Soushen ji* 10.6 and 13.18).

Gu Zhan of Wu commandery was once out hunting when, coming to a hill, he heard a human voice exclaiming, "Drat! I'm down this year." So he and his companions searched for the source of the sound. On top of the hill they found an opening leading into an ancient tomb, and inside the tomb there crouched an old fox. Spread before him was a ledger book to which he was pointing as if counting up entries. The hunters loosed their dogs, and they killed the fox.

When the men retrieved the fox and examined it, they saw that there were no teeth left in its mouth, and the fur on its head had all turned white. The register turned out to be a list of the names of women lovers the fox had intended to defile. Red checkmarks indicated those who had already been defiled. Over a hundred women's names were in the ledger, and Zhan's own daughter's was among them.

[96]

While Xi Zuochi of Xiangyang was serving as assistant magistrate in Jing-zhou, he once accompanied some of Huan Xuan's troops* on a hunting expedition. At the time there was much snow. At a point west of the city wall of Jiangling they saw a cloud of *qi* emanating from the snow on a field. When they went there to inspect, they saw a yellow creature and shot it; it died from the arrow wounds. Upon retrieving it, they found that it was an old male fox. On its ankle it was wearing an incense pouch made of fine silk.

[97]

During the Taiyuan period of the Jin [376–397], the Dingling† ruler Zhai Zhao‡ raised a macaque, keeping it in front of the courtesans' quarters. All the courtesans became pregnant at the same time, and each of them gave birth to a child with three heads. Each of these children began leaping about

---

*See Lewis, *China between Empires*, 69.

†Dingling 丁零 was the name both of a tribal federation and of a northern central Asian nomadic people. Members of this and other steppe ethnicities were often deployed as cavalry in Chinese armies during the period; see Graff, *Medieval Chinese Warfare*, 40–41.

‡This is probably the same figure as the Dingling leader Zhai Liao mentioned in *Jin shu* 9.232 and 81.2133 as the leader of a rebellion.

the moment it emerged from the birth canal. Only then did Zhao realize that this was the monkey's doing. He killed it and all the offspring, which set the courtesans wailing in unison. When Zhao inquired of them, they answered, "At first we saw a youth wearing a singlet of yellow silk and a white gauze cap, very adorable. He laughed and spoke just like a human being."

[98]

At the foot of Mount Linlü there is an inn. Each time passersby stayed there, they would grow sick or die. It was said that a gang of a dozen or so men and women, sometimes wearing black clothes, sometimes white, would invariably descend on the place to attack guests.

Once a certain Zhi Boyi stayed there. He lit a candle, sat down, and recited scriptures. At midnight a dozen or so people suddenly came in, sat down beside Boyi, and began playing dice and sixes* with one another. Boyi secretly looked at their reflections in a mirror: in fact, they were a pack of dogs. So he picked up the candle and stood, pretending to accidentally burn their clothes with it. This produced an odor of burnt fur. Boyi, who was packing a sword, grabbed one of these people and ran him through. At first the creature uttered a human cry, but once it had died, it turned into a dog. The others all fled.†

[99]

Late in the Wu period, a man from Linhai entered the mountains intent on bow hunting. He built a hut to stay in. During the night a man came to see him. He was a pole tall, wearing a yellow gown with a white sash. The

---

*Pubo 蒲博, which I take to be short for shupu 樗蒲 and liubo 六博. Both were games of chance and strategy played on boards with game pieces. See Dien, Six Dynasties Civilization, 382–386.

†The source for this Soushen houji story seems to have been Baopuzi neipian 17.300. Ge Hong's source, in turn, may well have been Fengsu tongyi, "Guaishen pian" 怪神篇 (modern ed. 353–354) or some similar text now lost. A somewhat similar story about this same protagonist, but involving a fox and with the protagonist's surname changed to Dao, appears as Soushen ji 18.15. In that story the "scriptures" chanted comprise both Daoist esoteric texts and Confucian classics. A clearly related story—perhaps we might call it a distant version of the same tale—is translated from Lieyi zhuan as item 20.

man said to the hunter, "I have a certain enemy. Tomorrow is the day we are due to do battle. If you would assist me, sir, I would reward you." The hunter replied, "Naturally I will help you, sir. What need is there for a reward?" The other responded, "Tomorrow at breakfast time, you should come out to the bank of the stream. My enemy will come from the north; I will meet him from the south. I will be the one wearing a white sash; he will be wearing a yellow sash." The hunter agreed to this.

Next morning the hunter indeed heard a noise from the northern bank like that of a terrific storm. Vegetation was flattened all about. Looking southward, he saw the same thing happening there. Then he saw two enormous serpents, each over ten poles long, engaging each other in the stream and coiling around one another. The one with shiny white scales was the weaker of the two, so the hunter drew and shot, and the serpent with shiny yellow scales died.

At sunset the hunter saw once more the man who had come the previous day. He took his leave and thanked the hunter by saying, "You may stay here for a full year and hunt. By next year you must be gone. Take care not to return here after that. If you do, misfortune will certainly befall you." The hunter said, "Fine."

So he stayed there for a year and hunted. He got lots of game, and his family grew quite wealthy.

Several years later, he suddenly remembered how much game he had obtained at that place but forgot what he had been told, so he went back there to hunt. There he saw the same man in the white sash, who said, "I told you not to come back, but you were unable to do as I said. My enemy's sons have now grown up, and they will now certainly seek vengeance against you. There is nothing I can do about it." When the hunter heard this, he was terrified. He tried to flee, but he saw before him three black-clad men, each eight feet tall. They all opened their mouths wide toward him. The hunter died immediately.

[100]

During the Yuanjia period [424–453], there were three men in Guangzhou who entered the mountains together to cut wood. Suddenly they saw in a rock crevice three eggs, each of them pint sized. They took them with the intent to boil them, but just as the water started to heat up, they heard a noise in the forest like that of wind and rain. In a moment a snake came toward them, of enormous girth* and four or five poles long. It approached, fished the eggs out of the water with its mouth, and went away. In no time at all the men perished.

[101]

Zhang Gou[33] of Wuxing was plowing his fields in the fifth month. He traveled back and forth in a small boat. He stored his food in a gourd on the boat, covering it with some brush. In the evening when he was hungry and went to take his meal, he found that the food was gone. This happened repeatedly. On a subsequent day he hid in the brush and kept watch, and so he observed a large snake coming to steal his food. Gou chopped the snake with his hoe, and it crawled off. Gou chased after it in his boat. He reached a hillside where there was a cave. The snake entered the cave, and a voice could be heard wailing, "Our so-and-so has been chopped!" Another voice said, "What should we do?" Another said, "Notify the Thunder Sire[†] and have him strike the bastard dead with thunder peals."

In a moment, clouds and rain joined to darken the sky, and it thundered repeatedly. Gou then climbed up onto a tree limb and screamed, "Heavenly Sire, I am destitute! I exhaust my strength working with the plow! That snake came and stole my food. The crime is the snake's! And yet you thunder at me? You must be an ignorant Thunder Sire, then! If you show yourself here, I'll chop your belly with my hoe!"

In another moment, the clouds and rain dissipated, and the thunder peals were redirected at the snakes' cave. Several dozen snakes were killed.

[102]

During the Xiankang period of the Jin [335–343], the regional inspector of Yuzhou, Mao Bao, was garrisoned in the [northern] capital city of Ye. At that time a soldier saw a white turtle for sale in the Wuchang market. It was four or five inches long, pure white, and adorable. So the soldier bought it,

---

*Literally "ten *wei* 圍 around"; I render the expression as recommended in Wilkinson, *Chinese History*, 554.

†Thunder Sire (Leigong 雷公) was one of an ensemble of atmospheric deities responsible for weather phenomena.

took it home, and raised it, keeping it in an urn. Each day it gradually grew larger until it reached a foot or so in length. Taking pity on it, the soldier carried it to a riverbank and released it into the water, watching it go.

Later, when Ye fell to Shi Hu,* Mao Bao fled Yuzhou. Those who were trying to escape across the river there were drowning in large numbers. At the same time, the man who had raised the turtle, wearing his armor and carrying his sword, was trying to get across the river as well. When the soldier entered the water, it felt to him as if he were standing on a rock, and the water came only to his waist. In a moment he began moving across the current. When he looked down in midstream, he saw beneath him the white turtle he had once released, its shell now six or seven feet long. When the turtle had carried the man safely to the eastern bank, it stuck out its head and gazed fixedly at him. Then it swam off. From midstream it turned back to look at him several times.

Xiao shuo 小說
ANECDOTES OF INSIGNIFICANT THINGS†
Compiled by Yin Yun 殷芸 (471–529)
135 extant items

[103]

On the north side of Mount Songgao is a large cave of unfathomable depth. People often visit there to sightsee. Once in the early Jin period a man accidentally fell into this cave. His companions, hoping that he had survived the fall, threw food down into the cave; the man who had fallen recovered

---

*The chronology mentioned here seems to be off, since Shi Hu (295–349) initially captured the city of Ye (near Anyang in modern Henan) in 313; as self-styled regent he made the city his capital in 335. Also, the presence of a Jin soldier in Ye during these years seems odd, since it was the capital of the Later Zhao, a northern state hostile to the Jin. On Ye in this period, see Dien, *Six Dynasties Civilization*, 19–24; and Lewis, *China between Empires*, 92–94.

†On this work, see Lin Chen, "Lu Xun xiansheng 'Gu xiaoshuo gouchen,'" 391–392; *SW,* 89; and the edition in Zhou Lengqie, *Yin Yun Xiao shuo*. Several items concerning the Han emperor Wu are translated in T. E. Smith, "Ritual and the Shaping of Narrative," 662–670. Item 16 is translated in Campany, "Return-from-Death Narratives," 103.

this food and, taking it as provision, began trying to find a way out. After perhaps ten days had passed, the cave suddenly widened out and he saw light. There was also a thatched hut where two men sat playing chess. Under their chessboard was a cup of clear beverage. The man who had fallen told them that he was hungry and thirsty, and one of the chess players said, "You may drink this." He did so and instantly felt ten times stronger. The chess players then asked, "Would you like to remain here?" The man declined. The players said, "Proceed west several dozen paces. There will be a well. In it are many strange creatures, but do not be afraid. Just throw yourself into it and you will emerge. If you get hungry, just pick up some of the material inside the well and eat it."

The man followed their instructions. In the well were many lamiae and dragons,* but when they saw him, they moved out of his way. He followed the course of the well and proceeded. In it was a substance like green paste. He ate some and no longer felt hunger. After perhaps half a year he finally emerged in Shu. He then returned to Luoyang and inquired of Zhang Hua. Zhang said, "That was a transcendents' palace. What you drank there was juice of jade, and what you ate was dragon cave stone marrow."

Xu Qi Xie ji 續齊諧記
MORE OF QI XIE'S RECORDS†
Compiled by Wu Jun 吳均 (469–520)
22 extant items

[104]

Yang Bao of Hongnong, byname Wenyuan, was a noted gentleman of the Later Han period. He was kind and caring by nature. When he was seven,

---

*Dragons (*long* 龍) and lamiae (*jiao* 蛟, sometimes less fittingly translated as kraken) were two closely related categories of powerful, water-associated creatures in Chinese lore. See *SW*, 249–250. They appear in several other stories in this volume, including 127, 128 [?], 129, 130, 131, and 202.

†On this work, see *LZG*, 406–414; Wang Guoliang, *Liuchao zhiguai xiaoshuo kaolun*, 173–205; Wang Guoliang, *Xu Qi Xie ji yanjiu*; and *SW*, 87–88. Items 8 and 17 are translated in *CCT*, 159–163; item 16 is translated in Campany, "Ghosts Matter," 27. On Wu Jun, see *CL*, 1369–1378.

he was once on the north side of Mount Huayin when he caught sight of a yellow sparrow that had been seized by an owl and then dropped beneath a tree. It was wounded in many places, writhing on the ground, and troubled by insects. Bao carried it home and placed it on one of the rafters in his home. That night he heard it emitting piercing cries. When he got up to look at the bird, he saw that it was being bitten by mosquitoes, so he placed it in a cloth-lined box and fed it chrysanthemum petals. After a hundred-odd days its feathers had grown back in, so Bao set it free to fly. It would fly off in the morning but return in the evening to spend the night in the cloth-lined box. This went on for several years.

Then one evening the sparrow arrived with a flock of others. They encircled the room and sang sadly, departing only after several days. That night at around the third watch, Bao was reading and had not yet gone to bed when a yellow-clad youth appeared, bowed twice to him, and said, "I am an envoy of the Queen Mother.* I had been sent to Penglai but, because of my carelessness, was caught by an owl. Thanks to your kindness, sir, I was rescued, and I am deeply grateful for your help. I have now been sent on a mission to the South Sea and can no longer remain here." In parting, the youth presented four jade rings to Bao, saying, "May your descendants be as pure as [the jade in] these rings, and may they rise to the rank of Three Dukes."† After this there were no more appearances [by the sparrow or the youth].

Bao's reputation for filial kindness became known throughout the empire, and his reputation and titles repeatedly climbed. His son Chen had a son, Bing; Bing had a son named Ci; and Ci had a son named Biao. All four generations were noted ministers, and the Yangs became a great clan in the eastern capital. During Chen's funeral a large bird descended. Everyone said that it had been summoned down by his perfect filiality.

[105]

Huan Jing, a native of Runan, for many years followed Fei Changfang about and studied under him.‡ Changfang [once] said to him: "On the ninth day

---

*That is, the Queen Mother of the West.

†The three paramount aides to the ruler. See Hucker, *Dictionary of Official Titles*, 399.

‡Fei Changfang was a noted practitioner of arts of healing and transcendence; see Campany, *To Live as Long as Heaven and Earth*, 161–168.

of the ninth month, there will be a calamity in your household. You must depart for home at once. Instruct each member of your family to fill a silk pouch with dogwood [leaves?] and tie it around his or her arm. Then, climb to a high place and drink chrysanthemum-blossom wine. In this way you can avoid this disaster." Jing did as he was told. His entire household climbed a mountain. That evening they returned home to find that all their chickens, dogs, oxen, and sheep had been slaughtered in one fell swoop. When Chang-fang heard of it, he remarked, "These must have served as substitutes."*

Nowadays people climb to a high place on the ninth day [of the ninth month] and drink wine, and women wear a pouch of dogwood at their waists. This custom probably originated from this incident.

*Alluded to here is the notion, important in popular religion in the period, that certain other persons, creatures, or objects might be used as "substitutes" (dai 代) to undergo punishment, pay off debts, or even die on one's behalf. (Examples may be seen in items 209 and 224.) Early medieval Daoist and Buddhist texts often criticize this notion, which attests to its ubiquity in popular practice. See Campany, *Signs from the Unseen Realm,* 40–43; and Campany, "Religious Repertoires and Contestation," 130–133.

Xuanyan ji 宣驗記 (alternate title: Mingyan ji 冥驗記 or Records of Manifestations from the Unseen Realm*)

RECORDS PROCLAIMING MANIFESTATIONS

Attributed to Liu Yiqing 劉義慶 (403–444)

48 extant items†

[106]

Zhang Rong of Bohai,‡ byname Meiyu: during the Xianning period of the Jin [275–280], his son's wife gave birth to a boy. At first the family noticed nothing odd about him. By the age of six he was surpassingly clever.

On one occasion Rong took his grandson to watch his shooting. Rong instructed someone to fetch the arrows and bring them back but was irritated by how long it was taking. His grandson said, "I'll get them myself!" Rong released an arrow at the same time that his grandson started running, and the boy reached the target at the same moment the arrow did; in a flash he had returned holding the arrow. Everyone present marveled at this.

On the second day after they returned home, the boy suddenly fell ill and died. Monks were summoned, and incense was lit. A Western§ monk said, "You should encoffin³⁴ your grandson immediately. He is a *rākṣasa* demon‖ and will otherwise devour and harm people." Having seen the episode with the arrows, the family hastened to seal [the corpse] in the coffin. Soon they heard the sound of something bumping around inside it, and

---

*This is a case where the alternate title given in some sources appears likely to be the correct one.

†Items 3 and 8 are translated in Campany, "The Real Presence," 241–243. Items 6 and 21 are translated in Campany, "The Earliest Tales of the Bodhisattva Guanshiyin," 87, 93–94. Item 18 is translated in Gjertson, *Miraculous Retribution,* 20–21. Item 24 is translated in Campany, "Notes on the Devotional Uses and Symbolic Functions of Sutra Texts," 51–52. Item 4 was translated in *SW,* 228–229, as being from *Soushen houji* but was incorrectly included in traditional editions of that text and is cited from *Xuanyan ji* in *TPYL* 950 and *Shilei fu zhu* 事類賦注 30 (see *XJS,* 708). On this work, see *WXS,* 325–326; *LZG,* 368–372; and *SW,* 77. On Liu Yiqing, see *CL,* 588–590.

‡Not to be confused with a figure of the same surname and given name (byname Siguang 思光), a native of Wu commandery who flourished in the Qi period (dying in 497) and wrote an anti-Buddhist tract, *Sanpo lun* 三破論; a biography appears in *Nan Qi shu* 41 and *Nan shi* 32.

§I.e., non-Chinese; the monk was of Indian or central Asian origin.

‖One of the many designations for demons imported with Buddhist texts—this type, the *luosha gui* 羅刹鬼, being particularly fierce. For an overview, see DeCaroli, *Haunting the Buddha.*

their grief turned to alarm. At once they processed with the coffin to the tomb and buried it.

Later the boy's form appeared several times. Rong performed the eight-fold abstinence,* and so it departed.

[107]

During the Jin Yixi period [405–418], in Chang'gan Monastery [35] in the capital there dwelled the monks Huixiang and Faxiang in adjoining chambers. One night during the fourth watch Huixiang yelled for Faxiang to come at once. When he rushed in, he saw Huixiang asleep on his back with his arms crossed tightly across his chest and his legs straight and stiff. Huixiang said, "Untie the rope around my arms and legs," and Faxiang replied, "There isn't any rope." Huixiang was then able to move. He said, "Just now a group of men came, bound my arms and legs, and beat me all over, demanding to know for what reason I had bitten lice." They had further told Huixiang that if he did not cease doing so, he would be forced between two stones and crushed.

From then on, Huixiang was scrupulous in observing this rule concerning lice. In other ways he was not particularly diligent.

[108]

Shen Jia of Wu commandery was imprisoned and sentenced to death. When he was about to be executed in the marketplace, he recited the name of [the bodhisattva] Guanshiyin† all day long, without flagging mentally or vocally. The executioner's sword broke, so he was released.

Another version says: Lu Hui of Wu was imprisoned and had received the death sentence. He instructed his family to make an image of Guanshiyin, hoping that their doing so would enable him to avoid dying. The executioner swung the blade three times, but each time it broke. There was an official inquiry, and the reply was sent up that it might have been due to the merciful power of Guanshiyin. So the image was inspected. Three in-

---

*Eightfold abstinence or *baguanzhai* 八關齋 is a way of referring to the cluster of observances mentioned in a note to item 4.

†As mentioned in the Introduction, devotion to this bodhisattva was an important element in Buddhist devotional life in early medieval China.

dentations, as if by a blade, were visible on its neck. A memorial was sent up [reporting this], and so Hui was spared.

[109]

A certain Mr. Zhou of Pei had three sons. All were unable to speak.

One day a man stopped at the home, asking for something to drink. When the man heard the sounds the sons were making, he inquired about it, and Mr. Zhou explained forthrightly. The visitor said, "You have committed a sin. You should go inside and reflect on it." Zhou wondered at the man's words and realized that he was no ordinary person. After a long while Zhou said, "I don't remember committing any sin." The visitor replied, "Try reflecting again on things you did in your youth." So Zhou went back inside.

After a while he reemerged and said, "I remember that near where I slept as a young boy there was a swallows' nest. In it were three baby swallows. The mother would return to the nest to feed them and then fly off again in search of food. I could reach down to it from my window, and when I stuck my finger into the nest the baby birds would open their mouths as if to receive food. So I took three caltrop nutlets* and fed one to each of the birds, and they died. When the mother returned and did not find her babies [alive], she uttered a mournful cry and flew away. I have often regretted this and reproached myself for it." The visitor then transformed, taking on the features of a monk, and said, "Since you have recognized this and confessed, the sin is now expunged!" At once Zhou heard his sons inside speaking normally. The monk vanished.

[110]

Wang Dao was a native of Henei.† He and his two brothers fell ill at the same time.

Beside their home was a magpie nest. Morning and night the birds fluttered about and sang very noisily. The brothers loathed the birds and dis-

---

*The nutlets of *Tribulus terrestris* (its name speaks volumes) resemble bulls' heads and have extremely sharp spines.

†This Wang Dao is presumably not to be confused with the famous Wang Dao (276–339) who served as top adviser to the ruler under the Eastern Jin, on whom see *SSHY*, 595.

cussed whether they should take care of the problem. So they did: they caught the birds, cut out their tongues, and killed them.

All three brothers were struck dumb.

Xuanzhong ji 玄中記
RECORDS FROM THE REALM OF THE OBSCURE*
Compiled by a Mr. Guo 郭氏 (perhaps Guo Pu 郭璞, 276–322)†
71 extant items

[111]

Foxes at fifty years of age can transform into women.[36] At one hundred they can become beautiful women or spirit mediums. Some of them become handsome men and have intercourse with women. They can know of affairs a thousand *li* away, and they are skilled at black magic and [other] demonic arts and can thus delude people and make them lose their senses. At a thousand years of age they attain communication with heaven and become celestial foxes.

[112]

When toads reach the age of one thousand years, they grow horns from their heads. He who can capture one and eat it will live a thousand years himself. These toads also eat mountain sprites.

[113]

The mountain sprite resembles a human, [but] it has one leg, three to four feet in length. It eats mountain crabs. It emerges at night and hides during

*On this work, see *LZG*, 269–279; *WXS*, 334; and *SW*, 93. On *xuan* or "the obscure," a highly resonant notion in early medieval times, see Zürcher, *The Buddhist Conquest*, 86–92; Mather, "The Controversy over Conformity and Naturalness"; Mather, "Individualist Expressions of the Outsiders"; and Ashmore, *The Transport of Reading*, 42–55.

†On Guo Pu see *CL*, 301–307.

the day, making it impossible for people to see it. But its cry can be heard at night. Thousand-year-old toads eat it.

[114]

The essence of jade becomes a white tiger. The essence of gold becomes a carriage and horses. The essence of copper becomes a young male or female[37] slave. The essence of lead becomes an old woman.

Xuyi ji 續異記
CONTINUED RECORDS OF MARVELS*
Compiler unknown; late sixth century
11 extant items

[115]

During the Later Han, Gentleman of the Palace Gate Xiao Shiyi was killed in the second year of the Yongyuan reign period of Emperor He [90–91 CE]. Several days earlier a dog belonging to his family had approached his wife and spoken these words: "Very bad fortune awaits you. Your family is about to be destroyed. What can be done?" His wife kept quiet about it and was not startled. The dog soon left of its own accord.

When Shiyi returned home, his wife began to imitate for him the dog's speech, and before she even finished speaking, assailants arrived to seize them.

[116]

Xu Miao was an attendant gentleman during the reign of the Jin emperor Wu [265–289]. [Earlier], when he held a regional-level post, his associates used to sense that although Miao was alone in his tent, he was nevertheless speaking with someone. A former fellow student of his peeked in one night

*On this work, see *LZG*, 431; and *SW*, 94.

but did not see him within. The sky was just beginning to brighten, so he opened a window. Upon doing so, he caught a glimpse of something flying out from beneath the screen and into an iron cauldron [outside]. He went to look and saw nothing in the cauldron other than some calamus roots and, beneath those, a large green grasshopper. Although he suspected that this might be a sprite, he had never seen reports of such a creature from ancient times to the present. So he only plucked off the grasshopper's wings.

That night the grasshopper entered Miao's dreams, saying, "I was harmed by your former fellow student. Our relationship is severed. Although I am not far away, to travel the distance between us would be as if traversing mountains and rivers." Upon having dreamed this, Miao was sorrowful. The fellow student knew what it meant and hinted at the reason. Miao at first hesitated to mention anything more about the matter but then said: "When I first arrived at this post, I saw a girl walk in dressed in green. Her hair was braided into two buns on the sides of her head, and she was extremely beautiful. I spoke to her flirtatiously, and she approached closer, so I became fond of her and lost myself in passion. I don't even know where she came from when she arrived here each time." He then told of his dream. The classmate set out his side of the story in detail.

Thenceforth he never again chased or killed grasshoppers.

[117]

Liu Zhao of Zhongshan, magistrate of Moling, earlier served as a supervisor in Jiankang in the third year of the Liang Tianjian period [504–505]. He was about to prepare some food with his understudies when he found a large turtle in the stove, a foot or more long. It was lying among the ashes but had not been harmed by the fire. Liu prepared a meal for it and then released it in Lake Lou.

Not long afterward he was promoted to serve as magistrate of Moling.

[118]

The governor of Lingling, Liu Xingdao of Guangling, after leaving office retired to his studio. He placed a bed against the western wall. Suddenly he saw an eye appear in the eastern wall. After a short while there were four; then he saw more and more of them, until eventually they seemed to fill the entire room. After a long time they subsided, without his knowing where they had gone. Then he saw hair beside his bed, more and more of it until a head emerged from the floor. It was the head of a *fangxiang*.* Then it suddenly vanished.

Liu was terrified. He fell ill and [never] left his bed again.

[119]

Zhu Fagong of Shanyin was once on a journey when he stopped to rest beneath a tangerine tree east of Tai city. Suddenly there came a girl of sixteen or seventeen, of stunning beauty. Dusk was drawing near. The girl sent a maidservant to speak with Fagong and see if he wanted her to spend the night with him. He agreed, and so she came. She gave her surname as Tan and said that she lived near the city wall. So they spent the night together. Come dawn she departed. The next evening she came again. This went on for several nights. She would leave each morning at first light, her maidservant always coming to escort her home. There was also a boy of five or six, very handsome and attractive. The girl said that he was her younger brother.

Then one morning as the girl was leaving him, her gown was open and he saw that she had a turtle's tail and feet. Only then did Fagong realize that she was a sprite. He intended to capture her, but when she came again that night and he lit a lamp so he could see her, she suddenly disappeared.

Fangxiang 方相 was the name of a type of masked exorcistic dancer who performed in seasonal festivals and religious processions to ward off maleficent spirits (see Bodde, *Festivals in Classical China,* chap. 4). The distinctive mask was made to look frightening to help banish demons. Demons themselves are often described in early medieval *zhiguai* texts as "looking like a *fangxiang*"; for examples, see item 210 and *SW,* 228n53.

Yi yuan 異苑
A GARDEN OF MARVELS*
Compiled by Liu Jingshu 劉敬叔 (fl. early fifth century)
382 extant items

[120]

In Yongjia commandery there is a place called Hundred Baskets Pool. The people of the commandery dammed a stream there so as to trap fish, and they slaughtered creatures as a sacrifice to pray for a plentiful catch. But, as it turned out, they caught nothing. Those involved were angry, resentful, and ready to quit. But that night they all dreamed of seeing an old man who said, "If you will kindly wait a short while, I will think over what is appropriate." The same night they suddenly heard a flipping sound. Startled, they got up as one and saw an enormous fish. They minced it up into slices and obtained enough to fill a hundred baskets.

This is why the pool is named Hundred Baskets.

[121]

Once at the outset of the Song Yuanjia period [424–453], a member of the Man people from Wuxi shot a deer and pursued it into a stone cavern. The cavern was barely large enough for one person to pass through. Upon entering, the Man hunter noticed steps off to one side, so he climbed these. The cavern then opened out into a broad space with flourishing mulberry and fruit groves. Passersby seemed friendly and did not think his presence odd. [On his way out] the man notched trees to mark the route.

Afterward people tried to find the place again, but no one ever succeeded in doing so.[38]

---

*On this work, which has been neglected by modern scholars out of all proportion to its size, see *LZG*, 372–382; *WXS*, 322–323; and *SW*, 78–80. The following items are translated in *SW*: 1.14 (217); 3.29 (190; see also Campany, *Making Transcendents*, 241); and 6.11 (226). Item 5.1 is translated in Miyakawa, "Local Cults around Mount Lu," 86.

Atop a mountain in the country of Gouyi in the west, there is a stone camel. Water emerges from beneath its belly. If one attempts to take this water with metal implements or with one's hands, it will flow away. Only by drawing the water with a gourd is it possible to obtain some to drink. The water causes people's bodies to become fragrant and pure, so that they ascend to become transcendents.

This country is numinous and mysterious. It is impossible to get there more than once.

On Mount Guimei in Nankang is a stone-walled enclosure. Inside it are sweet orange, tangerine, and pomelo trees. Those who arrive there and eat the fruit may follow their conscience and take only enough to satisfy their hunger. But those who pick some to take away with them encounter a large serpent, or else they fall down or lose their way. And any members of their families who eat the fruit will become ill.

There was once a man in Yangshan district of Shixing commandery who was out walking in the fields when he suddenly came across an elephant. The elephant wrapped him up with its trunk and took him deep into the mountains. There the man saw another elephant; it had a giant thorn in its foot. The man pulled out the thorn, whereupon the elephant stood up and pranced about as if it were happy. The first elephant then took the man back out. They arrived at a marshy area. The elephant used its trunk to dig up several ivory tusks from the mud.* Then it took the man back to the place where they had first met.

Now the crops in the area had often been plagued by elephants. People there called the animals "big guests." So the man said to the elephant, "My fields and crops are here. They are often trespassed upon by 'big guests.' If you think kindly of me, then please do not violate this area anymore." The

---

*Presumably to present to the man in thanks.

elephant stomped the ground as if agreeing. From that point on, his family's fields suffered no more incursions.

[125]

Early in the Longan era of the Jin,* He Danzhi of Donghai often traveled to the Guanzhong area. Once on his return trip he procured a dog. It was large bodied and unusual. Whenever he came or went, the dog always knew where he was.

Later, when Danzhi fell ill, so did his dog. The dog was with him right up until his death; it then drew one final breath and died as well.[39]

[126]

Lu Ji[†] once served some preserved fish to Zhang Hua. Many other guests were seated with them. Hua opened the serving vessel and said, "This is dragon meat." Everyone present scoffed. Hua said, "Try pouring some bitter wine on it. There will certainly be an anomaly." When this was done, a five-colored light arose.

Lu Ji went back to inquire of the fish seller. He said that among the rushes in his garden he had caught a fish of strange shape and appearance, and that he had used it to make preserved fish. Since the result was so delicious, he had presented some to Lu's household as a gift.

[127]

At the home of Zhang Yong there was a spring. A small dragon lived in it. Because of this, the family became very wealthy. After some years had passed, the dragon soared up into the sky during a rainstorm. Afterward the family's days of easy wealth were over.

A common saying has it, "One can live with a dragon but not recognize the divine dragon's efficacy."

---

*This era began in 397.
†Lu Ji (261–303) was an important political and literary figure; see *CL*, 611–628. Zhang Hua has been mentioned in other items above, as well as in the Introduction.

During the Jin Taiyuan period [376–397], in the West Monastery in Dong-yang, from a niche beneath the Seven Buddha Chamber a creature poked out its head. It resembled a deer. The monk Faxian approached it for a closer look. At this it belched forth a mass of mist and air, like clouds or fog.

On the seventh day of the fourth month of the fourteenth year of the [Song] Yuanjia period [27 May 437], its head again emerged. When people inspected the spot where it appeared, there was no hole or open-ing to be found. Each year there could be heard at this site a sound like thunder.

[129]

During the Jin Yixi period [405–418], there was an old lady named Zhao who sold wine for a living. One day the earthen floor of her home suddenly began to rumble. The old lady, regarding it as an anomaly, poured out a libation of wine for it every morning and evening. On one occasion she saw a creature emerge, its head resembling a donkey's, yet there was no hole in the floor.

When the old lady died, neighbors heard a sound like wailing coming from underground. Later on, someone dug up the floor and found a strange creature writhing there. They could not make out its size. After a short while it vanished.

This sort of creature is commonly known[40] as an earth dragon.

[130]

Li Zeng of Yongyang was traveling past a large stream when he saw two lamiae floating on its surface. He drew his bow and launched an arrow, hit-ting one of them. He then returned home.

Later, when he left the city once again, he saw a woman weeping, her tears drenching her clothes. She was holding his arrow. Zeng thought it strange. When he inquired of her, she said, "What need is there to ask? Your cruelty is about to be requited." She handed him the arrow and vanished. Filled with dread, Zeng fled, but before he could reach home, he died sud-denly on the road.

The Mian River bay in Jingzhou is very deep. A lamia in the water often killed people. Not a year went by without someone dying there while bathing or drawing water. During the Shengping period [357–362], Deng Xia (byname Yingyao) of Chen commandery was serving as governor of Xiangyang. He was pure of character, brave, and strong. Angered by the situation, he entered the water searching for the lamia. He caught it and dragged it ashore with his own hands. He was going to chop it to death when his mother said, "Lamiae are divine creatures. How can you bear to kill it? Try imprecating against it, instructing it not to cause any more trouble." So Xia uttered an imprecation and let it go. Ever since that time there have been no more disturbances.

Another version has it that Xia entered the water brandishing his sword. The lamia coiled itself around his feet. Xia, wielding his sword, cut it into several pieces. The flowing blood turned the water red. Xia was acknowledged as the bravest man of his day. Afterward there were no more lamia attacks.

Su Juan,[41] of Xinye, and his wife were farming, living in a hut near their fields. At every mealtime[42] a creature would come. Its form resembled that of a snake. It was seven feet and five inches long and very colorful. Thinking it strange, they fed it. This went on for several years, during which their crops were very bountiful.

Later the wife secretly beat the creature to death. Thereafter she contracted a severe eating disorder. Each day she would eat three bushels of food but still not be satiated. Soon she died.

Early in the [Song] Yuanjia period [424–453], the regional inspector of Yizhou sent three men into the mountains to cut firewood. They lost their way. They noticed a tortoise as big as a carriage wheel. Each of its four feet was resting on a smaller tortoise as it made its way along, and a hundred-odd yellow tortoises followed behind. The three men knocked their heads on the ground and asked to be shown the way out. The tortoise stretched its neck in a certain direction as if meaning to point with its head. So the men went in that direction and were able to find the way home.

One of the men for no good reason took one of the small tortoises along with him and cut it up to make broth, which he ate. Shortly afterward he died a sudden death. Only the men who had not tasted the broth avoided the illness.

[134]

Emperor Wu of the Song [reigned 420–422], named Yu, had Deyu as his byname and Jinu as his childhood name. When he was young, he was on campaign against the Di people in Xinzhou when he saw a giant serpent several dozen poles long. He shot and injured it.

The next day, when he went back into the area, he heard the sound of a mortar and pestle. When he went to look, he saw several youths in green garments preparing a medicine. He asked them why they were doing this, and they replied, "Our king was shot by Liu Jinu.* We are preparing this powder to administer to him." The [future] emperor asked, "If your king is divine, why does he not kill Jinu?" They replied, "Liu Jinu is a king. Unless he dies [by other means], he cannot be killed [by violence]."[43] The [future] emperor then shouted at them, causing them to scatter, and he collected the medicine and returned.

This is why people call this herb Liu Jinu.

[135]

The Temple of the Young Maiden at Qingxi is said to be that of the third younger sister of [the divine] Marquis Jiang.† Inside the temple is a thick grove of nut trees, in the tops of which birds often nest and raise their young.

During the Taiyuan era of the Jin [376–397], Xie Qing of Chen commandery shot several of the birds from horseback with his crossbow. At once he felt a piercing sensation in his body. That night he dreamed of a

*That is, by the future Emperor Wu.
†Marquis Jiang (Jiang hou 蔣侯) was an important regional god in the southeast. He is mentioned in several other stories in this volume.

girl shaking her sleeves and saying angrily, "I am the one who raised those birds. Why did you attack them?" Within a day Qing was dead.

Qing's personal name was Huan. He was the father of Xie Lingyun.*

[136]

During the Song [420–479],[44] Xiao Huiming was serving as governor of Wuxing. Within the borders of the commandery is Mount Bian, and at the foot of this mountain is a temple to Xiang Yu.[†] It was said that Xiang Yu often dwelled in the central hall of the commandery headquarters and heard cases. Other governors had therefore not dared to enter the central hall. Huiming said to a keeper of records, "Kong Jigong once was governor of this commandery, and I have never heard of his having had any misfortune." So he ordered a mat laid out as if to receive a guest. Shortly Huiming saw a man over a pole tall drawing a bow and launching an arrow at him. Then he saw him no more.

Because of this, Huiming's upper back broke out in sores. Within a week he was dead.

[137]

The wife of Chen Yu, byname Jundu, was of the Du clan in Lujiang. She often worshipped the Mother of Demons,[‡] playing women's music to delight the goddess. Then one night, when people gathered [in her home] to play their stringed and wind instruments, the instruments made no sound, and the singers sighed sorrowfully. She then dreamed that the Mother of Demons was agitatedly weeping, saying, "An evil man will soon come!" One of the family maidservants had been having relations with an outsider who

---

*A great lyric poet of the Six Dynasties period, Xie Lingyun (385–443) was descended from a noted northern émigré family of the southern aristocracy. See Chang and Owen, *Cambridge History of Chinese Literature*, 1:234–238; and Nienhauser, *The Indiana Companion to Traditional Chinese Literature*, 428–430.

†Xiang Yu was a famed military figure at the time of the establishment of the Han dynasty; after his death he became an important deity. See Loewe, *A Biographical Dictionary of the Qin*, 599–602.

‡The Mother of Demons (Guizimu 鬼子母) was a goddess who figured in Buddhist legend and whose worship (particularly by women) was imported with that religion beginning in around the third century. See Campany, *Signs from the Unseen Realm*, 115, for more.

placed a ladder against the wall to enter the house. This man stripped the vestments off the goddess and furthermore burned and broke her image into pieces before leaving.

[138]

In the world there is a goddess known as the Purple Maiden. From antiquity the story has been passed down that she was a concubine in a certain family, and that the head wife was jealous of her and always gave her vile tasks to perform. On the fifteenth day of the first lunar month she died of anger. That is why people now make images of her on that day. At night they welcome her at the privy or by the pigsty railing, invoking her with the words "Zixu's not here. (This was the husband's name.) Old lady Cao's gone home. (This was the head wife's name.) The little maiden can come out and play!" When the person holding the image feels it grow heavy, this means that the goddess has arrived. Wine and fruits are set out for her, and then one perceives that her face has brightened and flushed, and she starts jumping about. She can divine all sorts of affairs and can predict the year's silk harvest, and her prognostications often hit the mark. If the prediction is favorable, she dances about, and if unfavorable, she rolls her eyes.

A certain Mr. Meng of Pingchang never would believe this. When he came forward to take hold of the image himself, he was propelled right up out of the room and away, never to be seen again.

[139]

The Chen clan in Wushang had a daughter who had not yet married. In her clogs she went right up to the top of a tall sweetgum tree and, without a trace of fear, looked around and proclaimed, "I am to become a goddess. I will now depart for good. Only when black is on the left and yellow is on the right will I temporarily return." Her family members all turned out to look at her, but she only raised her hand in a gesture of farewell and then floated up higher and higher until she was out of sight.

No one understood what she had meant by "black" and "yellow." But every spring they sacrificed a black dog, and every fall a yellow dog, and set them out for her beneath the tree.

In Yuhang district there is a temple to Qiu Wang. There have always been many spirit anomalies there.

Early in the Long'an period of the Jin [397–402], a man of that district, Shu Bodao, was serving [elsewhere] as a subofficial functionary. He was granted a leave of absence and was at the harbor in Runan looking for passage home. He saw a crimson barge with a nobleman seated on it, so he asked for a ride on it. Soon it was as if he had fallen asleep. But he could still hear a sound like heavy rain. In a little while they had reached his home district. When he inquired of the boatman, he was told that the noble passenger was Qiu Wang. At this, Bodao bowed, apologized, and returned home.

During the Long'an era [397–402], there was a personage in Wuxing of around twenty years of age, surnamed Xie, who called himself the Sagely Sire. He had been dead for over a century when he suddenly showed up at the home of the Chen clan, saying, "This is my old residence. It should be returned to me. If not, I will burn you out." One night a fire indeed broke out, burning the home completely down. Bird feathers were stuck in the ground in a circle of several layers around the site.

The people thereupon established a temple for him.

During the Jin, Zheng Hui of Xin'an, when young, was ascending Qian Bridge when he dimly made out an old man before him. The man gave him a bag and said, "This is your life span. Take care not to lose it. If it breaks, this will be an evil omen." When he had finished speaking, he suddenly vanished. Hui opened the bag and stole a peek inside. It was a piece of charcoal. He kept this matter to himself, not even telling family members about it.

In the third year of Yongchu [422 or 423], at the age of sixty, he contracted a serious illness. He told his younger relatives, "My years are over. Look inside this bag and see for yourselves." The piece of charcoal was broken. He then died.

Qian You was a native of Yuyao in Guiji. On the second day of the fifth month of the fourth year of the [Song] Yuanjia era [21 March 427], he went outdoors at night and was seized by a tiger. Eighteen days later he returned home. He said that when the tiger had first taken him, they arrived at a government office and passed through a series of gates. He saw a man of imposing demeanor seated with his elbow propped on a table; around him were over thirty attendants. The man said to You, "I want to teach you methods for fortune-telling. That is why I had the tiger welcome you here. Do not be afraid." You remained there for fifteen days. Day and night they discussed the essential arts until he had been thoroughly taught all the methods.

When You had finished receiving the methods, it was time for him to be sent back, but he did not know the way home, so someone was dispatched to escort him back out through the gates. Then he found the way back and so was able to return. [Thenceforth] he was greatly skilled in divination; there was nothing so obscure that was not borne out [in his predictions]. A year later he died.

[144]

During the Jin, there was a temple to Yuan Shuang in Danyang district. He was the fourth son of Yuan Zhen.* Zhen was executed by Huan Xuanwu [Huan Wen].† Afterward [his corpse] disappeared, and numinous anomalies were noticed.[45] During the Taiyuan period [376–397], Shuang's‡ form appeared in Danyang, requesting that a temple be established for him. Work had not yet begun when there was a severe outbreak of tiger attacks. Members of families that had suffered attacks repeatedly dreamed that Shuang was pushing them urgently to start construction. The people set up a shrine hall, and the attacks then stopped.

---

*He is mentioned multiple times in *Jin shu*.

†An important military and political figure. See *SSHY*, 537; and Lewis, *China between Empires*, 64–66.

‡Yuan Zhen is said to have been the one executed, but the temple was dedicated to Yuan Shuang, so I assume that it was the latter's form that began appearing, demanding that a temple be established. Temples to multiple members of families deemed to have been wronged were not uncommon in the period.

Today clerics and laypersons in the area drum, dance, and offer sacrifices there on the last day of the second month, and on this day a storm will suddenly arrive. In the fifth year of the [Song] Yuanjia period [428–429], [on this day] the libations and prayers had just been set out when a villager named Qiu Du saw a creature behind the temple, its face human but its body that of a tortoise. It was clothed, and its seven apertures all seemed normal, but it reeked of wine. No one knew whether the spirit of Shuang had perhaps possessed this creature.

[145]

In western Yan district there is a temple to Lad Yang. In the district there was a man who had formerly served the god but who later went to the libationer Hou Chu seeking to enter the great Dao. It happened that Lou Wulong of Qiao commandery was also visiting Chu, so together they went to the god's shrine and burned the altar and accoutrements. Wulong asked for and took away with him a fan.

A year went by. One day Wulong heard the sound of a horseman riding up and calling out his name four times, then crying, "How is it that you still have not returned Lord Yang's fan?" When he had spoken these words, the horseman rode off again. Wulong then suffered paralysis and died.

[146]

After the Jin emperor Xuan had had Wang Ling executed, he was bedridden with illness. In the daytime he saw Ling approach him. The ruler cried out, "Yanyun* is detaining me!" Afterward bruises appeared on his body. Jia Kui also haunted him.† Within a few days he was dead.

When Ling had first been seized, as he was being taken past Jia Kui's temple, he yelled, "Jia Liangdao, I, Wang Ling, am a loyal servant of the Wei house! Surely you, on account of your divinity, know this!" That is why Kui helped him.

---

*Wang Ling's byname.

†Jia Kui (byname Liangdao, 174–228) was a noted official. Because of his fondness for the city of Xiang (in modern Henan), his ghost was often seen there, and the people built a temple for him (see *TPGJ* 292.7, quoting a stele dedicated to him).

During the Jin there lived Zou Zhan, a native of Nanyang. He began seeing an apparition of a man who called himself Zhen Shuzhong and said nothing else. This happened repeatedly. After some time had passed, he realized what it meant, saying, "West of my house there is a mound of earth with broken tiles in it. There must be a dead person within. 'Zhen Shuzhong' 甄舒仲 means 'I am the person among the broken tiles west of your house' 予舍西土瓦中人也." Upon examination, this turned out to be true.

So he reburied the man in generous fashion. Afterward he dreamed that the man came to thank him.

During the Yongjia era of the Jin [307–313], Zhu Yan lived in the wilderness in Yongning. Once, on entering his house, he heard the tones of wind and stringed instruments, along with the sound of a child crying. That night he saw a formidable-looking man shouting at him to slaughter his dog.* Now Yan was, as a rule, quite courageous. He was not frightened by the apparition, nor did he move out of his residence.

Later he had no more trouble.

There was a man of Pei commandery named Qin Shu, a native of Xiaoxin village in Qu'e. During the Yixi period [405–418],[46] he was once returning from the capital. He had not yet gone twenty *li* when the sky grew dark and he lost his way. Seeing firelight in the distance, he headed toward it. He saw a young woman holding a candle emerge and say, "I am but a weak woman who lives alone. I cannot accept overnight guests." Shu said, "I would like to proceed on my way, but it's the dead of night and I can go no farther. I beg of you to let me stay in an outer area." The woman agreed. So Shu entered into a seating area. He was with the woman in the same room. Afraid that her husband might return, he did not dare fall soundly asleep. But the woman said, "Why be so suspicious? Don't worry. I'm not lying to

---

*Presumably as an offering. But a variant version has "to put out his fire," that is, to vacate the home.

you." She then set out food for Shu. The food items were all old. Shu said to her, "You have received me when you have not yet married out. I, too, have not yet taken a wife. I propose that we come together. Do you think we could take care of one another?" The woman laughed and said, "I regard myself as of little account. How could I hope to be your wife?" So he slept with her.

When morning came, Shu set out to leave. They both rose to say goodbye. The woman wept and said, "Having had this one glimpse of you, I will never see your face again." She gave him a pair of rings, tying them on his waist sash, and saw him out the door. Shu lowered his head and hurried off.

When he had gone several dozen paces, he turned to look at the place where he had spent the night and saw that it was a tomb. After several days the rings were gone, but his sash was still tied as before.

[150]

In the third year of the Jianyuan reign period of Liu Cong,* a libationer from Bingzhou, Huan Hui, met an old man on the road who asked him, "Cheng Ping of Legong—what office does he hold now? He and I go back a long way. Because of his skill at pure conversation, he was nominated as filial and incorrupt.† If you happen to run into him, please give him my regards." Hui asked his name and was told, "I am Ma Zixuan of Wu commandery." As soon as he had said these words, he vanished.

When Hui saw Cheng Ping, he told him about it. Ping sighed and said, "Yes, this man once existed. It must be fifty years now since he died."

When the palace attendant Xun Yanshu heard about this, he composed a prayer text‡ for [Ma] and ordered Ping to set out an offering of wine and food beside the road.

---

*Liu Cong was the second ruler of the Former Zhao regime from 310 to 318, but I am not sure which year this reign title corresponds to, and I suspect that it is incorrect. (The third year of the Jin Jianyuan period corresponds to 345.)

†On this official recommendation system, started during the Han period and continued under ensuing dynasties, see Dien, "Civil Service Examinations," 102. On "pure conversation" (*qingtan* 清談), on which much has been written, a good place to start is Lewis, *China between Empires*, 44–51. The term referred to a sort of learned, densely allusive verbal repartee much valued in early medieval times and taken as a mark of cultural refinement and elegance.

‡Such prayer texts (*zhuwen* 祝文), when written by noted, skilled authors, were highly valued literary artifacts; some examples survive from this period.

During the [Song] Yuanjia period [424–453], a one-legged ghost about three feet tall suddenly appeared to Song Ji[47] of Yingchuan. Song Ji [often] had the ghost perform services for him.

Ji [once] wanted to play dice with a neighbor but lacked the game pieces for it. The ghost took a knife and cut off a branch from the willow tree in the courtyard, carved the branch in the doorway area, and then charred the pieces. Although the black and white areas on the dice were clearly distinguished, the pieces were rather crude.

[152]

In the fourteenth year of the [Song] Yuanjia period [437–438], Xu Daorao suddenly saw a ghost that said that it was his ancestor. It was winter at the time, and the weather was quite clear and cold. The family had stored some rice under the house. The ghost said, "Tomorrow you should dry the grain in the sun. A heavy rain is coming, and there won't be another clear day for a while." Rao followed the ghost's suggestion; the ghost even helped him transport the grain. Afterward there did indeed come incessant rain. To those who saw the ghost, its form resembled that of a macaque.

Rao went to see a Daoist to get a talisman, which he hung in the window. When the ghost saw it, it just laughed, saying, "If you're using this to interdict me, I can still enter through the dog hole!"* But despite having said this, the ghost no longer entered the house. Several days passed. The ghost then sighed and said, "Xu Shubao is coming. It is not appropriate for me to see him." A few days later Shubao did indeed arrive. From then on there were no more appearances.

[153]

In the late Han, Wang Shixie of Cangwu died in Jiaozhi. So he was buried in the southern region. His tomb was often shrouded in mist, and occasionally numinous anomalies occurred there. Because it was far from the disorder of the time, it was not opened.

---

*It seems that many houses in this period had a hole in an exterior wall large enough to allow a dog but not an adult person to pass through. See Campany, *To Live as Long as Heaven and Earth*, 260; and *Jin shu* 49.1385.

Then during the Xingning era of the Jin [363–366], Wen Fangzhi of Tai-yuan served as regional inspector in the area. He personally rode out on horseback and opened the tomb. On his way back he fell from his horse and died.

[154]

The wife of Chen Wu of Yan district was widowed while still young and lived with her two sons. She loved to drink tea.

Inside her residence there was an ancient tomb. Each day when she prepared tea to drink, she would first make an offering of it.[48] Her sons, annoyed by this, one day said, "How can an old tomb know you've gone to the trouble to make offerings?" They wanted to dig it up and remove it. But their mother stubbornly refused, and so they desisted. That same night the mother dreamed of a man who said, "I have resided in this tomb for over two centuries. Now I have been the beneficiary of your kindness. Your two sons have long wanted to destroy my dwelling, but fortunately you protected it. Moreover, you have served me fine tea. Although I am merely rotted flesh and bones,[49] how could I neglect to reward you generously?"[50] Then she awoke. The next morning at dawn she found one hundred thousand coins in her courtyard. They appeared to have been buried a long time, but the strings through the centers were all new. She picked them up and went in to tell her sons. The sons both looked ashamed.

From then on the family made even more lavish offerings.[51]

[155]

During the Longan period of the Jin [397–402], Yan Cong was having a new house built when one night he dreamed of a man who said to him: "Why, sir, have you destroyed my tomb?" Next morning he promptly excavated the area in front of his bed and found a coffin. Cong set out offerings and said, "Today I will relocate you to a nice spot and will build a separate small tomb for you there."

The morning after, a man appeared at the door seeking entry. He gave his surname as Zhu and his given name as Hu. He sat down, composed himself, and said, "I have lived here for forty years. I am deeply touched by your generous bestowal yesterday. Today is an auspicious day, so you may remove my coffin. Inside my headcloth box there are gold mirrors. I wish to contribute these." From the headcloth box inside the head of the coffin were indeed retrieved three gold mirrors. After presenting them to Cong, the figure suddenly disappeared.

[156]

During the Jin, the minister of works, Chi Fanghui,* had his wife buried on Mount Li. He commissioned a subofficial functionary in Guiji, one Shi Ze, to prepare the tomb. In doing so he leveled and razed many ancient tombs. When he broke open one especially large tomb, the grave goods within were rare and rich, and when the chamber was breached, the sound of drums and horns was heard.

[157]

Yingchuan native Zhuge Lü, byname Daoming: his tomb was on the west side of Mount Zhuangjiang in Yangzhou. Each time clouds and rain approached the tomb, the sound of stringed instruments and singing could be heard from within it.

[158]

In Ruyi district in Hailing, a seaside cliff near Dongcheng village collapsed, revealing an ancient tomb. In it was a square-headed lacquer coffin. On its top was an inscription in red: "Seven hundred years hence, I will fall into the water. In the third month of the twentieth year of Yuanjia [443], I will fall from a precipice. My coffin will drift on the water but will eventually return to come to rest here." The villager Zhu Hu and others, thinking this strange, opened the coffin. They beheld an old woman in her seventies. The white hair on her head was covered, and the hair at her temples was white as well, no different from that of a living person. Her hairpin, topknot, and attire were all as if new. Her grave furnishings, pillow, and shoes were all intact. Zhu Hu set out wine and dried meat as offerings beside the coffin.

That night Hu's wife dreamed that the old woman said to her, "My gratitude for what you have bestowed knows no bounds. But the walls of my dwelling have been broken open, and my body and bones lie exposed to

*On him, see *SSHY,* 510–511.

the damp. Here are a thousand pieces in cash. I beg you to use it to secure and protect me." With that she put down the coins and departed.

Upon awakening the next morning, they did indeed find the coins there. They used the money to rebury the woman, relocating her to the top of a nearby hill.

[159]

Ji Kang, byname Shuye,* a native of Qiao, when young was once sleeping during the daytime when he dreamed of a man over a pole tall who said that he was a court musician for the Yellow Thearch.† The man said that his bones were lying in the woods three *li* east of a nearby inn. Someone had exposed them, he said, and he asked Kang to rebury them, promising to reward him richly for the assistance. Kang went to the place in question and indeed found white bones there. The tibia was three feet long. He collected the bones and reburied them.

That night he dreamed again of the tall man. The man came to give him the Guangling tune.‡ When Kang awoke, he played the song on his zither, and it sounded marvelous. He forgot none of it. During the time of the duke of Gaogui [Cao Mao, r. 254–260], he was made grand master of palace leisure. Afterward, though, he was slandered by Zhong Hui and as a result was executed by Prince Sima Wen.

[160]

During the Jin, Zhang Mao, byname Weikang, a native of Guiji, once dreamed that he obtained an elephant. He inquired of Wan Ya[52] about it. Ya said: "You will become governor of a large commandery, but it will not end well. The elephant is a large beast. Based on its sound, 'beast' [*shou* 獸] indicates 'protector' [*shou* 守]. Hence the part about the large

---

*A famous literary and cultural figure of the third century. His dates of birth and death are debated. His surname is sometimes romanized as Xi. See *CL*, 1407–1419 (s.v. Xi Kang); and *SSHY*, 524.

†The Yellow Thearch or Huangdi 黃帝 was, in legend, a very ancient ruler credited with various important cultural inventions.

‡This "Guangling *san*" 廣陵散 was one of the most renowned zither tunes of medieval times and was forever associated with the figure of Ji Kang.

commandery.* But the elephant loses its body on account of its tusks.† This is what indicates that you will certainly be killed."

During the Yongchang period [322–323], Zhang Mao became governor of Wu. When Wang Dun unsuccessfully tried to wrest away the mandate and become ruler,‡ he indeed sent Shen Chong to kill Mao and seize the commandery.

[161]

During the reign of the Jin emperor Ming [r. 323–326], a man who was bringing a horse as tribute dreamed that the god of the [Yellow] River requested it. When he arrived, it turned out that the emperor had had the same dream. So the horse was thrown into the river as an offering to the god. Now the grand mentor Chu Bao had also been fond of this horse. The emperor told him, "It has already been given to the River god."

After Chu died, soldiers saw him ride by on this same horse.

[162]

During the Jin, Wen Qiao was near the jetty at Niuzhu when he heard the sound of music coming from under the water. The water's depth there was unfathomable, and it had long been said that many strange creatures lived below. So he put a lamp inside a rhinoceros horn and shone light down into the water. Soon he caught sight of underwater creatures reflecting his light back. They were all of strange form and anomalous shape. Some rode horses or carriages; some wore red gowns and caps.

That night Qiao dreamed of a man who said, "We are rightly separated from you by the boundary between the paths of the unseen and the seen.

*The office of governor of a district or commandery in this period was known as *taishou* 太守 or "grand protector." This comment focuses on the terms *shou* 獸 and *shou* 守, which, although pronounced differently at the time than they are in modern Mandarin, were homophones then, as they are now, but the same logic also seems to apply to each of the two-word compounds in question: *dashou* 大獸 (large beast) and *taishou* 太守 (grand protector), where *da* was pronounced something like *daj* and *tai* something like *taj*. For reconstructions of early medieval pronunciations I rely on Pulleyblank, *Lexicon*.

†In other words, elephants are killed for their ivory.

‡On these events, see Lewis, *China between Empires*, 63.

Why, then, did you shine the light on us?" Qiao was filled with dread by the dream. He died not long afterward.*

[163]

In the Taiyuan period [376–397], Wang Rong of Taiyuan[†] was named governor of Yulin. [On his way by boat to take up the post] he dropped anchor at Xinting and went to sleep there. He dreamed of a man who gave him seven mulberries; he placed them in his lapel. When he awoke, he really had them in his possession.

A diviner said: "The fruits are mulberry [*sangzi* 桑子]. From this point on, including males and females, young and old, [your family] will have seven burials [*sang* 喪] in all."

[164]

During the Jin, the regional inspector Huan Huo, a native of Jingzhou, was in his studio when he saw a man over a pole tall. Huo dreamed that the man said to him, "I am the god of Mount Long. I came here with no good intention. But since you are virtuous and unperturbable, I will leave of my own accord."

[165]

During the early Yixi period of the Jin [405–418], Huang Cai of Wushang was hunting for game along a riverbank. He saw a creature whose eyes emit-

---

*This story is similar to a passage in *Jin shu* 67.1795 (part of Wen's official biography), which is cited three times in *TPYL* (71.4b–5a, 885.2a–b, and 890.2a) and gives a version of the story that elaborates slightly on the cause of death (a "wind" [*feng* 風] caught after having a bad tooth pulled, shortly after this experience with the water creatures). One of these texts probably was based on the other—the *Jin shu* passage may well have been based on the *Yi yuan* tale (historians sometimes used *zhiguai* narratives as sources, but also vice versa). *TPGJ* 294.2 alludes to the story, citing a text simply titled *Zhiguai* 志怪, and other texts seem to as well; it seems to have become a stock example of the hazards of idly meddling with the boundary between the visible and normally invisible worlds (or, as the text put its, the *youming dao ge* 幽明道隔). On Wen Qiao, see also *SSHY*, 599–600; and *CL*, 1309–1312.

[†]Not to be confused with the more famous Wang Rong (234–305) who was one of the famous Seven Sages of the Bamboo Grove, on whom see *SSHY*, 589, nor with another Wang Rong (468–494, this Rong written differently) who was a noted fifth-century author, on whom see *CL*, 1208–1213.

ted penetrating light. Its eyes must have been spaced at least three feet apart, and it was shaped like an enormous bushel. Cai drew his bow and shot at it. The next moment, he heard the clamor of something rushing in alarm into the water and splashing about, but he could not tell exactly where the sound was coming from.

A year later he went with companions to a place called Zuluo Mound. It was about twenty *li* away from the previous spot by the river. They found a bone over three poles long. In it was lodged his arrow. So he told his companions, "This is the creature I shot last year. It must have died here." He retracted the arrow, and they returned home.

That night he dreamed of a tall man accusing him, saying, "I was there among the islands and streams, not at all concerned with human affairs, and then suddenly I was wrongly killed. I have had nowhere to lodge my complaint, but all this time I have been searching for you. Now I've finally got you." Cai awoke with a sharp pain in his abdomen. He fell ill and died.

[166]

During the Yixi reign period [of the Jin dynasty, 405–418], Shang Lingjun served as governor of Guiyang. He dreamed that a man came, bound him, and took him away; his bodily form and spirit were separated. But another person appeared and said, "Leave him for now. Before long, he'll serve in Hengyang. We can take him then." Shang woke with a start and afterward was depressed.

In the third year of the Yongchu period [422–423], he was appointed governor of Hengyang. Knowing that the principles of the unseen world are hard to dodge, he tried to decline the post, but he was unable to avoid taking it. As a result, he died in office there.

[167]

When Shang Zhongkan* was in Dantu, he dreamed of a man who said: "You, sir, are of a mind to succor creatures. If you could move me to a high, dry place, then your grace would extend even to a skeleton." The next day a

*The name might well be an error for Yin Zhongkan, a noted intellectual figure; see Zürcher, *The Buddhist Conquest of China*, 213.

coffin did indeed come floating down the river on the current. Zhongkan took it and reburied it atop a hill and made an offering of wine and food. That night in a dream he saw the same man return and bow to him in thanks.

Another version has it that Zhongkan was traveling beside the river when he saw a coffin floating by. He secured it and buried it there. A week later the ditch in front of his gate suddenly rose up to become an embankment. That night someone came to see Zhongkan, announcing himself as Xu Boyuan.[53] He said, "I am moved by your kindness, but I have nothing with which to repay you." So Zhongkan asked, "What does the embankment in front of my gate portend?" "When there is an embankment in the midst of water," the man replied, "it is called an island [*zhou* 洲] You will soon be put in charge of a province [*zhou* 州]." When he had spoken these words, he disappeared.

[168]

Jiang Daozhi was near a riverbank when he saw a wooden tablet floating on the water. He retrieved it and used it for grinding [ink?]. It was shaped rather like a fish. Inside it were Daoist talismans, spells, and papers. Daozhi took it everywhere with him for over twenty years.

Then one day it went missing. He dreamed of a man who said, "I was just traveling for a while on the Xiang River when I passed the temple to the Lord of the Xiang [River] and was detained there by his two consorts. Now I have returned. You can look for me by the riverside."

The next morning Daozhi went to the riverbank and saw a large net in which a carp had been caught. He bought the fish and cut it open. Inside he found the talismans, spells, and papers from before and realized that the man in his dream had thrown them away. Soon afterward there was a thunderstorm. A five-colored vapor ascended from his rooftop into the clouds.

Afterward, people who visited the temple to the Lord of the Xiang saw the fish-shaped tablet beside the Lord's two consorts.*

---

*That is, they saw the tablet, now included in a painted mural scene in the temple depicting the divine consorts.

During the [Song] Jingping period [423–424], Xun Maoyuan traveled to Nankang. That night he dreamed of a man with a horn on his head. He cast divination stalks for Maoyuan, then said, "Upon reaching the capital, you will certainly obtain an office [*guan* 官]." When Maoyuan asked which office, the man said, "An office that originates from water." Then Maoyuan awoke. He could not make sense of what he had been told, so he went back to sleep and dreamed again. In this dream the army* arrived at the Yangzhou water gate, and he fell into the water and died. When the coffin [*guan* 棺] had been prepared, he entered it to try it for himself, but it was uncomfortably small. He was then prepared for burial and interred beside the riverbank. He woke up with a start, depressed, and told his mother and elder brother about the dream.

When they reached the water gate, Maoyuan indeed fell into the river and died. The funeral rites were exactly as he had dreamed.

During the [Jin] Taiyuan period [376–397], Shen Ba, a native of Wuxing, dreamed that a young woman was coming and sleeping with him. His friends, secretly peeping in, saw only a female dog. Each time, it would wait for Ba to fall asleep, then come in and get on his bed with him. Thinking that it must be a sprite, the men killed it and ate it.

Afterward Ba dreamed of a black-clad person upbraiding him: "I had intended to join my affairs with yours in giving my daughter to you. If you were not compatible, you should have just said so. Why have you brought such disgrace? Please return her bones." The next morning Ba collected the bones and buried them on a hill. Afterward there were no more disturbances.

Late in the Taiyuan era of the Jin,† Xu Jizhi was once traveling in the countryside when he saw a girl gathering lotuses. She raised her hand and

---

*With which he must have been traveling in his dream.
†This era ended in 397 CE.

waved to Jizhi. Jizhi was pleased, so he invited her to stay with him, and from then on they became very familiar.

Jizhi grew emaciated. Sometimes he would speak of seeing floral chambers, deep spaces, fragrant mats, and ample banquets. Jizhi and the girl ate, drank, and made merry for several years.

His younger brother Suizhi once heard a crowd of voices coming from inside his chamber, so he crept up and peeked in. He saw several girls leaving by the back door, but one of them remained behind and hid in a basket. When Suizhi entered, Jizhi said angrily, "I was just on the verge of enjoying myself! Why did you burst in here? I'll not speak with you again!"[54] But his brother said, "There's someone inside the basket." Suizhi then opened the basket and saw a female monkey inside. So he killed her.

Afterward Jizhi's condition improved.

[172]

During the Yixi era [405–418], a maidservant in the household of the Xu clan of Donghai,[55] whose name was Lan, suddenly was stricken with a bout of extreme fatigue and seemed jaundiced, and she carried out her cleaning tasks differently than usual. The family secretly observed her and saw that the broomstick would come from the corner of her room to linger at her bed. So they took it and burned it.

The maidservant returned to normal.

[173]

During the Yixi period of the Jin [405–418], Sun Qi of Wushang was carrying documents[56] to the district seat. He had just reached a stone pavilion at sunset when it began to rain. He noticed a woman carrying a blue-green parasol. She was perhaps fifteen or sixteen years of age and was extraordinarily beautiful. She was clad entirely in purple.

That night, when lightning flashed and illuminated the room, he saw that she was a large fox. Qi drew his blade and struck, killing her. The parasol turned out to be lotus leaves.

[174]

During the Yixi period of the Jin [405–418], Zhao Yi, a native of Songyang in Yongjia district, was felling peach trees in the mountains with his oldest son, Xian. One of the trees bled when they cut it. Terrified, they stopped work.

Afterward the third child in the family suddenly disappeared. After ten days he suddenly returned. [Here is how it happened:] The family began hearing a voice in midair, sometimes singing, sometimes crying. Yi addressed it, saying, "Since you are a spirit, why don't you let us see you?" The reply came: "I am upright *qi*.* North of my† residence is a large sweet-gum tree. South of it is a lone mountain peak called Stone Tower. On all four sides it is a sheer drop-off. Neither man nor animal has ever set foot on it. I was a bit annoyed, and so I took this child and put him on a tree limb and then on top of Stone Tower." The whole family knocked their heads on the floor and pleaded. Only then was the child able to descend.

[175]

During the Yongchu reign period of the founding [Song] emperor [420–423], Zhang Chun served as governor of Wuchang. Once there was a bride there who had not yet ascended the carriage [to go to the wedding] when she suddenly was not herself. She went outside and began assaulting people, saying that she did not wish to marry a vulgar person. A spirit medium said that she was possessed by a demon, so they took the woman to the river-bank, beat drums, and pronounced special invocations to cure her. Chun considered this to be cheating and misleading the common people; he set a time limit by which the demon, if such it was, would have to be caught.

The following day a black snake came up to where the medium was. She‡ drove a large nail through its head. At midday a large turtle was observed coming up out of the river and lying in submission before the medium. The medium wrote a talisman on its back in vermilion, then sent it back into the river. At sunset a large white alligator emerged from the river, now sink-ing, now floating, with the turtle following behind it, forcing it forward. The alligator, knowing it was about to die anyway, approached boldly and

---

*By calling itself "upright *qi*" (*zhengqi* 正氣), the spirit is insisting on its own propriety and wishes not to be thought a malevolent demon or sprite.

†The residence referred to could instead be that of the human family where the conversation is taking place; the wording is unclear on this point.

‡The medium's gender is unspecified, but I am assuming here that the services of a female medium would probably have been sought for the exorcism of a female client.

first went in to say an insulting farewell to the woman. The woman then cried out in grief, saying that her chance for a good marriage had been ruined. Afterward she gradually recovered.

Someone asked the medium, "Demons possess one creature at a time. Why, in this case, were there three?" The medium said, "The snake was the communicator. The turtle was the intermediary. The alligator was the opponent."

They took all three creatures and showed them to Zhang Chun. Chun then recognized the incident as a numinous confirmation.* He had all three creatures killed.

[176]

Shu Shoufu of Yongkang was hunting deep in the mountains with others from his village when their dogs began howling and converged at a spot overgrown with lush vegetation. With astonishment the hunters beheld an old man beneath a tree. He was perhaps three feet tall, his hair and beard disheveled, his face wrinkled, his teeth gone. He was dressed all in brown. He could barely move. So they asked him, "What sort of person are you to be out here?" The man answered them frankly: "I have three comely daughters, each of them accomplished in the arts, on instruments, in singing, and in composing poems. In their idle hours they study the five classics." Shoufu and the others tied the man up and ordered him to call out his daughters. But the old man said, "My daughters live deep in a cavern chamber. Unless I myself go in and call to them, they cannot be moved to come out. Please untie me and I will call them." But the hunters would not release him.

In a moment he metamorphosed into a beast, brown and with four legs. The beast resembled a drum; then again, it also resembled a fox. Its head was three feet long, and from its forehead grew a single horn. Its ears stuck up higher than the crown of its head, but its face was just as it had been before. Shoufu and the others were terrified. Flustered, they untied and released the creature. It vanished at once.

---

*The governor, in other words, decided that the reported events and submitted evidence constituted miraculous or numinous confirmation (*lingyan* 靈驗) of what the spirit medium had said was happening.

Zhang Chen[57] of Le'an in Linhai died at twenty-something. Several days later they were about to prepare his corpse for burial when he revived. He said that he had been apprehended and taken to the celestial bureaus.* The supervisor there turned out to be his cousin, so he was able to break the regulations and escape.

When he first arrived, there was a young woman who had been apprehended and brought in at the same time; they stood waiting together outside the gate. When she saw that Chen's case was being dismissed and that he might be able to help her, she removed a golden armlet and other ornaments she was wearing and gave them to Chen for him to give to the supervisor to secure her release. So Chen made the request on her behalf and presented the items. After a long while someone emerged to say that things had been discussed with Chen and that Qiuying would be allowed to return with him. Qiuying was the woman's name. So they set off together. But after a while their feet grew sore and weary and they were unable to continue, and because it was growing dark, they stopped for the night in a small cave that was shaped like a roadside inn but had no innkeeper present. So Chen spent the night with this beauty, and they were able to talk further. She said, "My family name is Xu, and our home is in Wumen in Wu district. We live near the waterway. I fell from a date tree in front of our house, and that's how I ended up out here." In the morning they departed again, going their separate ways, and each of them revived.

Chen went on to become a district-level guard. When he was granted a leave, he left the capital. Passing through Wu, he stopped in Wumen, and, after asking around, he was able to find the Xu family home. After introducing himself to the head of the family, he asked, "Where is Qiuying?" "She has not yet gone out of the home to meet outsiders or received them here. How do you know her name?" came the reply. Chen then explained how they had met some time earlier as cloudsouls and that he had learned the young woman's name because she herself had mentioned it. The family head then realized what had happened and was greatly ashamed [of the mere fact that they had met], to say nothing of the fact that they had spent

---

*Tiancao 天曹, a general designation for the administrative structures believed responsible for processing the newly dead in the bureaucratic view of the afterlife pervasive at the time.

a night together. And if the neighbors found out about it, they would gossip about the family. So the head of the household had several servants brought out and shown to Chen, but each time he said, "That's not her." Only then did he ask Qiuying to come forth, and when she and Chen saw each other, it was obvious that they were like old acquaintances.

Saying that it must be Heaven's will, the Xu family gave her to Chen to marry. They had a son whom they named Heaven's Gift.

[178]

During the Yuanjia period of the Song [424–453], the wife (née Lin) of Wu Piao of Pei contracted an illness and died while pregnant. Because of the common taboo against putting a fetus in the womb on a funeral bier, it was deemed necessary to cut the fetus out.

The wife's nursemaid, pained at this, touched the corpse gently with her hand while saying this incantation: "If the Way of Heaven is efficacious, let this corpse not have to be cut asunder." In a moment the face of the corpse flushed with color. The nursemaid called for servants to help her. In a little while the child had emerged [from the birth canal]. The corpse then collapsed again.

[179]

In the Xianning period of the Jin [275–280], there was a man surnamed Peng, a native of Le'an in Poyang. For generations his family had made its living by bow hunting. Whenever he entered the mountains, he would always take his son with him. One day he suddenly stumbled, fell, and metamorphosed into a white deer. The son wept in sorrow, but[58] the deer bounded off and was no longer to be found. The son never hunted again.

When the grandson came along, he took up the occupation once more. Sometime later he shot a white deer one day. Between its horns was found a Daoist's seven-star talisman complete with his grandfather's names, place of residence, and a year and month. On seeing this, the grandson was filled with sorrow. He burned his bow and arrows and gave up hunting forever.

[180]

In the nineteenth year of the Taiyuan era of the Jin [394–395], Huan Chan, a native of Poyang, slaughtered a dog as an offering to [the god of] Mount

Sui, which was within his jurisdiction. The meat was boiled but was not completely done. The god grew angry and promptly issued a directive through a medium that said, "Since Huan Chan has insulted me with raw meat, it is fitting to punish him by requiring him to eat such himself."

That same year he was suddenly transformed into [periodically] acting like a tiger. Whenever he was in tiger mode,[59] he would leap in growling pursuit of any person he saw wearing a garment made of striped skin.*

[181]

Hu Daoxia said of himself that he was a native of Guangling. He was fond of music and matters concerning medical practice.† Because his body exuded an unpleasant odor, he always wore incense as a precaution. The only things he feared were fierce dogs.

Having ascertained his own death date, he admonished his disciples: "When my breathing stops, bury me at once. Do not let any dogs see my corpse." He died in Shanyang. When the mortuary preparations had been completed, [the mourners] became aware that the coffin seemed empty. When they opened it and looked inside, they did not find a corpse.

People at the time all said that he must have been a fox.

[182]

There was one Sun Xinu from Shangyu who wielded many sorts of magical skills. Early in the [Song] Yuanjia period, he led a rebellious incursion into the precincts of Jian'an. Later he appeared among the people. He could penetrate their bodies [for medical purposes] but cause it not to hurt. When he treated people's head colds, blood would run, but when he blew on the wounds, the bleeding would stop at once, and the wounds would quickly close up. Anyone who had suffered a tiger attack, snakebite, or poisoning would be healed when he applied protective spells. When he gave a long whistle into the air, birds would flock to him. At night he would say an

---

*This sentence might mean: "Whenever he began [transforming into] a tiger, if someone else clothed him in a garment made of striped skin, he would gain the ability to leap, growl, and pursue [game]."

†*Song shu* 207.5313 lists a one-scroll work of medical recipes attributed to him (or to someone with this name, at any rate).

imprecation against mosquitoes and flies, and they would all die in the area around him.

In the thirteenth year [of Yuanjia, 436], he was captured at Changshan by a local chief. Knowing that Xinu possessed magical arts and probably had rebellion on his mind, the chief had him fettered extra tightly and placed under heavy guard. But a few days afterward Xinu disappeared.

[183]

Yang Tong of Yuanjia was a master of vulgar arts* during the time of Sun Quan [r. 229–252]. He was once traveling alone by boat to Jianning when he anchored off an islet. That night a demon suddenly came, intending to strike him. Tong stood up and cried, "Who dares to approach Yang Tong?" The demon bowed its head, saying, "I didn't realize it was Ambassador Yang on board."†

Tong ordered the demon to pull the boat. The boat moved very swiftly, faster than if it had been under full sail. Upon reaching the district [of Jianning], he sent the demon away.

---

*"Master of vulgar arts" (*sushi* 俗師) is here a disdainful way of referring to someone who wields occult skills.

†The demon addresses him as Yang *shizhe* 陽使者, *shizhe* being (to my knowledge) a rare term of address in such a context, perhaps sometimes used for masters of occult arts and mediums.

Youming lu 幽明錄
RECORDS OF THE HIDDEN AND VISIBLE WORLDS*
Attributed to Liu Yiqing 劉義慶 (403–444)
266 extant items

[184]

On a hill in southern Pingdu district is a tomb. A traveler took some carp from the reservoir there.

Down the road he encountered the tomb's occupant, who said, "How dare you take my fish?" He seized them from the traveler's carriage and left.

[185]

In Guangling there was a tomb reputed to be that of Wang Jian of Jiangdu,†who had lived during the Han.

Once a villager was passing by when he noticed several dozen grindstones on the ground near it. He picked one of them up and took it home. That night someone knocked on his gate and very urgently insisted on getting the grindstone back. Next morning the villager took it back and laid it where it had been.

*On this work, see *LZG,* 356–368; *WXS,* 324; Wang Guoliang, *Liuchao zhiguai xiaoshuo kaolun,* 157–172, where a revised count of 259 extant items is proposed; *SW,* 75–77; and Zhang, *Buddhism and Tales of the Supernatural* (which I consulted in its earlier form as a 2007 doctoral dissertation; the published form appeared too late to be used in the present volume). On Liu Yiqing, see *CL,* 588–590. Items 29, 31, and 33 are translated in T. E. Smith, "Ritual and the Shaping of Narrative," 658–662. Items 39, 47, 83, 94, 204, 209, 223, and 252 are translated in *CCT,* 137–150. Items 58, 71, 74, and 125 are translated in Campany, "Return-from-Death Narratives," 111, 115–117, 101, and 117–118, respectively. Items 61, 93, 102, 105, 159, 162, 165, 185, 208, 216, 231, and 256 are translated in Campany, "Tales of Strange Events." Item 98 is translated in Campany, "Ghosts Matter," 25. Items 158, 217, 241, and 264 are translated in Campany, "To Hell and Back," 346–347, 350, and 353. Items 161 and 211 are translated in *SW,* 227–228.

†An official by this name appears in *Han shu* 19B.838; see Loewe, *Biographical Dictionary of the Qin,* 530.

In the fifth year of the Yongping reign period of Han Emperor Ming [62–63], Liu Chen and Ruan Zhao, natives of Yan district, traveled together to the Tiantai Mountains [in Zhejiang] to gather medicinal herbs.[60] They became lost and were unable to find the way back. After thirteen days, their provisions exhausted, they were on the verge of starvation when they noticed from afar a peach tree loaded with fruit at the top of the mountain. Given the sheer cliffs and deep ravines, there was no path to the summit, but by holding on to vines they were able to reach the top. Each of them devoured several peaches, at which point they felt completely satiated.

As they were descending the mountain, they took water in their cups to wash themselves and rinse their mouths when they noticed rape turnip leaves being carried down on the current. The leaves were quite fresh. Then a cup came floating down the stream carrying sesame seeds mixed with rice. "There must be people not far from here," they said, so they plunged into the water, swam upstream for two or three *li,* passed through the mountain, and emerged on the other side into a larger stream. Beside the stream were two young women of surpassing beauty. Seeing the two men emerge from the water with their cup, they smiled and said, "Masters Liu and Ruan, bring here the cup that we lost." Chen and Zhao did not recognize the women, yet the women addressed them by name as if they were old acquaintances and were happy to see them. The women asked, "How is it you arrived so late?" So the men went back with them to their home.

Their residence was roofed with bamboo.[61] Against the north and south walls were two large beds. The walls were draped with scarlet gauze curtains on which were hung gold and silver bells. At the head of each bed stood ten maidservants. The women ordered them as follows: "Masters Liu and Ruan have crossed mountains and valleys to get here. Although they just now dined on jade fruit, they must still be depleted and exhausted. Quickly prepare a meal for them."

They feasted on rice with sesame seeds, mountain-goat jerky, and beef, all of which were excellent. When the meal was finished, wine was served. Another group of girls entered, each bearing several peaches. Smiling, they said, "We present these to celebrate the arrival of your grooms." After the wine had been finished, music was performed. Liu and Ruan were happy and nervous by turns. Come nightfall, each of them retired to one of the beds to pass the night, and the young women joined them, speaking to them so soothingly that they forgot all their troubles.

After ten days[62] of this the men wanted to return home. The young women replied, "You were both led here by your good fortune from past lives. Why would you want to go back?" So the men stayed on another half year.

But when they saw from the plants and trees and heard from the calls of birds that spring had arrived, they were filled with sorrowful longing and begged even more urgently to be allowed to return home. The young women said, "If you are being led thus by your previous sins,[63] what can be done?" The young women summoned all the women who had attended previously, some thirty or forty in all, to a musical gathering to send off Liu and Ruan, pointing out to them the way back. And so they departed.

When they reached home, they found that their relatives and friends had all died and the buildings in the town had all changed; they recognized nothing. After inquiries, they located their seventh-generation descendants, who said that the story had been passed down that their ancestors had entered the mountains, become lost, and been unable to return.

In the eighth year of the Taiyuan period of the Jin [383–384], Liu and Ruan suddenly left again, no one knows for where.*

[187]

In the disorder at the end of the Han, there was a family fleeing their land for another commandery. They had a daughter aged five or six who was unable to walk the long distance. Unable both to escape and to take her with them, they spied an ancient tomb beside the road; it was broken open. So they lowered their daughter down into the tomb by a rope.

Only after more than a year had passed were they able to return. They looked for her remains in the tomb, intending to rebury them. Suddenly they found the daughter still alive. The father, astonished, asked his daughter how she had managed to survive, and she said, "In the tomb was a creature that extended its neck and swallowed *qi* each day at sunrise and sunset. I imitated what it was doing and no longer felt any hunger or thirst."

Members of the family searched the tomb to see what this creature might have been. It turned out to be a large tortoise.

*Centuries later this story became the subject of several dramas and noted paintings.

Dong Zhuo* placed his trust in spirit mediums. There were always some of them among his troops, exhorting him to pray and make offerings in order to obtain blessings.

One day, one of [the mediums] following Zhuo asked for some cloth. The quartermaster gave him a new cloth handkerchief. Then he asked for a brush. He then wielded it so as to write on the surface of the cloth. He drew something that looked like two mouths, one larger, the other smaller; they were connected together at the top of the kerchief. This he handed to Zhuo with the words, "Watch out for this!"

Later, Zhuo was killed by Lü Bu 呂布.† Only then did people realize that [the name] Lü Bu was what the medium had meant to indicate.

During Sun Quan's reign [229–252], the people of Nanzhou sent an envoy [to the Wu court] to present as tribute a rhinoceros-horn hair comb. As the envoy was passing by the Temple to the Lord of Mount Lu at Lake Gongting, he requested the god's blessing. The god issued a directive seeking the comb, and the container holding it was already sitting [on the altar] before the god. The envoy pleaded: "This comb is to be presented to the Son of Heaven. I must beg of you to be merciful." The god replied: "When you are approaching Shitou, I will return it to you." So the envoy departed.‡

When he reached Shitou, a three-foot-long carp jumped onto his boat. The envoy cut open its belly and retrieved the comb.

When Sun Quan contracted illness, a medium proclaimed: "There is a ghost wearing raw silk cloth. He seems to have the features of a former gen-

---

*A frontier general who was heavily involved in the events leading to the fall of the Later Han dynasty. For a convenient narrative, see de Crespigny, *Imperial Warlord,* 44–60.

†His name was what was being acted out by the medium: the surname Lü 呂 is written with a pair of mouths 口 connected, and the given name Bu 布 means "cloth." On these historical events, see Lewis, *China between Empires,* 32–33.

‡*Soushen ji* here has "The envoy, having no other choice, went on his way, knowing that losing the hairpin was a capital offense."

eral. His voice thundering, he is not once looking to either side but is heading directly into the palace."

That night, Quan saw Lu Su approach him. The material of his clothing was exactly as the medium had described.*

[191]

In Wu times,† Ge Zuo was governor of Hengyang. In his district a large raft lay stranded athwart the river. It was capable of producing demonic disturbances. The people built a temple to it. If travelers on the river made offerings at the temple, the raft would submerge itself; if they did not, it would remain afloat, destroying passing boats.

When Zuo was about to leave his post as governor, he assembled a large party of men with axes to go and rid the people of this burden. The night before the day they were due to arrive at the site, a murmuring of human voices was heard on the river. When the men went to look, the raft had moved several *li* downstream, coming to rest at a bend in the river.

From then on, travelers no longer had to worry about whether the raft would submerge or stay afloat. The people of Hengyang raised a stele for Zuo that said, "It was by his upright virtue and prayers that the divine logs were prevailed upon to move."

[192]

In Wu times, Chen Xian made his living as a merchant. He was once traveling by donkey when he came upon an empty dwelling. It was wide and tall and had a vermilion gate. Xian saw no one there, so he tethered the donkey and went inside to spend the night. After dark he heard a voice say, "Knave, have you no fear? Do you seek harm?" Then a man appeared directly before Xian, cursing him and saying, "How dare you enter my home!" In the dim moonlight Xian could make out that the man's face was covered with black spots, his eyes had no pupils, his lips were sunken in,

---

*Sun Quan (182–252) was the martial ruler from 229 to 252 of the eastern kingdom known as Wu during the Three Kingdoms period (220–280 CE); see de Crespigny, *Biographical Dictionary of Later Han*, 772–774. Lu Su (172–217) was an influential adviser to him; see ibid., 620–621.

†Wu was the last of the Three Kingdoms to fall, an event that occurred in 280 and led to the reunification of China by the Jin dynasty.

and his teeth had fallen out. In his hands he held a yellow thread. Xian fled the place and came to a nearby village. When he related what had happened, the old folk there said, "That place has long harbored a malicious ghost."

The next day, when he went to look again at the site of the residence, he saw that it was in fact a high grave mound.

[193]

During the Han,* there was a cave near Luoyang, the depth of which was unfathomable. A certain wife wished to murder her husband, so she said to him, "We have never been to see that cave." The husband, against his better judgment, went with her to see it. When they reached the mouth of the cave, the wife pushed him in. A long time passed before he hit the bottom. The wife afterward threw in food and other items, as if she meant to make offerings to him.

After his fall this man was unconscious for a long time, then revived. He found and consumed the food, which slightly improved his strength. He then searched on all sides for a passageway until he found an opening. He made his way forward by crawling, twisting and turning over the uneven floor. When he had gone several dozen *li,* the cave broadened, and he noticed a faint light. He then reached a large, wide, level area. After walking for over a hundred more *li,* he noticed that what he was walking on was like dust, but when he smelled it, it smelled like rice chaff. He tasted it, and it was delicious and more than sated his hunger, so he stuffed some in his clothing as provisions. He continued following the cave, eating this substance along the way. After it had run out, he passed by another substance that was like a paste, its flavor similar to that of the dust he had eaten earlier; so he collected some and went on.

There was no knowing how far he had traveled in the depths when he reached a flat, well-lit place, by which time he had eaten his remaining provisions. Here he entered a city. Its walls were straight and well tended; its palaces and offices were impressive, and its towers, pavilions, and dwelling spaces decorated with gold and jewels. Although there was no sun or moon here, the brightness surpassed that of the sun, moon, and stars. And the

*This dating is in error, since Zhang Hua, who appears as a character in this tale, lived from 232 to 300, after the Later Han had ended.

people were all thirty poles tall and wore garments made of feathers. They strummed strange music of a sort that had never been heard in the world before. He asked these people for help, and one of the elders among them directed him to proceed. He followed this directive and went farther, passing through nine places in all; in each of them the same thing happened. When he reached the last one, famished, an elder pointed him toward an enormous cypress tree in the middle of a courtyard. The tree was almost a hundred feet in circumference, and beneath it was a goat. He was instructed to kneel down and stroke the goat's beard. When he did so, the goat emitted a pearl, which the elder took. Again he stroked the beard, and again the elder took the pearl that was produced. He stroked again and was finally permitted to eat this pearl. Immediately his hunger went away.

He asked the names of the nine places he had traversed and requested to stay there and not leave. But he was told, "According to your allotted life span, you may not remain. When you return, ask Zhang Hua. He will know all the particulars of this place."

The man therefore continued following the cave passage until he emerged in Jiao commandery. He had been gone six or seven years. And so he returned to Luoyang, where he asked Zhang Hua about what he had seen and showed him the two kinds of substances he had obtained. Zhang Hua said: "The dust-like material is dragon saliva from beneath the Yellow River. The paste is mud from beneath Mount Kunlun. The nine places were the palaces of the nine grand masters of the earthbound transcendents.[*] The goat was the Fool's Dragon. To eat the first pearl it produced would have made your life span equal to that of heaven and earth. To eat the second would have extended your years considerably. The last one was good only for satiating hunger."

[194]

Ruan Deru[†] once saw a demon in the latrine. It was over ten feet tall, black with large eyes, wearing a black single-layer gown and a flat-topped cap, and was only inches away from him. Deru, his mind calm and his *qi* steady,

---

[*]On earthbound transcendents or *dixian* 地仙, see Campany, *To Live as Long as Heaven and Earth*, 75–78.

[†]This is Ruan Kan, a noted friend of Ji Kang. See *SSHY*, 539.

simply laughed and said, "People say that demons are loathsome. Now I can see that it's really true!"

The demon blushed with shame and withdrew.

[195]

In the second year of the Taixing period of the Jin [319–320], there was a man from Wu named Hua Long who loved to hunt. He raised a hunting dog named Diwei, which he took along with him wherever he went.

Once Long was on a riverbank cutting firewood, and the dog had wandered away for a while when Long was completely encircled in the coils of a huge snake. When the dog returned, it at once attacked and killed the snake. But Long lay unconscious. The dog was distraught and howled. It ran back to the boat, then ran back into the brush. Long's companions, wondering why the dog was acting this way, went to see what was amiss and found Long lying in a daze on the ground. So they took him home. For two days the dog would eat no food; only after Long regained consciousness did the dog accept food.

Long loved this dog dearly, just as one would a friend. Later he lost the dog. He kept up the search for two years before finally finding Diwei on a mountain.

[196]

During the Yonghe period of the Jin [345–357], at the home of Chen Xu of Xincheng district, a knocking was heard at the gate. Commandant Chen was notified. Then was heard the sound of horses and carriages, without any forms being visible. They came straight in, and then [a voice] asked to speak with the head of the household. It said: "It is appropriate that I come and live at your home, sir, for a period of time. We will bring each other good fortune." It commanded Xu to set up a couch and curtain in the studio. Whenever someone came to call, he would present offerings and seek what he wished [to know]. Whatever was said [in response] always proved accurate. Each time wine and food were presented, the person would be commanded to kneel, bow, and place the items inside the curtain without opening it or looking inside.

Now there was a person who suspected that this might be a creature of the fox genus. So, as he was kneeling there, he suddenly tried to grab it.

The creature retreated behind the couch and cried angrily, "How dare you suspect and test the commandant!" This person felt a sharp pain in his heart and was on the verge of death when the head of the household [Xu] apologized and knocked his head on the floor on the man's behalf. After a while the man felt the pain subside. After this, no one dared to offend the creature.

Xu's family members, for their part, suffered no illnesses. Every affair worked out to their advantage, and they otherwise experienced no great profit or loss.

[197]

When Huan [Wen], as commander in chief,* was quelling Zhe Qi, the adjutant He, while on an expedition in the marches, urinated on the skull of a dead person. After his return he was napping during the day and dreamed of a woman who said to him: "You are a person of distinction. How is it you have defiled me with your urine? Tonight I will make you aware of [the seriousness of your offense]."

Now at the time there was a ferocious tiger in the area, and no one dared to go out at night. He [the adjutant] habitually used the walls in a certain cave as a urinal. That night he went there again to urinate. The tiger, enraged by his urine, bit off his penis, and he died.

[198]

Xu Sun† was orphaned when young and did not know the location of his ancestors' tombs. Once he felt a strange sensation in his heart, then suddenly saw an ancestor of his, who said, "I died over thirty years ago. If I could now obtain a proper burial from you, it would mean that you possess the utmost in filiality and love." He then raised a marker in the ground, saying, "You can look for me beneath this spot."

Xu therefore performed funeral rites for him. The master of the burial ceremony said, "This tomb will produce a marquis and some minor district elders."

---

*On Huan Wen's important role in the history of the period, see Lewis, *China between Empires*, 64–66.

†An important figure in later Daoist history; see Boltz, *A Survey of Taoist Literature*, 70–78. He figures in other early *zhiguai* tales as well, one of them being *Youming lu* 106 (LX 270).

During the Jin Taiyuan period [376–397], Gao Heng of Le'an was governor of Wei commandery and was stationed at Shitou. His grandson Yazhi said that while he was in the stable, a god had descended to him, calling himself Old Man Whitehead and leaning on a staff that emitted enough light to illuminate the whole room. He behaved familiarly with Yazhi and set out on an overnight journey with him; in one evening they went to Jingkou and returned again by morning.

Later, Yazhi and his father were killed by Huan Xuan.*

The Jin emperor Wu was once cooling off from the heat beneath the northern window of the palace when he suddenly saw a man wearing a white-lined robe of plain yellow silk. His entire body was dripping wet, and he announced himself as the god of the pond in the Floriate Grove garden, giving his name as Lord of Dripping Overflow. He told the ruler, "If you treat me well, I will reward you." The emperor, however, was already in his cups. He drew the sword he always wore at his waist and stabbed the figure, but his sword hit nothing. The god was enraged and cried, "If I am not to be received as an honored guest but instead treated in this way, I will cause you to know where it is you are living."

In a little while the emperor died. Many said that this misfortune was brought on by this spirit.

During the Yixi period [405–418], a board, two feet by over twenty, suddenly appeared in Nie Lake in Jiangcheng and came to rest on the bank of the river. Gatherers of water caltrop and fishermen availed themselves of it and saved themselves thereby.

Later several persons rode it downriver into the lake. They tried cutting it with knives, and blood at once came forth, the board sank, and several of the people drowned.

---

*On Huan Xuan, son of Huan Wen and, like his father, a noted military commander, see Lewis, *China between Empires,* 69.

Early in the Longan reign period of the Jin emperor An [397–402], a commoner from Qu'e named Xie Sheng was boating on a lake, gathering water caltrop, when he saw a lamia coming toward his boat. He turned the boat so as to avoid it, but the lamia followed him, so Sheng used his prong to kill it. Fearful, he returned home. A year went by without mishap.

In the Yuanxing period there was a severe drought. Sheng and several companions were walking beside the same lake when he spotted his prong on the ground nearby. He picked it up and said, "This is my prong." When the others asked him why it was there, he told them the truth. Walking several more steps, he felt a sharp pain in his heart. He returned home but was dead the same night.

During the Jin, Zhu Huangzu[64] served his relatives with utmost filiality. His mother developed a serious ailment, and he bowed his head to the ground in his courtyard. In a moment the Heavenly River* opened and brightened, and down came an old gentleman, accompanied by a child, carrying a box. He presented the mother with two medicinal pellets to swallow, and when she did so, her ailment suddenly vanished. So they stayed the night. During that night, over the guest quarters there was a five-colored column of vapor reaching up to the heavens, and the music of zithers and voices could be heard clearly. Huangzu went out to look. Sitting within the canopy of the Dipper, at its four corners and at the crown, were large pearls shaped like geese, scintillating with light. The old man told him, "In the third month, you should row up the River to us."

When the time arrived, Huangzu set out. He saw a gate inscription that read "Gate of the Virtuous and Blessed." Inside it was a body of water called Drunkspring Pond, in which there were lotus flowers as big as cartwheels.

Huan Miao was a native of Runan commandery. He once presented four black ducks to be used in a ritual. His eldest son dreamed of four black-clad

---

*The Milky Way. See Schafer, *Pacing the Void*, 257–269.

men pleading for their lives. Upon waking, he suddenly saw the ducks about to be slaughtered, so he saved them, buying meat as a replacement.

In his next dream the four men came to thank him, then departed.

[205]

Lü Qiu of Dongping had fine features and a handsome visage. Traveling by boat, he came to Qu'e Lake, where he encountered an unfavorable wind and could not proceed. He dropped anchor beside a patch of sedge. He saw a girl piloting a boat and gathering water caltrop. She was entirely clad in lotus leaves. So he asked her, "If you are not a demon, why are you clothed in this way?" Appearing afraid, she answered:

> Have you not heard of lotus garments?
> With a belt of fragrant grass, you arrived so quickly.
> Will you leave just as abruptly?

So saying, still looking fearful, she reversed her boat, adjusted her oars, and made off. From a distance Qiu shot her. She turned out to be[65] an otter. What had formerly seemed to be her boat turned out to be a mass of leaves of aquatic fern, artemisia, and mare's tail, along with aquatic grasses.

Qiu then noticed an old woman standing on the shore as if waiting for someone. When she saw Qiu passing by in his boat, she called out to him, "Sir, just now did you happen to see a girl picking caltrops on the lake?" Qiu answered, "She's right behind me." He shot the woman and again obtained an old otter.

Those who live beside this lake say that on the lake there frequently appears a girl picking water caltrop, her beauty surpassing that of a mere human, and that sometimes she goes to people's homes, and that many are those who have had relations with her.

[206]

When Liu Bin was serving in Wu commandery, there was a certain woman in Lou district who suddenly was borne aloft on a storm one night and wound up inside the walls of the capital city. She herself was only aware of being away from home for a brief moment, and her clothes were not wet.

She was aware of being atop a gate and asking to have this message passed [to Liu]: "I am a messenger of Heaven. You, Governor, should rise and come to welcome me. If you do, you will have much wealth and honor; if you do not, you will meet with disaster." Liu asked where she had come from, but she herself did not know.

About twenty days after this, Liu was indeed executed.

[207]

In Jingkou there was a young man of the Xu clan whose family was very destitute. He habitually collected driftwood from the riverside. One day he suddenly saw a whole procession of boats coming down the river, spread out all across it. Making their way across the waves, they anchored opposite Xu, and a messenger was sent over to him to say, "A celestial lady is to become Master Xu's wife today." Xu fled to the corner of his room and hid himself and would not come out; but his mother, older brother, and younger sister finally forced him to emerge.

Before he reached the boats, it was first ordered that a bath be prepared for Master Xu in a private chamber. The fragrance in the bathwater was not such as is usually found in this world. He was then presented with a gift of silk clothing. But Xu felt only terror. He merely sat on the edge of the bed with his legs crossed at the knees, and so that night the union was not consummated.

Afterward the girl was furious. She sent a messenger to request the return of the clothes and other items that had been given as gifts, and she herself withdrew. Everyone in his household resented and cursed him, and he died of shame.

[208]

Cai Xing of Jinling suddenly went mad. He would sometimes break out into song or would talk and laugh with invisible others around him. One of his interlocutors would say, "Which woman should I get next?" Another would say, "You already have plenty at home!"

One night later on, a dozen or more people were heard entering the home of Liu Yuzhi in the same village. Brandishing a blade, Yuzhi emerged from the rear door to see a black man, who shouted, "I am the supervisor of the lake, come to call on you, and now you mean to kill me?" Then the one in black called out, "Comrades, will none of you help me?" Yuzhi swung his blade wildly. He thus obtained a large turtle and a fox.

Zhenyi zhuan 甄異傳 (alternate title: *Zhenyi ji* 甄異記)
SELECTED ANOMALY ACCOUNTS*
Compiled by Dai Zuo 戴祚 (fl. late fourth century)
19 extant items

[209]

Zhang Kai of Xincheng in the second year of the [Jin] Jianwu period [344–345] was returning from outside the city to his home when he saw someone lying beside the road. When he inquired, the man said, "My foot is injured, and I cannot continue. My home is in Nanchu. I have nowhere else to turn." Kai took pity on him. He was transporting some goods in a second carriage; he abandoned these and took the man as a passenger.

When they reached Kai's home, however, the man did not appear grateful. Instead, he told Kai, "Earlier I wasn't really injured. I was just testing you." Kai, angry, retorted, "Who are you, sir, to toy with me in this way?" But the man replied, "I am a demon! I came on orders from the Northern Pavilion† to apprehend you. When I noticed your seniority, I couldn't bear to seize you, so I feigned injury and lay by the roadside. When you ditched your goods to carry me, I was in all sincerity impressed by the gesture. And yet I am here on orders and am not free to do as I please. What can be done?" Kai, frightened, asked the demon to stay. He set out a suckling pig and wine as an offering for it. The ghost having enjoyed the meal, Kai then wept and begged for his life. The demon said, "Is there anyone with the same given name as you?" Kai replied, "There is an immigrant named Huang Kai." "Go and visit him, and I will go there too," said the demon. When Kai reached

---

*On this work, see *WXS*, 321; *LZG*, 340–341; and *SW*, 67–68. Items 3 and 8 are translated in *CCT*, 125–128. Item 9 is translated in Campany, "Return-from-Death Narratives," 118.

†One of the multiple destinations of the dead, who were often imagined as journeying northward upon their demise.

the man's home, the man came out to see him, at which point the demon placed a red marker on the host's head, then stabbed him in the heart with a small dagger. When the host felt the dagger, the demon withdrew it, then said to Kai, "You, sir, have a noble physiognomy. Don't feel sorry for this man. I broke the regulations in order to save you. But the ways of the spirits are obscure and secret. Do not speak of this to others."

Kai then departed. The host suffered from a pain in his heart and died that same night. Kai lived to the age of sixty and reached the rank of grand master for splendid happiness.

[210]

When Yu Liang* was governing Jingzhou, he once went to the privy and saw inside it a creature resembling a masked exorcist, its eyes bright red, its body glowing, slowly emerging from the ground. Liang rolled up his sleeves and struck at it. There was a sound as his hand hit it. It then sank back into the ground.

Because of this, he contracted an illness and died.

[211]

In the fifth year of the [Jin] Taiyuan period [380–381], the commoner Wu Qing of Xuzhou was commissioned to serve in a military offensive. The draftees were sacrificing roosters to bring good fortune. Suddenly the cooked rooster head on Qing's plate began to crow. The sound lasted a long time.

Later, the expedition crushed the rebels. Their leader, Shao Bao, had been in the vanguard of the formation and had been killed. But there was only a pile of rigored corpses; none among the enemy could be recognized. But Qing spotted one corpse clad in a white brocade gown and suspected that it might be the rebel leader. So he pulled the body out of the pile, and when inquiries were made, it turned out that he had indeed found Shao Bao's head.

For this contribution Qing was awarded the governorship of Qinghe. So, for him to have risen to such a high position from such humble origins, the

---

*Yu Liang (289–340) was an important figure in Eastern Jin politics; see *SSHY*, 608.

apparent baleful omen of the rooster head ended up being converted into an auspicious sign.

[212]

Sima Yi of Jinwu had a concubine named Biyu who excelled at playing stringed instruments and singing. During the [Jin] Taiyuan period [376–397], he fell seriously ill. He warned Biyu, "After I die, you are not to remarry. If you remarry, I will kill you." She replied, "I respectfully receive your command."

After the burial a neighboring family wanted to acquire Biyu. As she was about to leave for their home, she saw Yi ride in through the gate on horseback, draw a bow, and shoot her through the throat. She felt a sharp pain in her throat; the look on her face changed, and she suddenly expired. Ten or more days later she revived. She could not speak, and her four limbs looked as if she had been beaten. After a year she began to be able to speak again, but not clearly.

In her appearance Biyu had never been beautiful at all. She had all along been chosen for her voice. Once she had undergone this misfortune, she was never able to remarry.

[213]

Zhang An, a native of Wuxing, was ill. At one point he began to feel that there was a creature atop his bedcovers, and his illness then grew much worse. Mustering his strength, An raised up the bedcovers and trapped the creature. It transformed into a bird resembling an owl.

He soon recovered from his case of malaria.

[214]

Zhang Boyuan, a native of Pei, died of illness when he was eight. At the foot of a big mountain he saw a dozen-odd children pushing a large wagon. The wagon was several poles tall. Boyuan joined the other children in pushing it. Just then a violent wind arose, stirring up a cloud of dust. Boyuan clung to a mulberry branch. He heard voices calling out to him, so he turned back. And so he revived. In his hair were still bits of sand and dust.

Later, as an adult, he was once traveling near Mount Tai* when he recognized the mulberry tree. It was just like the one he had seen while he was dead.

[215]

Wang Sigui of Changsha served as magistrate of Haiyan. One day he suddenly saw a functionary. He asked, "Who are you?" The functionary said, "I am ordered to summon you as recorder, sir," producing a summons placard and placing it before the bench. The functionary spoke again: "The appointed time is far off yet, not until the tenth month. If you do not believe me, look up at the sky at noon on the fifteenth of the seventh month. You will see something."

Sigui ordered the members of his family to watch the skies on that date. They heard the sound of wailing, and in the air they saw people hanging banners and arranging things, all as if for a funeral procession.

[216]

Hua Yi of Guangling resided in Jiangling. Seven years after his death he returned to his family home. At first, family members only heard his voice but did not see his form. They begged to be allowed to see him. He replied, "I am suffering now and cannot yet bear to be seen by you." When they asked why, he said, "Although my original allotted life span was not long, it was not yet exhausted when I died. I am guilty of having administered excessive punishments while I was alive, as well as having killed servants and slaves. For this I had my life counts reduced." Then he said,[66] "I have received orders to go to Changsha. I will return here on my way back." He did indeed return at the promised time. He admonished his two sons, "Since I died early, you two must be diligent and self-disciplined. If the family perishes, what sorts of sons will you turn out to have been?" He also upbraided his older brother for not admonishing his two sons more severely.

*A sacred mountain in Shandong province in the northeast that had long been believed to be a destination of the dead.

His countenance was very disturbed. He then said, "Meng Yu's name has already been added to the register of the dead.* His days are numbered."

At the time, Yu was healthy and strong, but at the time Yi had predicted, Yu suddenly died.

[217]

Xiahou Wengui, a native of Qiao commandery, resided in the capital. A year after his death he manifested his form and returned home riding a calf-drawn carriage and attended by several dozen retainers, calling himself governor of Beihai. His family set out food for him. As they watched, the food and drink would disappear, but after they took away the vessels, they would be full again as before. Family members wailed and wept, but Wengui said, "Do not wail. I will come again soon." He would return every month or so, sometimes staying half a day. The red-clad outriders he always brought with him were small bodied; they would sit and wait on the fence or in a side room, one never quite knew where. But whenever it was time for Wengui to depart, and the family members would call out to the outriders to get up, they would fall into place in orderly fashion, not like strange creatures.

Wengui had a grandson who was several years old and of whom he was very fond. When he called for the child to be brought to him, his attendant ghosts brought the child forward, but the boy could not tolerate the *qi* of ghosts, and so he fainted away unconscious. At this, Wengui asked for water and spit some on him, and the boy regained consciousness.

Seeing a peach tree in the courtyard, Wengui remarked, "I planted this tree. My, how well it has grown." His wife asked, "People say that the dead fear peach wood. How is it you are not afraid of it?"† Wengui replied, "A southeast branch from a peach tree, one that is two feet eight inches long and pointing toward the sun—we do detest these; but others we do not fear." He saw some garlic husks on the floor and ordered that they be cleared away. Judging from this, it would seem that he detested garlic but feared peach wood.

---

*The registers of the dead (*silu* 死錄) were lists of the names of those who had died or were due to do so soon.

†Peach wood was generally believed to ward off unwelcome spirits. The ghost here is suggesting a revision of this common wisdom.

Yang Chounu of Henan often pulled up calamus in Zhang'an Lake. On one such occasion it was approaching sunset when he saw a young woman, scantily clad and with a comely face. She was in a boat gathering calamus. Her home was by the lakeside. The onset of darkness prevented him from returning home, so he dropped anchor and stayed on at the woman's place. He borrowed some eating utensils. On the plates were dried fish and raw vegetables. After having eaten, they amused themselves and laughed. Chounu teased her with a song, to which the woman replied, "My home is on the western shore of the lake. The sun has set and daylight has faded. Having had the good fortune to meet such a kind gentleman, I have begun, unawares, to have feelings for you."*

They quickly extinguished the light and lay down together. Chounu noticed that she exuded a rank odor and had very short fingers. Only then did he begin to suspect that she was a sprite. The creature, able to recognize people's intentions, quickly fled out the door. Metamorphosing into an otter, it ran straight into the water.

Zhi guai 志怪
ACCOUNTS OF ANOMALIES†
Compiled by Zu Taizhi 祖台之 (fl. ca. 376–410)
15 extant items

[219]

During the Longan period [of the Jin (397–402)], Chen Kui set a fish trap near the bank of the Jiang River. When the tide receded, he found a woman in the trap. She was six feet long, beautiful, and wore no clothes. Once the water had receded, she had become unable to move and lay there on the sand. She did not respond when spoken to. Someone had come along and violated her.

---

*This reply is in five-character unrhymed verse and so may be intended to represent the song she sang in response.

†On this work, see *LZG*, 335; *WXS*, 319; and *SW*, 63–64.

That night she appeared to Kui in a dream, saying, "I am a 'river-yellow.'* Yesterday I lost my way and blundered into your trap. On top of that, I was violated by someone. I will now report this to the god† in order to have that man killed." Kui did not dare move.

When the tide came back in, the creature went off into the water. As for the rapist, he soon was stricken with illness.

[220]

There was a gentleman officer in Wu who was heading home on leave from the capital. Upon reaching the dam at Qu'e, he saw an attractive woman and called to her to come and join him for the night. The gentleman removed a golden clasp from his arm and fastened it to hers in hopes that she might return that evening, but she did not.

The next day he sent a man to look for her. The woman was nowhere to be found. But, passing by a pigpen, the man suddenly caught sight of a sow with a golden clasp on one of its forelegs.

Other Assorted Accounts

[221]

Xiahou Hong[67] claimed that he could personally see ghosts and converse with them, but no one believed him. Suddenly one day, the horse often ridden by the West-quelling general Xie Shang died. It so happened that Hong at this time was visiting Shang. Shang was extremely morose, so Hong told him, "How would you like it if I were to revive your horse for you?" Shang, who had never believed Hong, replied, "If you can resurrect this horse, then you must truly be able to communicate with spirits." At this, Hong got down from his couch. After a long while he returned and told Shang, "It's just that the temple god loved your horse, and so he took it. Just

---

*Jianghuang 江黃, a term apparently attested only here and seemingly a generic term for a type of anomalous water creature.

†Probably not the gods in general but the god of the Jiang River.

now, when I went to see him and requested it, at first he was stubborn and would not agree, but afterward he allowed it. The horse will revive right away." Shang went and sat down beside his dead horse, firmly disbelieving this in his mind and thinking what Hong had said very strange. In a moment his horse came galloping in through the gate; everyone present saw it, and there were none who were not astonished. When it arrived at the place where its own carcass was, it promptly vanished, while at the same time the carcass began to move. In a little while it was back on its feet, neighing. Shang was greatly relieved at this.

Xie [also] said to Hong, "It is my lifelong punishment not to have any male descendants." For a little while Hong made no reply; then he said, "Just now I saw a minor spirit, but he can under no conditions discuss the reasons for this."

Sometime later, Hong ran across a ghost riding along in a new carriage, followed by about a dozen retainers. The ghost wore an azure gown made of silk cloth. Hong stood before the procession and seized the draft calf by the nose. The personage on the carriage said to Hong, "Why are you detaining me?" Hong answered, "There is a matter I wish to ask you about. The West-quelling general Xie Shang has no son. This gentleman has an excellent reputation; his ancestral sacrifices must not be allowed to be cut off." The expression on the face of the person in the carriage changed, and he replied, "The man you have mentioned, sir, is my son. In his youth he had an affair with one of the family slaves. He swore to her that he would not marry another, but then he broke his oath. Now this slave has died, and she has filed a plaint against him in the heavens.* This is why he has no son." Hong spoke of all of this to Xie Shang, who responded, "Those events really did happen in my youth."

In Jiangling, Hong saw a great demon carrying a spear, followed by several lesser demons. Hong was frightened and got off the road to avoid them. After the greater demon had passed by, Hong grabbed one of the smaller ones and asked, "What being is this?" "A *dasha*† from Guangzhou," the demon replied. "What is it doing with this spear?" "It attacks people

---

*The wronged dead were thought to have the power to file a plaint (*su* 訴) against the offending party. If it was found to have merit, the plaint would result in the illness, injury, or death of the guilty party. Such plaints often figured in ghost stories and were much feared. See Cohen, *Tales of Vengeful Souls*; and Bokenkamp, *Ancestors and Anxiety*.

†Literally, a "big killer."

with this spear. If a person gets hit by it in the heart or stomach, he will certainly die; if he gets hit anywhere else, it's not fatal." Hong asked, "Is there a method for curing this illness?" The demon answered, "Lay a black chicken over the person, and he will recover." Hong then asked, "Where are you headed now?" The demon said, "We're headed into Jingzhou and Yangzhou." That same day an illness of the heart and stomach indeed broke out [in those regions], and everyone who contracted it was dying. So Hong told people to slaughter black chickens and cover the sick with them, and in this way eight or nine out of every ten were saved. The custom today of laying a black chicken on oneself when sick stems from Hong.

[222]

The monk Zhu Sengyao obtained a divine incantation[68] and was especially good at restraining demons. A girl in the household of the prince of Guangling was made ill by a demon. Yao was summoned to cure her.

Upon entering the [outer] door, he opened his eyes wide in a glare and yelled in a loud voice, "Old demon! Rather than fixing your thoughts on cultivating the path, you dare to attack people!" Within the inner quarters the girl could be heard wailing, "Someone's killing my husband!" Beside her the demon said, "My life is over now! How it grieves me!" It then blubbered and sobbed with sorrow. It spoke again: "There's no way to fight against this spirit!" Bystanders heard it all.

The demon then transformed into an old tortoise and crawled out into the courtyard. Sengyao ordered a slave to kill it.

[223]

During the Jin, Yuan Wuji of the Chen kingdom was residing in Dongping. At the beginning of the Yongjia era [307–313], an epidemic broke out in the area, and of his family of over a hundred persons, almost all died. Fleeing the central family residence, he was compelled to live in makeshift quarters out in the fields. There, in a small hut, he and his brothers slept together on plank beds covered with several mats. They would sleep at night, and then during the day they would place the beds outside,[69] and in this way they managed to dwell there. But the brothers were uneasy and fearful and thus unable to sleep.

Later they saw a lady arrive before the door of the hut. Realizing that Wuji and the others were not asleep, she remained outside the door. It was not yet near dawn, but the moon was bright, and they could see her outside. She wore a variegated robe and white makeup. In her tied-up hair atop her head she wore a floral pin and a silver and ivory comb. Wuji and the others began chasing her. At first she ran around the hut several times, causing all the ornaments to fall out of her hair; Wuji picked them up. Then she ran off through a gate toward the south. Beside the road was a well. The lady jumped into it. Wuji and the others returned and went to sleep.

In the morning they could see that the pin and comb were real objects. Reaching down into the well, they found a catalpa coffin rotted away by the water. So Wuji changed [the lady's] coffin and clothing for new. He returned her items to her and reburied her in a high and dry location.

After that [the epidemic] ceased.

[224]

During the Wei, Liu Chifu dreamed that Marquis Jiang was summoning him to serve as recorder. When the appointed day was drawing near, he went to the temple to set forth a plea: "My mother is old, my son is weak: these are affecting and extenuating circumstances. I beg you out of mercy to release and forgive me from this obligation. Wei Guo of Guiji is very accomplished and is devoted to the service of spirits. I beg your leave to nominate Guo as my own replacement." He knocked his head on the ground till blood ran.

The temple invocator responded:* "I especially wish to appoint you. Who is Wei Guo, that you should recommend him?" Chifu pleaded further, but to no avail. Soon afterward he died.

[225]

During the Xianning era† a son of Chamberlain for Ceremonials Han Bo, a son of Chamberlain for the Capital Wang Yun of Guiji, and a son of Grand

---

*The god, Marquis Jiang, is responding through the invocator (*miao zhu* 廟祝).

†*FYZL* adds "of the Song," and LX also writes the line thus, but there was no such reign era of the Liu Song dynasty. Xianning was a reign era of the Western Jin, corresponding to the dates 275–280.

Master for Splendid Happiness Liu Dan traveled together to the temple of Mount Jiang. In the temple were several comely images of women.* Inebriated, each of the young men pointed to one of the images and picked her out, in jest, to be his wife.

That night each of the three men had the same dream. In the dream Marquis Jiang sent a message: "The girls in my family are base and homely, but you have seen fit to look upon them with favor. Let us set a date soon on which you will be received here." Each of the men felt that the dream must indicate something extraordinary, and when they discussed it with one another, they realized that they had each dreamed precisely the same thing.

At this they were terrified. They prepared the three sacrificial animals† and went back to the temple to apologize for their sin and beg for forgiveness. Again they dreamed that Marquis Jiang personally descended and said: "It was you gentlemen who looked upon [my daughters] and desired a liaison. The agreed-upon time is nigh. How can I permit things to be suddenly changed just because of your regret?"

Shortly afterward all three of them died.

---

*These would have been images of the daughters of Marquis Jiang, the god worshipped in this temple.
†Bull, pig, and lamb.

ENDNOTES

1. *TPYL* gives his name as 宋董; LX as 宋謹; and *TPGJ* as Song Dong 宋董.

2. Both *TPYL* and *TPGJ* have 非苴杖即削杖, indicating two types of staffs hung outside households in mourning and carried in funeral processions.

3. *TPGJ* gives his name as You Xianchao 游先朝; I follow *TPYL*.

4. The wording of *TPYL* suggests that it is Xie Zong who is doing this, but *TPGJ* makes clear that others are involved, and this fits subsequent details in the *TPYL* quotation better, so I supply this phrase here.

5. *TPYL* 882 and *YWLJ* have Lord Dusuo addressing these words to the strangely attired visitor; *TPYL* 968 and *Qimin yaoshu* have the visitor addressing them to the god.

6. Here I follow the Scripta Sinica edition of *TPGJ*. Other, printed editions, as well as LX, mention here the *Classic of Odes* as the book Sheng studied.

7. Instead of "thigh," *TPYL* 819 has "the upper back."

8. All sources have 至一大冢木中有好婦; I am treating *zhong mu* 冢木 as an error for *zhongmu* 冢墓, "tomb." That all sources share the error (if error it is) shows that the *TPYL* compilers quoted from the *Sanguo zhi* text and not from an independently transmitted version of *Lushi yilin*, a text probably otherwise lost by the early tenth century.

9. *BTSC* writes Zhi 支 as his given name and misprints his place of origin.

10. *BTSC* breaks off at this point.

11. The *Lieyi zhuan* version writes his name as Jiang Yan 江嚴.

12. The *Lieyi zhuan* version says that the jade was crimson colored and had the shape of a bird.

13. Some versions have Dangyang.

14. Some versions put this statement in the mouth of Dong Zhaozhi.

15. *TPYL* gives his name as Wang Qiongzhi 王瓊之 and his native place as Guangling.

16. *TPYL* 867 has "buffalo"; *TPYL* 41 and *TPGJ* have "goats" (and *TPGJ* has not three but three hundred of them). *TPGJ* has the master drinking water from the pool; the other two early witnesses have him leading Yu Hong to the waterfall. *TPYL* 41 places the encounter on Mount Tiantai.

17. Thus *FYZL*. *TPYL* 377 instead records the following commentarial insertion here: "He was born along with Heaven and Earth and does not perish; that is why he is called "the Dependable." *FYZL* also quotes this commentarial line but attaches it as a gloss of the next name ("the Numinous").

18. Following the emendation in the Scripta Sinica online edition of *TPGJ*, which here restores the word *dao* 道 (thus forming the expression *daoren* 道人) on the basis of a Ming-era textual witness.

19. Emending *TPGJ*, which has 黃白, in accordance with the electronic Scripta Sinica edition, based on a Ming edition.

20. On *dongfu* 東府, see *Hanyu dacidian* 4.834a.

21. *TPYL* 767 gives his name as Hu Zi 胡茲.

22. A variant version has "Afterward it would make sounds like a buffalo."

23. *TPGJ* has "monks" here, not "nuns."

24. Here reading *xiong* 胸 with *Yi yuan* 6.38 rather than *nao* 腦 with *TPGJ* and LX.

25. Following Lu Xun's emendation.

26. Reading *chang* 嘗 with LX, not *chang* 常 with *TPYL*.

27. *BTSC* gives his name as Xiahou Zuhuan 夏侯祖歡.

28. *TPYL* has "Neither of them married."

29. Preferring *TPGJ*'s *lian* 殮 to LX's *lian* 歛.

30. In many editions of Ren Fang's *Shuyi ji* the protagonist's name is printed as Wu Helong 吳合龍, a variant easily enough explained as a copying error. I here follow all the other versions of the story in rendering the name as Wu Kan 吳龕.

31. This sentence appears in the *Youming lu* and *Xu Qi Xie ji* versions; I add it here.

32. Following *TPYL* and Li Jianguo. *FYZL* unsurprisingly puts it more strongly: "Maohui then began to put his faith in the Buddha and practiced the religion energetically."

33. Some versions give his name as Zhang Xun 荀.

34. Reading *lian* 殮—which can mean to prepare for burial or more specifically to seal the corpse in the coffin—for the *lian* 歛 given in *TPGJ* and LX.

35. LX and *TPYL* have 長年寺; *TPGJ* has 長干寺. I follow *TPGJ*.

36. Some versions have "lascivious women."

37. Different versions vary on the gender.

38. The last sentence is based on the *Wuling ji* version.

39. The last sentence is based on *TPYL*, which differs slightly from the text given in the *XJTY* edition of *Yi yuan*.

40. Following *TPGJ* 360, one would understand this to be the designation arrived at by the persons digging up the floor. *TPGJ* 418 and the *XJTY* edition add the graph 俗 before 謂, and I translate accordingly.

41. Some versions have Su Xiang 巷.

42. One version has "each time they went into the fields"; another has "each time they drank."

43. *Shuyi ji* here has "The [future] emperor asked, 'What deity is [your king]?' but the youths made no reply." The final line of this story appears only in *Shuyi ji*.

44. The *XJTY* edition opens with 晉武太始初, but Taishi 太始 was a reign era under the Han emperor Wu and not during the Jin. *TPGJ* and *TPYL* place the events in the Song but do not specify a ruler or era. I follow them.

45. Combining the readings in both editions, each of which seems problematic. The *XJTY* edition has "Afterward [his corpse] disappeared, [and there were] numinous anomalies" (便失所在靈恠). The *Shuo ku* edition has "Afterward numinous anomalies were noticed in the area" (便覺所在靈恠).

46. This date is given in *TPYL*; other versions lack it.

47. *TPYL* gives his surname as Chen 陳.

48. *YWLJ* has "she would always first place it on top of the tomb" (輒先以著墳上).

49. Reading *qian* 淺 for *YWLJ*'s *qian* 潛 and *XJTY*'s *quan* 泉 here.

50. *YWLJ* has 敢忘翳桑之報; *XJTY* has 豈忘翳桑之報. I follow *XJTY*. "Reward you generously" is literally "recompense as [in the case of the man from] Yisang," an allusion to a passage in the *Zuo Annals* (*Zuo zhuan* 左傳, 魯宣公二年). My thanks to Susan Huang for help with the reference.

51. *YWLJ* has 自是設饌愈謹; *XJTY* has 從是禱酹愈至. The meaning is roughly the same.

52. Some texts give his name as Wan Tui 推.

53. For Yuan 元, the Scripta Sinica online version of *Han Wei liuchao biji xiaoshuo daguan*, as well as the *Shuo ku* edition, have Xuan 玄.

54. Reading 勿 for 忽.

55. *TPYL* here has Beihai 北海.

56. Preferring *TPGJ*'s *wenshu* 文書 to the *XJTY* edition's *fushu* 父書.

57. Some editions give his name as Zhang Fan 汎.

58. *TPGJ* omits the preceding phrase.

59. Reading 時 for 始.

60. Here following *TPGJ*.

61. Here following *TPYL*.

62. *FYZL* has "half a year."

63. Thus *FYZL*, which LX here follows: 罪牽君當可如何. *TPYL* has simply 當如何.

64. *TPYL* 999 gives his surname as Mo 末.

65. LX misprints 印 for *YWLJ*'s 即.

66. Here preferring *TPGJ*'s *yun* 云 over LX's *qu* 去.

67. *TPGJ*, *TPYL* 884, and *Soushen ji* give the name thus; *TPYL* 897 has Sun Hong 孫弘.

68. Thus *TPGJ*; *TPYL* has "divine talisman" (*shenfu* 神符).

69. Preferring the *TPGJ* text here to that in *FYZL* and LX.

TEXTUAL SOURCES

Item
Number

1   LX 333; *TPYL* 718.7b.

2   LX 537; *FYZL* 13.383b. I translate from *FYZL*.

3   LX 538–539; *FYZL* 85.910a.

4   LX 541; *FYZL* 85.910a. The story is repeated in closely similar wording but without attribution in *Xu gaoseng zhuan* 續高僧傳 (*T* 2060) 28.686.

5   LX 393; *TPGJ* 276.44; *TPYL* 400.9b. Translation based on *TPYL*.

6   LX 394; *TPGJ* 368.5; *TPYL* 707.4a.

7   LX 394; *TPGJ* 368.6; *TPYL* 698.5a.

8   LX 215–217, based on a note in *Shishuo xinyu* 世說新語, chapter *"Fangzheng-pian"* 方正篇; summary in *Mengqiu zhu* 蒙求注 1. I have benefited from the translation in *SSHY,* 159–161, adopting almost wholesale Mather's rendition of the verses. A version appears in *Soushen ji* 16.22 (quoted in *TPGJ* 316.4 and *TPYL* 884.3b–4b), and another, shorter version is attributed to *Soushen houji* (quoted in *TPYL* 30.9a–b).

9   LX 218; cited in a note in *Shishuo xinyu* 世說新語, chapter *"Paidiao pian"* 排調, and previously translated in *SSHY,* 409. A version appears in Gan Bao's official biography in *Jin shu* 82.2150, translated in *SW,* 146–147. Another appears in *Soushen houji;* see *XJS,* 557–558.

10   LX 218; *YWLJ* 89.1531; *TPYL* 957.3b. Also appears as *Soushen houji* 7.6 in traditional arrangements of that text. The wording is virtually identical across versions; I translate from LX.

11   LX 218–219; *TPYL* 931.9b–10a. Another version is quoted in *TPGJ* 468.16 from a text simply titled *Zhi guai* 志怪. (LX 424 collects this as item 12 under his miscellaneous rubric *Za guishen zhiguai* 雜鬼神志怪.) This version ends differently: Xie Zong puts the three turtles in a basket and shows them to his uncle, a high-ranking official.

12   LX 136; *TPYL* 884.2b–3a; *TPGJ* 316.2, which slightly truncates the ending.

13   LX 137; *TPYL* 934.2b. Longer versions appear in *Hou Han shu* 82B.2749 and *Soushen ji* 2.1, the latter of which is partially quoted in *FYZL* 31.525.

14 LX 139; *Qimin yaoshu* 10.239; *CXJ* 28.672; *YWLJ* 86.1466; *TPYL* 968.6a. LX lists *TPYL* 882 as a source, but I have not located the story there.

15 LX 141; *TPYL* 762.6a; *TPGJ* 400.7. A version appears as *Soushen ji* 18.2 and is cited from that text in *TPYL* 472 and 882 and in *YWLJ* 64, among other places.

16 LX 143, cited in a commentary to *Wenxuan* 31 and in *TPYL* 884.3a. A version is attributed to *Soushen ji* (2.14) in *TPGJ* 284.4 and other sources.

17 LX 143; *TPYL* 710.11a.

18 LX 144, based on *TPYL* 51.6a–b. Another version appears in *Soushen ji* 4.20.

19 LX 144–145, based on *TPGJ* 316.5. A similar version appears as *Soushen ji* 16.21 and is quoted from that work in *FYZL* 75 and in *TPYL* 375 and 693.

20 LX 146, based on *TPYL* 253.6a–b. A version of the story attributed to *Xu soushen ji*, with a differently surnamed protagonist, is translated as item 98.

21 LX 147; *BTSC* 158.6a–b; *YWLJ* 95.1658; *TPYL* 885.3b, 911.7a. Another version appears in *Soushen ji* 18.25.

22 LX 385; *Sanguo zhi* 13.396; *TPYL* 819.2a–b, 887.5b–6a.

23 LX 412; *TPGJ* 316.7 Another version appears in *Zhi guai* by Zu Taizhi (item 2, LX 208), cited in *TPYL* 718.

24 LX 413–414; *TPGJ* 383.7. Another version appears in *Soushen ji* 15.6.

25 LX 414; *TPGJ* 383.9; *BTSC* 127.6a. I translate from *TPGJ*.

26 LX 415; *TPYL* 345.9b. Discussed in *SW,* 231.

27 LX 416; *TPGJ* 318.13; *TPYL* 743.2b–3a.

28 LX 417; *TPYL* 805.8a. Another version appears in *Lieyi zhuan* 44 (LX 146, based on *TPGJ* 401.13).

29 LX 231–232; my translation follows the version cited in *TPGJ* 473.8. All but a few variants appearing in the following other locations go unremarked in my notes: *YWLJ* 97.1689; *TPYL* 479.7b, 643.9b–10a; *CXJ* 20.493. Another version appears in *Soushen ji* 20.8. Previously translated in *CCT,* 134–135; my translation differs.

30 LX 233–234; *TPGJ* 426.8; *FYZL* 32.532; *TPYL* 888.7a.

31 LX 234; *TPGJ* 461.28.

32 LX 234; *TPYL* 743.6a; *TPGJ* 218.5. Translation based on Scripta Sinica version of *TPGJ* (incorporating a Ming-era variant and differing slightly in other ways from *TPYL*, which LX takes as the base text).

33 LX 234–235; *TPYL* 816.7a; *BTSC* 129.9a. The last sentence is an appended note.

34 LX 235; *TPYL* 883.7b; *TPGJ* 321.2. Translation based on *TPGJ*.

35 LX 235; *TPYL* 30.2a–b, 825.4b.

36 LX 235; *TPGJ* 318.8; *TPYL* 353.1b–2a. The versions are identical except for synonymous graphic variants.

37 LX 235–236; *TPYL* 598.8a.

38 LX 227, based on a citation in *Taiping huanyu ji;* I have not located this item in that work. Partial version in *Shuijing zhu* 29.2447–2448, citing *Shenyi zhuan* 神異傳. A version appears in *Soushen ji* 13.8; *Shen lu* is more detailed and adds an ending omitted in *Soushen ji.*

39   LX 227, citing *Taiping huanyu ji* as the source. I have not found this item in editions of this work to which I have access.

40   Collected in LX 223 as *Shenguai lu*, based on *Mengqiu zhu* 2 and *TPYL* 559.7a (both of which cite *Shenguai zhi*). Quoted without attribution in *TPGJ* 391.7, where the protagonist is said to have served as general under the Tang, so this may be a Tang-period tale (see *SW,* 97), but it might also have originated earlier.

41   *TPGJ* 467.5.

42   *TPGJ* 295.5.

43   LX 399–400; *TPYL* 710.11a–b. A slightly different version is attributed to *Shengui zhuan* 神鬼傳 in *TPGJ* 293.10. A shorter version appears in item 78.

44   LX 400; *TPYL* 41.2a–b (citing *Shenyi jing* 神異經), 867.3a; *TPGJ* 412.32. Translation based on *TPGJ.*

45   *HWCS* ed. 3a–b; *TPYL* 377.6b; *FYZL* 5.307; *TPGJ* 482.16. I translate from the collated version in Zhou Ciji, *Shenyi jing yanjiu,* 17–18.

46   *HWCS* ed. 11b–12a; *TPYL* 377.6b, 845.2b; *FYZL* 5.307c; *YWLJ* 72.1247, 98.1698; Zhou Ciji, *Shenyi jing yanjiu,* 61. There are no significant differences in the main body of the text across these versions, but at certain points *YWLJ* 72, *TPYL* 377, and *FYZL* include commentarial passages. Zhou Ciji does not provide these, nor does he list *FYZL* and *YWLJ* as sources for this item. I include the commentarial passages in the translation.

47   LX 166; *TPYL* 966.2b–3a, 490.5a; *CXJ* 28.680; *YWLJ* 86.1474. A less detailed version appears in *Soushen ji* 17.12.

48   LX 167; *TPGJ* 400.6; *TPYL* 811.4b, also 387.5a (partial); *FYZL* 28.496. Translated from LX. A summary version of the last portion, but structured differently, also appears in Ren Fang's *Shuyi ji* (*HWCS* ed. 1.10b) and is translated and discussed in the Introduction.

49   LX 168; *TPGJ* 294.11.

50   Whether the story initially was included in the text with this title compiled by Zu Chongzhi, or the one by Ren Fang, or both, is unclear. I translate from the text given by LX (170–171, = *Shuyi ji* 18). Versions of the story are quoted from one of the two texts titled *Shuyi ji* in *TPYL* 936.2b, 955.6a (where it is Ren Fang's text that is cited); and *YWLJ* 9.168, 88.1521. Versions are quoted from *Shuzheng ji* 述征記 in *TPYL* 66 and *FYZL* 28. *FYZL* is quoted in turn in *TPGJ* 467.2.

51   LX 172; *TPYL* 990.5a. A more developed version is preserved in a quotation from *Guang gujin wuxing ji* 廣古今五行記 in *TPGJ* 322.13. This was a Tang work compiled by Dou Weiwu 竇維鋈.

52   LX 172; *FYZL* 32.532.

53   LX 173; *TPYL* 400.9a.

54   LX 177–178, based on *TPYL* 905.4b and *TPGJ* 437.16. *YWLJ* 94.1639 quotes a truncated version.

55   LX 177; *FYZL* 32.527b; *TPGJ* 360.19 (which attributes the story to *Soushen ji*). *TPYL* 942.7a–b cites a version from *Guang wuxing ji.*

56	LX 175–176; *TPGJ* 296.2.
57	LX 178; *TPGJ* 325.9.
58	LX 179; *TPYL* 559.3a–b.
59	LX 179–180; *TPGJ* 325.6.
60	LX 180; *TPGJ* 377.3.
61	LX 181–182. Translation based on *FYZL* 46.639c–640a and its quotation in *TPGJ* 324.15. *TPYL* 767.3b is a summary of part of the story. *Yi yuan* 6.31 (*XJTY* ed. 6.9a) also preserves part of the same narrative.
62	LX 182; *TPGJ* 325.7.
63	LX 182–183; *TPGJ* 325.8. Translated from *TPGJ*.
64	LX 183; *TPGJ* 325.5. A version of the first paragraph also appears as *Yi yuan* 6.37, and of the second paragraph as *Yi yuan* 6.38. Other material on the Yellow Father demon may be found in *Hou Han shu* 57.1841 and in a *Shenyi jing* 神異經 passage translated in item 45.
65	LX 183–184; *TPGJ* 326.2.
66	LX 184; *TPGJ* 383.10. Translated from the Scripta Sinica edition of *TPGJ*.
67	LX 184–185; *TPGJ* 325.14.
68	LX 185; *TPYL* 897.6b.
69	LX 185–186; *TPYL* 766.9a (citing *Yi ji* 異記).
70	LX 186–187; *FYZL* 46.640a.
71	LX 187; *TPYL* 753.4a. *TPGJ* 325.13 cites a similar version, with some variations in the ghost's letter, from *Zhugong jiushi* 渚宮舊事.
72	LX 187–188; *TPGJ* 323.15.
73	LX 188; *BTSC* 87.9a.
74	LX 188–189, based largely on *TPYL* 916.7b. Portions are quoted in *YWLJ* 63.1130–31 and 90.1564. A version similar to that quoted in *TPYL* appears in Ren Fang's *Shuyi ji* as item 1.78 (1.13b–14a in *HWCS* ed.). A version is also quoted in *Sandong qunxian lu* 三洞群仙錄 16, where it is attributed to *Suiyi ji* 遂異記 [*sic*].
75	LX 189; *TPYL* 757.6a.
76	LX 189; *TPYL* 696.2b. A similar version is partially quoted in *BTSC* 129.21a. A longer version, with a second part not evidenced in these sources, is quoted from *Guang gujin wuxing ji* in *TPGJ* 324.10.
77	LX 190; *TPGJ* 276.49; *TPYL* 399.9a–b, 479.7a. LX also lists a citation in *Baikong liutie* 23, which I have not consulted.
78	LX 190; *BTSC* 133.12a. A longer version of the same story appears in item 43.
79	LX 190; *BTSC* 87.9a. An only slightly different version is quoted in *TPYL* 532.8a–b.
80	LX 191; *TPGJ* 318.10.
81	LX 191; *TPGJ* 322.11.
82	LX 192; *TPYL* 912.4a.
83	LX 192; *TPYL* 910.4a. *TPGJ* 131.17 also quotes a version of the story from *Shuyi ji*, giving the protagonist's name as 伍寺之. It reads as if it were a summary of the tale, but it also contains other differences (such as the mention

of a serpent in place of the tiger mentioned in *TPYL*). I do not list all the variants.

84   LX 192; *TPGJ* 327.2.

85   *HWCS* ed. 1.1a–b. I have not located citations of this passage elsewhere.

86   *HWCS* ed. 1.11b. Not located in collectanea.

87   *HWCS* ed. 1.13b. I have not located this item in collectanea, but three significantly different versions of the story are cited—all from *Nankang ji* 南康記 by Deng Deming 鄧德明—in *TPYL* 48.8a, 559.6b–7a, and 941.3b–4a (this last version is much longer and quite different).

88   *HWCS* ed. 1.11b. A version appears in traditional editions of *Soushen houji* (1.11) but is nowhere cited from it (by that title or the alternate *Xu soushen ji*) in collectanea (see *XJS*, 705). Several works (including *TPYL* 46) cite a version from a *Xuancheng ji* 宣城記 by Ji Yi 紀義 that adds a final sentence about the continued performance of music beside this spring.

89   *HWCS* ed. 2.20a is the basic translation text. Other versions, no two completely alike, also appear in Zu Chongzhi's *Shuyi ji* 86 (LX 192, based on *BTSC* 77.10a); *Youming lu* (LX 286, based on multiple sources; a truncated form of this version is also cited in *Bencao gangmu* 本草綱目 52 in the section "Human puppets" [*renkui* 人傀]); *Yi yuan* 2.23; and *Xu Qi Xie ji* 20 as quoted in *TPYL* 703.6a (Wang Guoliang, *Xu Qi Xie ji yanjiu*, 63).

90   *HWCS* ed. 2.3a; *TPGJ* 410.8; *TPYL* 968.6b.

91   *XJS*, 495–496; *FYZL* 46.639 (cited in turn in *TPGJ* 319.4); *TPYL* 884.5b.

92   *XJS*, 503. *TPYL* 981.7a cites it from *Xu soushen ji*.

93   *XJS*, 583. Cited from *Xu soushen ji* in *TPYL* 248.

94   *XJS*, 540. Cited from *Xu soushen ji* in *TPGJ* 462.9.

95   *XJS*, 535–536. Cited from *Xu soushen ji* in *TPYL* 909.7b.

96   *XJS*, 535. Cited from *Xu soushen ji* in *TPYL* 909.7b. A slightly less detailed version appears as *Youming lu* 110 (LX 270; cited in *TPYL* 704.5b).

97   *XJS*, 531. Cited from *Xu soushen ji* in *TPGJ* 446.3.

98   *XJS*, 536–537. Cited from *Xu soushen ji* in *TPYL* 717.5b and 905.6a–b; cited from *Soushen ji* in *YWLJ* 94.

99   *XJS*, 541–542. Cited from *Xu soushen ji* in *TPYL* 832.4b; *TPGJ* 131.2; *FYZL* 64.772.

100   *XJS*, 522. Cited from *Xu soushen ji* in *TPYL* 885.5a and *TPGJ* 457.3. Cited from *Soushen ji* in *TPYL* 934 and *TPGJ* 131.12.

101   *XJS*, 499–500. Cited from *Xu soushen ji* in *Kaiyuan zhanjing* 102 and *TPYL* 13 and 764. Cited in a truncated version from *Soushen ji* in *TPGJ* 456.30.

102   *XJS*, 552–554. Cited from *Xu soushen ji* in *YWLJ* 96.1668 and *TPYL* 479.9a–b and 931.8b–9a.

103   LX 117–118; *TPGJ* 197.4. *Youming lu* 64 is a more compressed version. The story was erroneously included in traditional editions of *Soushen houji*; see *XJS*, 701.

104   Translated from the emended text in Wang Guoliang, *Xu Qi Xie ji yanjiu*, 26–29. Another version appears in *Soushen ji* 20.4.

105   Translated from the emended text in Wang Guoliang, *Xu Qi Xie ji yanjiu*, 39–40. Attested in *YWLJ* 4.81, 89.1541; *TPYL* 991.4a; and *Jing Chu suishi ji*, 50–51. *Shuijing zhu* 21.1785–1787 indicates that a version of the story was preserved in an inscription at a temple beside Ge Lake. See also Campany, *To Live as Long as Heaven and Earth*, 161–168, 407–412.

106   LX 435; *TPGJ* 357.5.

107   LX 435–436; *TPYL* 951.5a. A closely similar version is quoted from *Sanjiao zhuying* 三教珠英 in *TPGJ* 99.1. Translation based on LX and *TPYL* except where noted.

108   LX 437; *TPGJ* 111.12.

109   LX 438–439; *TPYL* 922.3a–b. LX cites *Shilei fu zhu* 事類賦注 19. A similar version is cited from *Mingyan ji* 冥驗記 in *Foguo huanwu chanshi biyanlu* 佛果圜悟禪師碧巖錄 [*T* 2003, 10.225b11–17] by the monk Zhongxian 重顯 (980–1052); this source is not listed in LX.

110   LX 439; *TPYL* 740.7a, which attributes the story to an otherwise unknown *Lingyan ji* 靈驗記. *TPGJ* 132.6 (not cited by LX) quotes the story from a *Xuanyan zhi* 宣驗志, also otherwise unknown but very similarly titled to *Xuanyan ji* (substitution of *zhi* 志 for *ji* 記 and vice versa in mentions of titles is common). *TPGJ*, however, dates these events to an unspecified reign period in the Tang.

111   LX 378; *CXJ* 29.717; *TPGJ* 447.1. LX also cites *TPYL* 990, but I have not found this item there.

112   LX 379; *TPYL* 949.1b; and other sources.

113   LX 379; *TPYL* 886.6a. Partial quotation in *TPGJ* 397.3.

114   LX 380; *TPYL* 812.7b (partial), 813.5a (partial), 886.6a, 912.1b (partial). The last-listed citation reads: "The essence of lead and tin becomes a fox."

115   LX 403; *TPGJ* 141.2.

116   LX 403–404; *TPGJ* 473.16.

117   LX 404; *TPGJ* 118.9.

118   LX 405; *TPGJ* 141.14.

119   LX 405; *TPGJ* 469.8.

120   1.18 (*XJTY* ed. 1.4a); *TPYL* 69.6b. Item numbers in *Yi yuan* consist of chapter number followed by the serial position of the item in that chapter—here, item 18 in chapter 1.

121   1.24 (*XJTY* ed. 1.5a). I have not been able to locate this item in collectanea. *TPYL* 54.5b preserves a closely similar text from *Wuling ji* 武陵記 on which I partially draw.

122   2.20 (*XJTY* ed. 2.3b–4a); *YWLJ* 94.1630; *TPYL* 901.7b.

123   2.22 (*XJTY* ed. 2.4a); *TPYL* 966.2b, 966.6b, 971.2a.

124   3.21 (*XJTY* ed. 3.4b); *TPYL* 479.6b–7a.

125   3.24 (*XJTY* ed. 3.5a); *TPYL* 905.5a.

126   3.33 (*XJTY* ed. 3.6b–7a). *TPYL* 929.3a cites the passage but attributes it to *Jin shu*, and indeed the story is found in *Jin shu* 36.1075.

127 3.34 (*XJTY* ed. 3.7a); *TPYL* 472.2b.

128 3.35 (*XJTY* ed. 3.7a–b); *TPYL* 889.3b. Faxian is the subject of a brief biography in *Gaoseng zhuan* 13.411b; this story does not appear there.

129 3.36 (*XJTY* ed. 3.7b). *TPGJ* 360.12 cites the story from *Yi yuan; TPGJ* 418.4 cites a similar tale from *Zhugong jiushi* 渚宮舊事.

130 3.38 (*XJTY* ed. 3.7b–8a); *TPGJ* 469.11.

131 3.39 (*XJTY* ed. 3.8a–b). *TPYL* 386.7b cites only an abbreviated version of the story from *Yi yuan; TPYL* 62 cites another, similar version from *Jingzhou ji* 荊州記 by Sheng Hongzhi 盛弘之. The same incident is recounted (in mostly different wording) in *Jin shu* 81.2132.

132 3.41 (*XJTY* ed. 3.8b); *TPYL* 849.6a; *TPGJ* 131.18.

133 3.49 (*XJTY* ed. 3.10a–b); *TPGJ* 131.8.

134 4.13 (*XJTY* ed. 4.3a–b); alternate version in Ren Fang's *Shuyi ji* 1.84 (*HWCS* ed. 1.15b). *Bencao gangmu* 15 cites a version from Li Yanshou's 李延壽 *Nan shi* 南史, and the story is still found there (*Nan shi* 1.1–2). Translation based on *XJTY* except where noted.

135 5.10 (*XJTY* ed. 5.3b); *TPGJ* 295.6; *TPYL* 350.2a.

136 5.19 (*XJTY* ed. 5.5b–6a); *TPGJ* 295.13. *TPYL* 416 quotes an almost identically worded story from *Song shu* 宋書. I do not find a similar story in today's *Song shu* (although Xiang Yu's numinous presence in the commandery headquarters near Mount Bian is mentioned at *Song shu* 54.1532), but a version of the story is preserved in *Nan shi* 18.499.

137 5.15 (*XJTY* ed. 5.4b); *TPGJ* 292.10.

138 5.16 (*XJTY* ed. 5.5a); *TPGJ* 292.16; *TPYL* 30.2b–3a, 884.1b–2a; *Jing Chu suishi ji*, 20–21.

139 5.17 (*XJTY* ed. 5.5a–b); *TPGJ* 293.6; *TPYL* 957.7a–b; *YWLJ* 89.1539.

140 5.11 (*XJTY* ed. 5.3b); *TPGJ* 295.8. Another story about this temple is recorded in *Guang gujin wuxing ji* as quoted in *TPGJ* 131.7.

141 5.12 (*XJTY* ed. 5.4a). *TPGJ* 295.18 attributes the story to the ninth-century *Youyang zazu* 酉陽雜俎, and it is translated from that text in Reed, *Chinese Chronicles of the Strange*, 40.

142 5.14 (*XJTY* ed. 5.4a–b); *TPYL* 871.5a–b. The translation is based on *TPYL*, to which the *XJTY* text of *Yi yuan* is identical except for one added clause, the protagonist's death at the age of eighty-three, and an indication of a variant of his given name.

143 5.21 (*XJTY* ed. 5.6b); *TPGJ* 292.13; *TPYL* 726.6b–7a. Translated from *TPYL*. All three versions are worded similarly, with only minor differences (such as a one-day variation in the date).

144 5.9, comparing *Shuo ku* (5.2a) and *XJTY* (5.3a–b) eds. *TPGJ* 294.5 has yet another variant in the problematic passage about his spirit. Another story about Yuan Shuang appears in *TPGJ* 426.7.

145 5.18 (*XJTY* ed. 5.5b). *TPGJ* 295.9 is identical except for having 如去 "as if departing," rather than 而去, in the penultimate sentence.

146   6.1 (*XJTY* ed. 6.1a); *TPYL* 95.7a. A more detailed version appears in *Yuan-hun zhi* 冤魂志; see Cohen, *Tales of Vengeful Souls*, 48–49. See also *Jin shu* 1.19, where the Ling of Wang Ling (172–251) is written 凌; and *SSHY*, 591.

147   6.4 (*XJTY* ed. 6.1b–2a). Versions are cited from *Jin shu* in *TPYL* 883 and *TPGJ* 276.14, and indeed the story is found in *Jin shu* 92.2380.

148   6.6 (*XJTY* ed. 6.2b); *TPGJ* 318.3.

149   6.20 (*XJTY* ed. 6.6a–b). *TPGJ* 324.1 cites the story from *Zhenyi lu* 甄異錄, and *TPYL* 718.8a cites it from *Zhenyi zhuan* 甄異傳. The latter is only a summary.

150   6.8 (*XJTY* ed. 6.3a); *TPGJ* 318.4. Mentioned in Campany, "Ghosts Matter," 25.

151   6.35 (*XJTY* ed. 6.11a); *TPYL* 754.7a.

152   6.39 (*XJTY* ed. 6.11a–b); *TPGJ* 323.9.

153   7.3 (*XJTY* ed. 7.1b); *TPYL* 559.5a.

154   7.4 (*XJTY* ed. 7.1b–2a); *YWLJ* 82.1411.

155   7.5 (*XJTY* ed. 7.2a). I have yet to find this story attributed to *Yi yuan* in any other source. A version with only slightly different wording (but omitting the last clause) appears as *Youming lu* 147 (LX 281), quoted in *BTSC* 135.2b.

156   7.6 (*XJTY* ed. 7.2a–b). I have yet to find this story in any other text.

157   7.7 (*XJTY* ed. 7.2b); *BTSC* 94.6a.

158   7.11 (*XJTY* ed. 7.3a–b); *TPYL* 399.9a.

159   7.14 (*XJTY* 7.4a); so far I have found this text nowhere else, although there are several other stories about the spectral sources of Ji Kang's musical compositions.

160   7.15 (*XJTY* ed. 7.4b). The same story in somewhat different wording is also preserved in a *Jin yangqiu* 晉陽秋 as cited in *Shishuo xinyu* 世說新語 (see *SSHY*, 253) and in *Jin shu* 78.2064–2065.

161   7.17 (*XJTY* ed. 7.4b–5a). A version in virtually identical wording is attributed to *Kong Yue zhiguai* 孔約志怪 in *TPGJ* 276.25 and is collected as item 7 of that text in LX 218.

162   7.19 (*XJTY* ed. 7.5a–b). I have not yet found any text in which this version is quoted, but other versions of the tale survive in various places, as mentioned in a footnote to the translation.

163   7.23 (*XJTY* ed. 7.5b–6a); *TPGJ* 276.13.

164   7.24 (*XJTY* ed. 7.6a); cited in *TPGJ* 276.30 from either *Shuyi ji* or *Zhenyi zhuan*, depending on the *TPGJ* edition. Collected in LX as *Shuyi ji* 19 (171).

165   7.25 (*XJTY* ed. 7.6a–b); *TPYL* 350.1b–2a.

166   7.27 (*XJTY* ed. 7.7a); *TPGJ* 276.29. The *XJTY* ed. has phrases that do not appear in *TPGJ*, which is more truncated.

167   7.28 (*XJTY* ed. 7.7a–b). I find no version worded thus in collectanea. *Soushen houji* 93 (*XJS*, 584) has a similar, differently worded story about the protagonist Yin Zhongkan 殷仲堪 (d. 399 or 400), a well-known figure (see *SSHY*, 604) who did indeed serve as governor of Jing province under the Eastern Jin. A much more truncated version is attributed in *TPGJ* 276.28 to *Meng jun* 夢雋.

168   7.29 (*XJTY* ed. 7.7b). I have not yet found this story elsewhere.

169   7.31 (*XJTY* ed. 7.8a–b); *TPYL* 396.3a.

170   8.5 (*XJTY* ed. 8.2b); *TPGJ* 438.8.

171   8.8 (*XJTY* ed. 8.3a); *TPGJ* 446.4.

172   8.9 (*XJTY* ed. 8.3b); *TPGJ* 368.3; *TPYL* 765.2b.

173   8.10 (*XJTY* ed. 8.3b); *TPGJ* 442.16.

174   8.11 (*XJTY* ed. 8.3b–4a); *TPGJ* 415.5.

175   8.13 (*XJTY* ed. 8.4a–b). The story in similar wording is attributed to *Youming lu* in *TPYL* 932.7a, which is the primary basis for the version in LX, item 236 (307). A partial quotation from *Youming lu* is also preserved in *FYZL* 31.526c. A rather similar version is quoted in *TPGJ* 468.11 from *Guang gujin wuxing ji*.

176   8.22 (*XJTY* ed. 8.6b–7a); *TPYL* 889.3a–b.

177   8.25 (*XJTY* ed. 8.8a–b). A much briefer version is preserved as *Zhenyi zhuan* 9 (LX 158), based on *TPYL* 718.5b–6a: "Zhang Chen 章沈 of Lean died of illness, but before he was sealed in his coffin he revived. He said that he had been taken to a celestial bureau. The supervisor happened to be his cousin, who broke the rules so that he could leave. [On his way out] he saw a woman who had been brought there at the same time. She removed two pairs of golden bracelets and gave them to Shen to be presented to the supervisor, and in this way she was able to return as well, and the two of them grew quite close. The woman said that her home was in Wu and that her name was Xu Qiuying 徐秋英. Afterward Shen made inquiries and found the woman. And so her parents gave her to him in marriage."

178   8.34 (*XJTY* ed. 8.9b); *TPYL* 361.9b. Lewis (*The Flood Myths of Early China*, 93) comments on the story as it relates to beliefs about dangers posed by deceased children.

179   8.37 (*XJTY* ed. 8.10a–b). Slightly different versions are cited from *Yi yuan* in *TPYL* 906.6b, *TPGJ* 443.11, and *CXJ* 29.715. Another version is attributed to *Lieyi zhuan*, collected as item 30 in LX (142–143) and quoted from *Lieyi zhuan* in *TPYL* 888.3b.

180   8.40 (*XJTY* ed. 8.11a); *TPYL* 892.2b.

181   8.41 (*XJTY* ed. 8.11a–b); *TPGJ* 447.11; *TPYL* 909.6b; *CXJ* 29.717.

182   9.18 (*XJTY* ed. 6a); *FYZL* 61.749.

183   9.19 (*XJTY* ed. 9.6b–7a); *TPYL* 737.3a.

184   LX 242; *TPYL* 936.6a.

185   LX 242; *TPYL* 762.8a.

186   Translation based on a comparison of the text given in LX (247–248) with those in *TPYL* 41.2b–3a and *FYZL* 31.521. Summaries are also preserved in *TPGJ* 61.7 and *YWLJ* 7.138. Li Jianguo (*XJS*, 717–718) thinks that the tale might have once been included in *Soushen houji*. A version was reworked into chapter 7 of the Daoist hagiographic compilation *Lishi zhenxian tidao tongjian* 歷世真仙體道通鑑. My translation differs from that in *CCT*, 137–139.

187   LX 251; *TPYL* 559.2b–3a.

188 LX 252; *TPYL* 735.4b; *BTSC* 136.10a.

189 LX 253; *TPYL* 688.5a–b, 936.6a. A version appears as *Soushen ji* 4.11.

190 LX 253; *TPGJ* 317.18.

191 LX 254; *TPGJ* 293.3. A version appears as *Soushen ji* 11.13.

192 LX 254; *TPGJ* 317.16.

193 LX 255–256, which is based on a large number of citations, including *FYZL* 31.520–521; *CXJ* 29; *YWLJ* 94.1634; *TPYL* 39, 803.8a, 902.7b–8a; and *TPGJ* 197.10. Traditional compilations of *Soushen houji* include a version as item 1.2, but Li Jianguo (*XJS*, 773) deems it mistakenly attributed to that text.

194 LX 257; *TPGJ* 318.20; *TPYL* 186.7a, 883.8a. Another version appears in *Xiao shuo* 101 (LX 115).

195 LX 263; *TPYL* 905.7a; *TPGJ* 437.1. A version appears as *Soushen ji* 20.10 but is not attributed to that work in any early collection (see *XJS*, 696–697).

196 LX 264–265; *TPGJ* 294.10.

197 LX 270; *TPYL* 892.3b.

198 LX 271; *TPYL* 519.3a.

199 LX 276; *TPGJ* 294.12. An identical version appears in *Soushen houji* (*XJS*, 525–526) and is cited from *Xu soushen ji* in *TPYL* 805.

200 LX 278; *TPYL* 882.6a–b; *TPGJ* 294.20 (a summary version). Another version in *Xiao shuo* 27 (LX 97) lacks the final sentence. Translated from LX. A similarly themed story about the Jin emperor Wu is preserved in *Youming lu* 133 (LX 278).

201 LX 279; *TPYL* 767.1b.

202 LX 281; *TPYL* 930.6a; *TPGJ* 131.5.

203 LX 283; *TPYL* 999.3a, 699.4a (lacks the story's end).

204 LX 286; *TPGJ* 276.48.

205 LX 287; *YWLJ* 82.1407.

206 LX 294; *TPYL* 885.8a–b; *TPGJ* 360.21.

207 LX 297; *TPGJ* 292.14.

208 LX 305; *TPGJ* 469.10.

209 LX 155–156; *TPGJ* 321.9. Discussed in Campany, "Ghosts Matter," 22.

210 LX 156–157; *TPGJ* 321.6. Another version with a slightly different ending appears in *Soushen ji* 9.13.

211 LX 157; *TPGJ* 461.27; *TPYL* 885.8b.

212 LX 157; *TPGJ* 321.7.

213 LX 158–159; *TPYL* 743.3a.

214 LX 159; *TPYL* 955.6b.

215 LX 159; *TPGJ* 322.15.

216 LX 159–160; *TPGJ* 322.16.

217 LX 160. LX, which I translate, is based largely on *TPGJ* 325.16 except for one minor insertion based on *TPYL* 967.7a. Summaries of the part of the story concerning peach wood are preserved in *Qimin yaoshu* 10.238–239 and *YWLJ* 86.1469.

218   LX 160; *TPGJ* 468.15. *Youming lu* 171 (LX 288; *TPYL* 999.5b, 980.2b; *YWLJ* 82.1407) preserves a more compressed version.

219   LX 209; *TPYL* 68.5a.

220   LX 219; *BTSC* 135.10a; *TPYL* 903.5a. A version is preserved in *Soushen ji* 18.18, quoted in *TPGJ* 439.20.

221   From a not clearly specified *zhiguai* text collected by Lu Xun under his "miscellaneous" category (*Za guishen zhiguai*, LX 425–426). Cited in *TPYL* 897.6a from "a *zhiguai* collection" 志怪集 and in *TPGJ* 322.2 from "*zhiguai* records" 志怪錄; partially cited from "a *zhiguai* text" 志怪 in *TPYL* 884.7b and from *guaizhi* 怪志 in *YWLJ* 93.1619. A less detailed version appears as *Soushen ji* 2.17. Translated from LX.

222   Collected by Lu Xun in his "miscellaneous" category (*Za guishen zhiguai*, LX 424). Cited in *TPYL* 932.6b from an otherwise unknown *Mr. Xu's zhiguai* 許氏志怪; also cited (with slight differences of wording) in *TPGJ* 468.14 simply from "a *zhiguai* text." Translated from LX.

223   Collected by Lu Xun under his "miscellaneous" category (*Za guishen zhiguai*, LX 427). *TPGJ* 322.20 cites a version of this story from "*zhiguai* records"; *FYZL* 95.927–928 cites it from "a *zhiguai* collection." I translate from LX except where noted.

224   Entered by LX under his *Za guishen zhiguai* (LX 428), this story is cited in *FYZL* 67.798 from a *zhiguai zhuan* 志怪傳 and in *TPGJ* 293.2 from "*Soushen ji, Youming lu, Zhi guai,* and other books" 搜神記、幽明錄、志怪等書. Another version appears as *Soushen ji* 5.2.

225   Entered by LX in *Za guishen zhiguai* (LX 428), this story is cited in *FYZL* 75.851 from a *zhiguai zhuan* 志怪傳 and in *TPGJ* 293.2 from "*Soushen ji, Youming lu, Zhi guai,* and other books." Another version appears as *Soushen ji* 5.3.

WORKS CITED

Allen, Sarah M. *Shifting Stories: History, Gossip, and Lore in Narratives from Tang Dynasty China.* Cambridge, MA: Harvard University Press, 2014.

———. "Tales Retold: Narrative Variation in a Tang Story." *Harvard Journal of Asiatic Studies* 66 (2006): 105–143.

Ashmore, Robert. *The Transport of Reading: Text and Understanding in the World of Tao Qian (365–427).* Cambridge, MA: Harvard University Press, 2010.

Baopuzi neipian 抱朴子內篇 by Ge Hong 葛洪. *Baopuzi neipian jiaoshi* 抱朴子內篇校釋. Ed. Wang Ming 王明. 2nd ed. Beijing: Zhonghua shuju, 1985.

Barrett, T. H. *The Woman Who Discovered Printing.* New Haven, CT: Yale University Press, 2008.

Bencao gangmu 本草綱目. Accessed via Hanji dianzi wenxian ciliao ku 漢籍電子文獻資料庫 (Scripta Sinica) electronic edition, http://hanchi.ihp.sinica.edu.tw.proxy.library.vanderbilt.edu/ihp/hanji.htm. Accessible only through university libraries.

Benn, James A. *Burning for the Buddha: Self-Immolation in Chinese Buddhism.* Kuroda Institute Studies in East Asian Buddhism 19. Honolulu: University of Hawai'i Press, 2007.

Berkowitz, Alan. "Biographies of Recluses: Huangfu Mi's *Accounts of High-Minded Men.*" In *Early Medieval China: A Sourcebook,* ed. Wendy Swartz, Robert Ford Campany, Yang Lu, and Jessey J. C. Choo, 333–349. New York: Columbia University Press, 2014.

———. *Patterns of Disengagement: The Practice and Portrayal of Reclusion in Early Medieval China.* Stanford, CA: Stanford University Press, 2000.

Birrell, Anne. *Chinese Myth and Culture.* Cambridge: McGuiness China Monographs, 2006.

———. *The Classic of Mountains and Seas.* Harmondsworth: Penguin, 1999.

Bodde, Derk. "Dominant Ideas in the Formation of Chinese Culture." *Journal of the American Oriental Society* 62 (1942): 293–299.

———. *Festivals in Classical China.* Princeton, NJ: Princeton University Press, 1975.

———. "Myths of Ancient China." In *Mythologies of the Ancient World,* ed. Samuel N. Kramer, 367–408. Garden City, NY: Doubleday, 1961.

———. "Some Chinese Tales of the Supernatural." *Harvard Journal of Asiatic Studies* 6 (1941): 338–357.

Bokenkamp, Stephen R. *Ancestors and Anxiety: Daoism and the Birth of Rebirth in China.* Berkeley: University of California Press, 2007.

———. "The Peach Flower Font and the Grotto Passage." *Journal of the American Oriental Society* 106 (1986): 65–77.

Boltz, Judith M. *A Survey of Taoist Literature: Tenth to Seventeenth Centuries.* Berkeley: Institute of East Asian Studies, University of California, 1987.

Boucher, Daniel. "Sutra on the Merit of Bathing the Buddha." In *Buddhism in Practice,* ed. Donald S. Lopez Jr., 59–68. Princeton, NJ: Princeton University Press, 1995.

Brashier, K. E. "Han Thanatology and the Division of 'Souls.'" *Early China* 21 (1996): 125–158.

Campany, Robert Ford. "Buddhist Revelation and Taoist Translation in Early Medieval China." *Taoist Resources* 4, no. 1 (1993): 1–29.

———. "Chinese Accounts of the Strange: A Study in the History of Religions." PhD diss., University of Chicago, 1988.

———. "Chinese History and Writing about 'Religion(s)': Reflections at a Crossroads." In *Dynamics in the History of Religions between Asia and Europe: Encounters, Notions, and Comparative Perspectives,* ed. Marion Steinicke and Volkhard Krech, 273–294. Leiden: Brill, 2011.

———. "The Earliest Tales of the Bodhisattva Guanshiyin." In *Religions of China in Practice,* ed. Donald S. Lopez Jr., 82–96. Princeton, NJ: Princeton University Press, 1996.

———. "Ghosts Matter: The Culture of Ghosts in Six Dynasties *Zhiguai.*" *Chinese Literature: Essays, Articles, Reviews* 13 (1991): 15–34.

———. "Living Off the Books: Fifty Ways to Dodge *Ming* 命 in Early Medieval China." In *The Magnitude of* Ming: *Command, Allotment, and Fate in Chinese Culture,* ed. Christopher Lupke, 129–150. Honolulu: University of Hawai'i Press, 2005.

———. "Long-Distance Specialists in Early Medieval China." In *Journeys West and East,* ed. Eric Ziolkowski, 109–124. Wilmington: University of Delaware Press, 2005.

———. *Making Transcendents: Ascetics and Social Memory in Early Medieval China.* Honolulu: University of Hawai'i Press, 2009.

———. "Notes on the Devotional Uses and Symbolic Functions of Sutra Texts as Depicted in Early Chinese Buddhist Miracle Tales and Hagiographies." *Journal of the International Association of Buddhist Studies* 14 (1991): 28–72.

———. "On the Very Idea of Religions (in the Modern West and in Early Medieval China)." *History of Religions* 42 (2003): 287–319.

———. "The Real Presence." *History of Religions* 32 (1993): 233–272.

———. "Religious Repertoires and Contestation: A Case Study Based on Buddhist Miracle Tales." *History of Religions* 52 (2012): 99–141.

———. "Return-from-Death Narratives in Early Medieval China." *Journal of Chinese Religions* 18 (1990): 91–125.

———. Review of *A Chinese Bestiary: Strange Creatures from the Guideways through Mountains and Seas,* by Richard Strassberg. *Journal of Chinese Religions* 32 (2004): 260–261.

———. Review of *In Search of the Supernatural: The Written Record,* by Kenneth DeWoskin and J. I. Crump. *China Review International* 4 (1997): 118–121.

———. Review of *Libro dei monti e dei mari (Shanhai jing): Cosmografia e mitologia nella Cina antica,* by Riccardo Fracasso, and *The Classic of Mountains and Seas,* by Anne Birrell. *Journal of Chinese Religions* 28 (2000): 177–187.

———. *Signs from the Unseen Realm: Buddhist Miracle Tales from Early Medieval China*. Honolulu: University of Hawai'i Press, 2012.

———. *Strange Writing: Anomaly Accounts in Early Medieval China*. Albany: State University of New York Press, 1996.

———. "'Survival' as an Interpretive Strategy: A Sino-Western Comparative Case Study." *Method and Theory in the Study of Religion* 2 (1990): 1–26.

———. "Tales of Strange Events." In *Early Medieval China: A Sourcebook*, ed. Wendy Swartz, Robert Ford Campany, Yang Lu, and Jessey J. C. Choo, 576–591. New York: Columbia University Press, 2014.

———. "To Hell and Back: Death, Near-Death, and Other Worldly Journeys in Early Medieval China." In *Death, Ecstasy, and Other Worldly Journeys*, ed. John Collins and Michael Fishbane, 343–360. Chicago: University of Chicago Press, 1995.

———. *To Live as Long as Heaven and Earth: A Translation and Study of Ge Hong's "Traditions of Divine Transcendents."* Berkeley: University of California Press, 2002.

———. "Two Religious Thinkers of the Early Eastern Jin: Gan Bao and Ge Hong in Multiple Contexts." *Asia Major*, 3rd ser., 18 (2005): 175–224.

Chan, Alan K. L., and Yuet-Keung Lo, eds. *Interpretation and Literature in Early Medieval China*. Albany: State University of New York Press, 2010.

———, eds. *Philosophy and Religion in Early Medieval China*. Albany: State University of New York Press, 2010.

Chan, Leo Tak-hung. *The Discourse on Foxes and Ghosts: Ji Yun and Eighteenth-Century Literati Storytelling*. Honolulu: University of Hawai'i Press, 1998.

Chang, Kang-i Sun, and Stephen Owen, eds. *The Cambridge History of Chinese Literature*. 2 vols. Cambridge: Cambridge University Press, 2010.

Chiang, Sing-chen Lydia. *Collecting the Self: Body and Identity in Strange Tale Collections of Late Imperial China*. Leiden: Brill, 2005.

Chittick, Andrew. "The Development of Local Writing in Early Medieval China." *Early Medieval China* 9 (2003): 35–70.

———. "Pride of Place: The Advent of Local History in Early Medieval China." PhD diss., University of Michigan, 1997.

Cohen, Alvin P. *Tales of Vengeful Souls: A Sixth Century Collection of Chinese Avenging Ghost Stories*. Taipei: Institut Ricci, 1982.

Davis, Natalie Zemon. *Fiction in the Archives: Pardon Tales and Their Tellers in Sixteenth-Century France*. Cambridge: Cambridge University Press, 1987.

DeCaroli, Robert. *Haunting the Buddha: Indian Popular Religions and the Formation of Buddhism*. Oxford: Oxford University Press, 2004.

de Crespigny, Rafe. *A Biographical Dictionary of Later Han to the Three Kingdoms (23–220 AD)*. Leiden: Brill, 2007.

———. *Imperial Warlord: A Biography of Cao Cao, 155–220 AD*. Leiden: Brill, 2010.

DeWoskin, Kenneth. *Doctors, Diviners, and Magicians of Ancient China: Biographies of "Fang-shih."* New York: Columbia University Press, 1983.

———. "The Six Dynasties *Chih-kuai* and the Birth of Fiction." In *Chinese Narrative: Critical and Theoretical Essays*, ed. Andrew H. Plaks, 21–52. Princeton, NJ: Princeton University Press, 1977.

DeWoskin, Kenneth, and J. I. Crump Jr. *In Search of the Supernatural: The Written Record*. Stanford, CA: Stanford University Press, 1996.

Dien, Albert E. "Civil Service Examinations: Evidence from the Northwest." In *Culture and Power in the Reconstitution of the Chinese Realm, 200–600,* ed. Scott Pearce, Audrey Spiro, and Patricia Ebrey, 99–121. Cambridge, MA: Harvard University Press, 2001.

———. "Custom and Society: *The Family Instructions of Mr. Yan.*" In *Early Medieval China: A Sourcebook,* ed. Wendy Swartz, Robert Ford Campany, Yang Lu, and Jessey J. C. Choo, 494–510. New York: Columbia University Press, 2014.

———. "Instructions for the Grave: The Case of Yan Zhitui." *Cahiers d'Extrême-Asie* 8 (1995): 41–58.

———. *Pei Ch'i shu 45: Biography of Yen Chih-t'ui.* Bern: Herbert Lang, 1976.

———. *Six Dynasties Civilization.* New Haven, CT: Yale University Press, 2007.

———, ed. *State and Society in Early Medieval China.* Stanford, CA: Stanford University Press, 1990.

———. "Yen Chih-t'ui (531–591+): A Buddho-Confucian." In *Confucian Personalities,* ed. Arthur F. Wright and Dennis Twitchett, 44–64. Stanford, CA: Stanford University Press, 1962.

———. "The *Yuan-hun chih* (Accounts of Ghosts with Grievances): A Sixth-Century Collection of Stories." In *Wen-lin: Studies in the Chinese Humanities,* ed. Chow Tse-tung, 211–228. Madison: University of Wisconsin Press, 1968.

Diény, Jean-Pierre. "Le *Fenghuang* et le phénix." *Cahiers d'Extrême-Asie* 5 (1989–1990): 1–13.

Dorofeeva-Lichtmann, Vera. "Conception of Terrestrial Organization in the *Shan hai jing.*" *Bulletin de l'Ecole Française d'Extrême-Orient* 82 (1995): 57–110.

———. "Mapping a 'Spiritual' Landscape: Representing Terrestrial Space in the *Shan hai jing.*" In *Political Frontiers, Ethnic Boundaries, and Human Geographies in Chinese History,* ed. Nicola di Cosmo and Don Wyatt, 35–79. London: RoutledgeCurzon, 2003.

———. "Topographical Accuracy or Conceptual Organization of Space? Some Remarks on the System of Locations Found in the *Shan hai jing.*" In *Current Perspectives on the History of Science in East Asia,* ed. Kim Yung-Sik and Francesca Bray, 165–179. Seoul: Seoul National University Press, 1999.

Douglas, Mary. *Purity and Danger: An Analysis of the Concepts of Pollution and Taboo.* 2nd ed. London: Routledge & Kegan Paul.

Drège, Jean-Pierre. *Les bibliothèques en Chine au temps des manuscrits.* Paris: Ecole Française d'Extrême-Orient, 1991.

Dudbridge, Glen. *Books, Tales and Vernacular Culture: Selected Papers on China.* Leiden: Brill, 2005.

———. *A Portrait of Five Dynasties China from the Memoirs of Wang Renyu (880–956).* Oxford: Oxford University Press, 2013.

———. *Religious Experience and Lay Society in T'ang China: A Reading of Tai Fu's "Kuang-i chi."* Cambridge: Cambridge University Press, 1995.

———. "Tang Sources for the Study of Religious Culture: Problems and Procedures." *Cahiers d'Extrême-Asie* 12 (2001): 141–154.

Farmer, J. Michael. *The Talent of Shu: Qiao Zhou and the Intellectual World of Early Medieval Sichuan.* Albany: State University of New York Press, 2007.

Fengsu tongyi 風俗通義 by Ying Shao 應劭. *Fengsu tongyi jiaozhu* 風俗通義校注. Ed. Wang Liqi 王利器. 2 vols., continuously paginated. Beijing: Zhonghua shuju, 1981.

Foster, Lawrence Chapin. "The *Shih-i chi* and Its Relationship to the Genre Known as *Chih-kuai hsiao-shuo.*" PhD diss., University of Washington, 1974.

Fracasso, Riccardo. *Libro dei monti e dei mari (Shanhai jing): Cosmografia et mitologia nella Cina antica*. Venice: Saggi Marsilio, 1996.

Giles, Herbert A., trans. *Strange Stories from a Chinese Studio*. Shanghai: Kelly & Walsh, 1936.

Gjertson, Donald E. "The Early Chinese Buddhist Miracle Tale: A Preliminary Survey." *Journal of the American Oriental Society* 101 (1981): 287–301.

———. *Ghosts, Gods, and Retribution: Nine Buddhist Miracle Tales from Six Dynasties and Early T'ang China*. Asian Studies Committee Occasional Papers Series 2. Amherst: University of Massachusetts, 1978.

———. *Miraculous Retribution: A Study and Translation of T'ang Lin's "Ming-pao chi."* Berkeley: Institute of Buddhist Studies, 1989.

Goodman, Howard L. *Ts'ao P'i Transcendent: The Political Culture of Dynasty-Founding in China at the End of the Han*. Seattle: Scripta Serica, 1998.

Graff, David A. *Medieval Chinese Warfare, 300–900*. New York: Routledge, 2002.

Greatrex, Roger. *The Bowu zhi: An Annotated Translation*. Stockholm: Skrifter utgivna av Föreningen för Orientaliska Studier, 1987.

Groot, J. J. M. de. *The Religious System of China*. 6 vols. Leiden: Brill, 1892–1910.

Han shu 漢書. Beijing: Zhonghua shuju, 1962.

Han Wei congshu 漢魏叢書. Comp. Cheng Rong 程榮. Printed in 1592. Place of publication and printing house unknown; copy held at the Joseph Regenstein Library (East Asia Collection), University of Chicago.

Hanyu dacidian 漢語大辭典. Ed. Luo Zhufeng 罗竹风. Shanghai: Shanghai cishu chubanshe, 1986.

Hargett, James M. "會稽: Guaiji? Guiji? Huiji? Kuaiji?" *Sino-Platonic Papers* no. 234. March 2013.

Holcombe, Charles. *In the Shadow of the Han: Literati Thought and Society at the Beginning of the Southern Dynasties*. Honolulu: University of Hawai'i Press, 1994.

Hou Han shu 後漢書. Beijing: Zhonghua shuju, 1965.

Hsieh, Daniel. *Love and Women in Early Chinese Fiction*. Hong Kong: Chinese University Press, 2008.

Hucker, Charles O. *A Dictionary of Official Titles in Imperial China*. Stanford, CA: Stanford University Press, 1985.

Huntington, Rania. *Alien Kind: Foxes and Late Imperial Chinese Narrative*. Cambridge, MA: Harvard University Press, 2003.

———. "Ghosts Seeking Substitutes: Female Suicide and Repetition." *Late Imperial China* 26 (2005): 1–40.

Hureau, Sylvie. "Buddhist Rituals." In *Early Chinese Religion*, pt. 2, *The Period of Division (220–589 AD)*, ed. John Lagerwey and Lü Pengzhi, 1207–1244. Leiden: Brill, 2010.

Inglis, Alister D. *Hong Mai's "Record of the Listener" and Its Song Dynasty Context*. Albany: State University of New York Press, 2006.

Jin shu 晉書. Beijing: Zhonghua shuju, 1974.

Jing Chu suishi ji 荊楚歲時記 by Zong Lin 宗懍. In *Suishi xisu ziliao huibian* 歲時習俗資料彙編. Taipei: Yiwen yinshuguan, 1970. Accessed via Hanji dianzi wenxian ciliao ku 漢籍電子文獻資料庫 (Scripta Sinica) electronic edition, http://hanchi.ihp.sinica.edu.tw.proxy.library.vanderbilt.edu/ihp/hanji.htm. Accessible only through university libraries.

Kaltenmark, Max. "La légende de la ville immergée en Chine." *Cahiers d'Extrême-Asie* 1 (1985): 1–10.

———. *Le Lie-sien tchouan*. Peking: Université de Paris, Centre d'études sinologiques de Pékin, 1953.

Kang, Xiaofei. *The Cult of the Fox: Power, Gender, and Popular Religion in Late Imperial and Modern China*. New York: Columbia University Press, 2005.

Kao, Karl S. Y., ed. *Classical Chinese Tales of the Supernatural and the Fantastic: Selections from the Third to the Tenth Century*. Bloomington: Indiana University Press, 1985.

Kern, Martin. "Introduction: The Ritual Texture of Early China." In *Text and Ritual in Early China*, ed. Martin Kern, vii–xxvii. Seattle: University of Washington Press, 2005.

Kieschnick, John. *The Eminent Monk: Buddhist Ideals in Medieval Chinese Hagiography*. Honolulu: University of Hawai'i Press, 1997.

Knapp, Keith N. "Confucian Views of the Supernatural." In *Early Medieval China: A Sourcebook*, ed. Wendy Swartz, Robert Ford Campany, Yang Lu, and Jessey J. C. Choo, 640–651. New York: Columbia University Press, 2014.

———. *Selfless Offspring: Filial Children and Social Order in Early Medieval China*. Honolulu: University of Hawai'i Press, 2005.

Knechtges, David R. "Culling the Weeds and Selecting Prime Blossoms: The Anthology in Early Medieval China." In *Culture and Power in the Reconstitution of the Chinese Realm, 200–600*, ed. Scott Pearce, Audrey Spiro, and Patricia Ebrey, 200–241. Cambridge, MA: Harvard University Press, 2001.

Lagerwey, John. *China: A Religious State*. Hong Kong: Hong Kong University Press, 2010.

Lagerwey, John, and Lü Pengzhi, eds. *Early Chinese Religion*. Pt. 2, *The Period of Division (220–589 AD)*. 2 vols. Leiden: Brill, 2010.

Lewis, Mark Edward. *China between Empires: The Northern and Southern Dynasties*. Cambridge, MA: Harvard University Press, 2009.

———. *The Construction of Space in Early China*. Albany: State University of New York Press, 2006.

———. *The Flood Myths of Early China*. Albany: State University of New York Press, 2006.

Li Fengmao 李豐楙. *Liuchao Sui Tang xiandaolei xiaoshuo yanjiu* 六朝隋唐仙道類小說研究. Taipei: Taiwan xuesheng shuju, 1986.

Li Jung-shi, trans. *Biographies of Buddhist Nuns: Pao-chang's Pi-chiu-ni chuan*. Osaka: Tohokai, n.d.

Lin Chen 林辰. "Lu Xun xiansheng 'Gu xiaoshuo gouchen' de jilu niandai ji suoshou geshu zuozhe 魯迅先生'古小說鈎沈' 的輯錄年代及所收各書作者." *Wenxue yichan xuanji* 文學遺產選集 3 (1960): 385–407.

Lin Fu-Shih. "Chinese Shamans and Shamanism in the Chiang-nan Area during the Six Dynasties Period (3rd–6th century A.D.)." PhD diss., Princeton University, 1994.

Lippiello, Tiziana. *Auspicious Omens and Miracles in Ancient China: Han, Three Kingdoms and Six Dynasties*. Monumenta Serica Monograph Series 39. Sankt Augustin: Monumenta Serica Institute, 2001.

Liu Yuanru 劉苑如. *Chaoxiang shenghuo shijie de wenxue quanshi: Liuchao zongjiao xushu de shenti shijian yu kongjian shuxie* 朝向生活世界的文學詮釋: 六朝宗教敘述的身體實踐與空間書寫. Taipei: Xinwenfeng, 2010.

———. "Xingjian yu mingbao: Liuchao zhiguai zhong guiguai xushu de fengyu—yi ge 'daoyi wei chang' moshi de kaocha 形見與冥報: 六朝志怪敘述的諷喻——一個'導異

為常'模式的考察." *Bulletin of the Institute of Chinese Literature and Philosophy (Zhongyang yanjiuyuan zhongguo wenzhe yanjiu jikan* 中央研究院中國文哲研究集刊) 29 (2006): 1–45.

Loewe, Michael, ed. *A Biographical Dictionary of the Qin, Former Han & Xin Periods (221 BC-AD 24)*. Leiden: Brill, 2000.

———, ed. *Early Chinese Texts: A Bibliographical Guide*. Berkeley: Society for the Study of Early China and the Institute of East Asian Studies, University of California, 1993.

Lu Xun [Lu Hsun]. *A Brief History of Chinese Fiction*. Trans. Yang Hsien-yi and Gladys Yang. Beijing: Foreign Languages Press, 1976.

Lu Zongli. *Power of the Words: Chen Prophecy in Chinese Politics, AD 265–618*. Oxford: Peter Lang, 2003.

Ma, Y. W., and Joseph S. M. Lau, eds. *Traditional Chinese Stories: Themes and Variations*. New York: Columbia University Press, 1978.

Makita Tairyō 牧田諦亮. *Rikuchō kōitsu Kanzeon ōkenki no kenkyū* 六朝古逸觀世音應驗記の研究. Kyoto: Hyōrakuji shoten, 1970.

Mather, Richard B. "The Controversy over Conformity and Naturalness during the Six Dynasties." *History of Religions* 9 (1969–1970): 160–180.

———. "Individualist Expressions of the Outsiders during the Six Dynasties." In *Individualism and Holism: Studies in Confucian and Taoist Values*, ed. Donald Munro, 199–215. Ann Arbor: Center for Chinese Studies, University of Michigan, 1985.

Mathieu, Rémi, ed. *À la recherche des esprits: Récits tirés du "Sou shen ji."* Paris: Gallimard, 1992.

———. *Démons et merveilles dans la littérature chinoise des Six Dynasties: Le fantastique et l'anecdotique dans le "Soushen ji" de Gan Bao*. Paris: Editions You-Feng, 2000.

———. *Étude sur la mythologie et l'ethnologie de la Chine ancienne*. 2 vols. Paris: Institut des Hautes Etudes Chinoises, 1983.

McCraw, David R. "Along the Wutong Trail: The Paulownia in Chinese Poetry." *Chinese Literature: Essays, Articles, Reviews* 10 (1988): 81–107.

McDermott, Joseph P. *A Social History of the Chinese Book: Books and Literati Culture in Late Imperial China*. Hong Kong: Hong Kong University Press, 2006.

Miyakawa Hisayuki. "Local Cults around Mount Lu at the Time of Sun En's Rebellion." In *Facets of Taoism: Essays in Chinese Religion*, ed. Holmes Welch and Anna Seidel, 83–102. New Haven, CT: Yale University Press, 1979.

Nan Qi shu 南齊書. Beijing: Zhonghua shuju, 1972.

Nan shi 南史. Beijing: Zhonghua shuju, 1975.

Nattier, Jan. *Once upon a Future Time: Studies in a Buddhist Prophecy of Decline*. Berkeley: Asian Humanities Press, 1991.

Nienhauser, William H., Jr., ed. *The Indiana Companion to Traditional Chinese Literature*. Bloomington: Indiana University Press, 1986.

———. *Tang Dynasty Tales: A Guided Reader*. Singapore: World Scientific Press, 2010.

Nugent, Christopher M. B. *Manifest in Words, Written on Paper: Producing and Circulating Poetry in Tang Dynasty China*. Cambridge, MA: Harvard University Press, 2010.

Nylan, Michael. "Ying Shao's *Feng su t'ung yi:* An Exploration of Problems in Han Dynasty Political, Philosophical and Social Unity." PhD diss., Princeton University, 1982.

Otto, Rudolf. *The Idea of the Holy*. London: Oxford University Press, 1958.

Pearce, Scott, Audrey Spiro, and Patricia Ebrey, eds. *Culture and Power in the Reconstitution of the Chinese Realm, 200–600*. Cambridge, MA: Harvard University Press, 2001.

Pulleyblank, Edwin G. *Lexicon of Reconstructed Pronunciation in Early Middle Chinese, Late Middle Chinese, and Early Mandarin*. Vancouver: University of British Columbia Press, 1991.

Qimin yaoshu 齊民要術 by Jia Sixie 賈思勰. Congshu jicheng 叢書集成 ed. Shanghai [?]: Shangwu yinshuguan, 1939.

Reed, Carrie. *Chinese Chronicles of the Strange: The "Nuogao ji" by Duan Chengshi*. New York: Peter Lang, 2001.

———. "The Lecherous Holy Man and the Maiden in the Box." *Journal of the American Oriental Society* 127 (2007): 41–55.

———. "Motivation and Meaning of a 'Hodge-Podge': Duan Chengshi's *Youyang zazu*." *Journal of the American Oriental Society* 123 (2003): 121–145.

———. "Parallel Worlds, Stretched Time, and Illusory Reality: The Tang Tale 'Du Zichun.'" *Harvard Journal of Asiatic Studies* 69 (2009): 309–342.

———. *A Tang Miscellany: An Introduction to "Youyang zazu."* New York: Peter Lang, 2003.

Sanguo zhi 三國志. 2nd ed. Beijing: Zhonghua shuju, 1982.

Santangelo, Paolo, and Yan Beiwen. *Zibuyu, "What the Master Would Not Discuss," according to Yuan Mei (1716–1798): A Collection of Supernatural Stories*. 2 vols. Leiden: Brill, 2013.

Schafer, Edward H. *Pacing the Void: T'ang Approaches to the Stars*. Berkeley: University of California Press, 1977.

Schiffler, John W. "Chinese Folk Medicine: A Study of the *Shan-hai Ching*." *Asian Folklore Studies* 39 (1980): 41–83.

Schipper, Kristofer. *L'empereur Wou des Han dans la légende taoïste: Han Wou-ti nei-tchouan*. Paris: Ecole Française d'Extrême-Orient, 1965.

Shaughnessy, Edward L. *Rewriting Early Chinese Texts*. Albany: State University of New York Press, 2006.

Shih, Robert. *Biographies des moines éminents (Kao seng tchouan) de Houei-kiao*. Louvain: Université de Louvain, Institut Orientaliste, 1968.

Shinohara Koichi. "Two Sources of Chinese Buddhist Biographies: Stupa Inscriptions and Miracle Stories." In *Monks and Magicians: Religious Biographies in Asia,* ed. Phyllis Granoff and Koichi Shinohara, 119–228. Oakville, ON: Mosaic, 1988.

Shiyi ji 拾遺記 by Wang Jia 王嘉. *HWCS* ed.

Shuijing zhu 水經注 by Li Daoyuan 酈道元. Ed. Yang Shoujing 楊守敬 and Xiong Huizhen 熊會貞. 3 vols., continuously paginated. Nanjing: Jiangsu guji chubanshe, 1989.

Shuo ku 說庫. Comp. Wang Wenru 王文濡. Reprint, Taipei: Xinxing shuju, 1963 [1915].

Simmons, Richard VanNess. "The *Soushen houji* Attributed to Tao Yuanming (365–427)." MA thesis, University of Washington, 1986.

Smith, Barbara Herrnstein. "Narrative Versions, Narrative Theories." *Critical Inquiry* 7 (1980): 213–236.

Smith, Thomas E. "Record of the Ten Continents." *Taoist Resources* 2 (1990): 87–119.

———. "Ritual and the Shaping of Narrative: The Legend of the Han Emperor Wu." PhD diss., University of Michigan, 1992.

Song shu 宋書. Beijing: Zhonghua shuju, 1974.

Stevenson, Daniel B. "Tales of the Lotus Sutra." In *Buddhism in Practice,* ed. Donald S. Lopez Jr., 427–451. Princeton, NJ: Princeton University Press, 1995.

Sterckx, Roel. *The Animal and the Daemon in Early China*. Albany: State University of New York Press, 2002.

Strassberg, Richard. *A Chinese Bestiary: Strange Creatures from the Guideways through Mountains and Seas.* Berkeley: University of California Press, 2002.

Swartz, Wendy. "Classifying the Literary Tradition: Zhi Yu's 'Discourse on Literary Compositions Divided by Genre.'" In *Early Medieval China: A Sourcebook,* ed. Wendy Swartz, Robert Ford Campany, Yang Lu, and Jessey J. C. Choo, 274–286. New York: Columbia University Press, 2014.

Swartz, Wendy, Robert Ford Campany, Yang Lu, and Jessey J. C. Choo, eds. *Early Medieval China: A Sourcebook.* New York: Columbia University Press, 2014.

Taves, Ann. *Religious Experience Reconsidered: A Building-Block Approach to the Study of Religion and Other Special Things.* Princeton, NJ: Princeton University Press, 2009.

Tian, Xiaofei. *Beacon Fire and Shooting Star: The Literary Culture of the Liang (502–557).* Cambridge, MA: Harvard University Press, 2007.

———. "Book Collecting and Cataloging in the Age of Manuscript Culture: Xiao Yi's *Master of the Golden Tower* and Ruan Xiaoxu's Preface to *Seven Records.*" In *Early Medieval China: A Sourcebook,* ed. Wendy Swartz, Robert Ford Campany, Yang Lu, and Jessey J. C. Choo, 307–323. New York: Columbia University Press, 2014.

———. *Tao Yuanming and Manuscript Culture: The Record of a Dusty Table.* Seattle: University of Washington Press, 2005.

———. *Visionary Journeys: Travel Writings from Early Medieval and Nineteenth-Century China.* Cambridge, MA: Harvard University Press, 2011.

Todorov, Tzvetan. *The Fantastic: A Structural Approach to a Literary Genre.* Trans. Richard Howard. Ithaca, NY: Cornell University Press, 1975.

Tokuno, Kyoko. "The Book of Resolving Doubts Concerning the Semblance Dharma." In *Buddhism in Practice,* ed. Donald S. Lopez Jr., 257–271. Princeton, NJ: Princeton University Press, 1995.

Tsai, Katherine. *Lives of the Nuns: Biographies of Chinese Buddhist Nuns from the Fourth to Sixth Centuries.* Honolulu: University of Hawai'i Press, 1994.

Tsien, Tsuen-hsuin. *Written on Bamboo and Silk: The Beginnings of Chinese Books and Inscriptions.* 2nd ed. with an afterword by Edward L. Shaughnessy. Chicago: University of Chicago Press, 2004 [1962].

Twitchett, Denis. *Printing and Publishing in Medieval China.* New York: Frederic C. Beil, 1983.

Unger, Ulrich. "Die Fragmente des *So-Yü.*" In *Studia Sinica-Mongolia: Festschrift für Herbert Franke,* ed. Wolfgang Bauer, 373–400. Wiesbaden: Franz Steiner, 1979.

Vervoorn, Aat. *Men of the Cliffs and Caves: The Development of the Chinese Eremetic Tradition to the End of the Han Dynasty.* Hong Kong: Chinese University Press, 1990.

Wang Guoliang 王國良. *Liuchao zhiguai xiaoshuo kaolun* 六朝志怪小說考論. Taipei: Wenshizhe chubanshe, 1988.

———. "*Mingxiang ji* xiao kao 冥祥記小考." *Dong Wu zhongwen xuebao* 東吳中文學報 3 (1997): 271–284.

———. *Mingxiang ji yanjiu* 冥祥記研究. Taipei: Wenshizhe chubanshe, 1999.

———. *Soushen houji yanjiu* 搜神後記研究. Taipei: Wenshizhe chubanshe, 1978.

———. *Xu Qi Xie ji yanjiu* 續齊諧記研究. Taipei: Wenshizhe chubanshe, 1987.

———. *Yan Zhitui Yuanhun zhi yanjiu* 顏之推冤魂志研究. Taipei: Wenshizhe chubanshe, 1995.

Wang Qing 王青. *Xiyu wenhua yingxiang xia de zhonggu xiaoshuo* 西域文化影響下的中古小說. Beijing: Zhongguo shehui kexue chubanshe, 2006.

Wilkinson, Endymion. *Chinese History: A New Manual.* Cambridge, MA: Harvard University Press, 2012.

Woolley, Nathan. "The Many Boats to Yangzhou: Purpose and Variation in Religious Records of the Tang." *Asia Major,* 3rd ser., 26, no. 2 (2013): 59–88.

Wu, Laura Hua. "From *Xiaoshuo* to Fiction: Hu Yinglin's Genre Study of *Xiaoshuo.*" *Harvard Journal of Asiatic Studies* 55 (1995): 339–371.

Yu, Anthony C. "'Rest, Rest, Perturbed Spirit!' Ghosts in Traditional Chinese Fiction." *Harvard Journal of Asiatic Studies* 47 (1987): 397–434.

———. *State and Religion in China: Historical and Textual Perspectives.* Chicago: Open Court, 2005.

Zeitlin, Judith. *Historian of the Strange: Pu Songling and the Chinese Classical Tale.* Stanford, CA: Stanford University Press, 1993.

Zhang Zhenjun. *Buddhism and Tales of the Supernatural in Early Medieval China: A Study of Liu Yiqing's (403–444) "Youming lu."* Leiden: Brill, 2014.

Zhao Xiaohuan. *Classical Chinese Supernatural Fiction: A Morphological History.* Lewiston, NY: Edwin Mellen, 2005.

———. "*Xiaoshuo* as a Cataloguing Term in Traditional Chinese Bibliography." *Sungkyun Journal of East Asian Studies* 5 (2005): 157–181.

Zhou Ciji 周次吉. *Shenyi jing yanjiu* 神異經研究. Taipei: Wenshizhe chubanshe, 1986.

Zhou Junxun 周俊勛. *Wei Jin nanbeichao zhiguai xiaoshuo cihui yanjiu* 魏晉南北朝志怪小說詞彙研究. Chengdu: Ba Shu shushe, 2006.

Zhou Lengqie 周楞伽, ed. *Yin Yun Xiaoshuo* 殷芸小說. Shanghai: Guji chubanshe, 1984.

Zürcher, Erik. *The Buddhist Conquest of China: The Spread and Adaptation of Buddhism in Early Medieval China.* 3rd ed. Ed. Stephen F. Teiser. Leiden: Brill, 2007 [1959].

FURTHER READINGS

Publication information is given in the Works Cited chapter.

Translations and Studies of Anecdotal Literature

WORKS SPANNING MANY PERIODS

Chang, Kang-i Sun, and Stephen Owen, eds. *The Cambridge History of Chinese Literature.*
Kao, Karl S. Y., ed. *Classical Chinese Tales of the Supernatural and the Fantastic: Selections from the Third to the Tenth Century.*
Lu Xun [Lu Hsun]. *A Brief History of Chinese Fiction.*
Ma, Y. W., and Joseph S. M. Lau, eds. *Traditional Chinese Stories: Themes and Variations.*
Zhao Xiaohuan. *Classical Chinese Supernatural Fiction: A Morphological History.*
———. "*Xiaoshuo* as a Cataloguing Term in Traditional Chinese Bibliography"

LATE WARRING STATES, HAN, AND THE EARLY MEDIEVAL PERIOD (TO 618 CE)

Birrell, Anne. *The Classic of Mountains and Seas.*
Campany, Robert Ford. "The Earliest Tales of the Bodhisattva Guanshiyin."
———. "Ghosts Matter: The Culture of Ghosts in Six Dynasties *Zhiguai.*"
———. "The Real Presence."
———. "Return-from-Death Narratives in Early Medieval China."
———. *Signs from the Unseen Realm: Buddhist Miracle Tales from Early Medieval China.*
———. *Strange Writing: Anomaly Accounts in Early Medieval China.*
———. "Tales of Strange Events."
———. *To Live as Long as Heaven and Earth: A Translation and Study of Ge Hong's "Traditions of Divine Transcendents."*
———. "Two Religious Thinkers of the Early Eastern Jin: Gan Bao and Ge Hong in Multiple Contexts."
Cohen, Alvin P. *Tales of Vengeful Souls: A Sixth Century Collection of Chinese Avenging Ghost Stories.*

DeWoskin, Kenneth. *Doctors, Diviners, and Magicians of Ancient China: Biographies of "Fang-shih."*

————. "The Six Dynasties *Chih-kuai* and the Birth of Fiction."

DeWoskin, Kenneth, and J. I. Crump Jr. *In Search of the Supernatural: The Written Record.*

Gjertson, Donald E. "The Early Chinese Buddhist Miracle Tale: A Preliminary Survey."

Greatrex, Roger. *The Bowu zhi: An Annotated Translation.*

Mathieu, Rémi, ed. *À la recherche des esprits: Récits tirés du "Sou shen ji."*

————. *Démons et merveilles dans la littérature chinoise des Six Dynasties: Le fantastique et l'anecdotique dans le "Soushen ji" de Gan Bao.*

————. *Étude sur la mythologie et l'ethnologie de la Chine ancienne.*

Zhang, Zhenjun. *Buddhism and Tales of the Supernatural in Early Medieval China: A Study of Liu Yiqing's (403–444) "Youming lu."*

TANG PERIOD (618–907 CE)

Allen, Sarah M. *Shifting Stories: History, Gossip, and Lore in Narratives from Tang Dynasty China.*

————. "Tales Retold: Narrative Variation in a Tang Story."

Dudbridge, Glen. *Religious Experience and Lay Society in T'ang China: A Reading of Tai Fu's "Kuang-i chi."*

————. "Tang Sources for the Study of Religious Culture: Problems and Procedures."

Gjertson, Donald E. *Miraculous Retribution: A Study and Translation of T'ang Lin's "Ming-pao chi."*

Hsieh, Daniel. *Love and Women in Early Chinese Fiction.*

Nienhauser, William H., Jr. *Tang Dynasty Tales: A Guided Reader.*

Reed, Carrie. *Chinese Chronicles of the Strange: The "Nuogao ji" by Duan Chengshi.*

————. "Motivation and Meaning of a 'Hodge-Podge': Duan Chengshi's *Youyang zazu.*"

————. "Parallel Worlds, Stretched Time, and Illusory Reality: The Tang Tale 'Du Zichun.'"

————. *A Tang Miscellany: An Introduction to "Youyang zazu."*

Woolley, Nathan. "The Many Boats to Yangzhou: Purpose and Variation in Religious Records of the Tang."

FIVE DYNASTIES (907–960), SONG (960–1279), AND BEYOND

Chan, Leo Tak-hung. *The Discourse on Foxes and Ghosts: Ji Yun and Eighteenth-Century Literati Storytelling.*

Chiang, Sing-chen Lydia. *Collecting the Self: Body and Identity in Strange Tale Collections of Late Imperial China.*

Dudbridge, Glen. *A Portrait of Five Dynasties China from the Memoirs of Wang Renyu (880–956).*

Giles, Herbert A., trans. *Strange Stories from a Chinese Studio.*

Huntington, Rania. *Alien Kind: Foxes and Late Imperial Chinese Narrative.*

————. "Ghosts Seeking Substitutes: Female Suicide and Repetition."

Inglis, Alister D. *Hong Mai's "Record of the Listener" and Its Song Dynasty Context.*

Santangelo, Paolo, and Yan Beiwen. *Zibuyu,"What the Master Would Not Discuss," according to Yuan Mei (1716–1798): A Collection of Supernatural Stories.*

Zeitlin, Judith. *Historian of the Strange: Pu Songling and the Chinese Classical Tale.*

Early Medieval Social, Cultural, Political, and Military History

Chan, Alan K. L., and Yuet-Keung Lo, eds. *Interpretation and Literature in Early Medieval China.*

———, eds. *Philosophy and Religion in Early Medieval China.*

Dien, Albert E. *Six Dynasties Civilization.*

———, ed. *State and Society in Early Medieval China.*

Graff, David A. *Medieval Chinese Warfare, 300–900.*

Holcombe, Charles. *In the Shadow of the Han: Literati Thought and Society at the Beginning of the Southern Dynasties.*

Knapp, Keith N. *Selfless Offspring: Filial Children and Social Order in Early Medieval China.*

Lewis, Mark Edward. *China between Empires: The Northern and Southern Dynasties.*

Pearce, Scott, Audrey Spiro, and Patricia Ebrey, eds. *Culture and Power in the Reconstitution of the Chinese Realm, 200–600.*

Swartz, Wendy, Robert Ford Campany, Yang Lu, and Jessey J. C. Choo, eds. *Early Medieval China: A Sourcebook.*

Tian, Xiaofei. *Beacon Fire and Shooting Star: The Literary Culture of the Liang (502–557).*

———. *Tao Yuanming and Manuscript Culture: The Record of a Dusty Table.*

———. *Visionary Journeys: Travel Writings from Early Medieval and Nineteenth-Century China.*

Wilkinson, Endymion. *Chinese History: A New Manual.*

INDEX

Dongfang Shuo, 33
Dongyang Wuyi, 24
dragons (including *jiao* or lamiae), *103, 126, 127, 129, 130, 131, 193, 202*
dream: communication through, *29, 68, 77, 83, 116, 137, 144, 147, 154, 155, 158, 159, 161, 162, 164, 165, 167, 168, 170, 204, 225;* interpreted, *5, 147, 160, 163, 167, 169, 197;* prediction in, *53;* real object obtained in, *23*

earth god, *24, 73, 79, 83*
ellipses, 21
encamped families, *35, 57*
exorcism, *13, 222*

fangxiang, 77, *210*
Fei Changfang, 69–70
Fengsu tongyi, xiv
fiction, xxiv, xxvi
filial piety, *104, 198, 203*
fox spirits, *20, 37, 82, 95, 96, 111, 173, 176, 181, 196, 208*
frugal burial, *53*

Gan Bao, xxvii–xxx, xlii, 12
Ge Hong, xli, 64
ghost, *34, 51, 68, 76, 79, 80, 106, 150, 161, 190, 216, 217, 221;* avenges wrong, *70, 93, 146, 197;* causes epidemic, *223;* guards tomb, *184, 185, 192;* haunts household, *61;* heals living supplicant, *69;* helps living persons, *1, 12, 75, 151, 152;* marriage or union with, *8, 9, 16, 19, 22, 149;* punishes living person for breaking agreement, *212;* requests frugal burial, *72;* substances feared by, *217;* term for, xxxvii; tricked by person, *67;* writes letter to living person, *71. See also* reburial
god, *46, 89, 140;* accompanies human, *199;* covets person's belonging, *189, 221;* of lake, *3;* mates with human, *92, 207, 225;* of mountain, *33, 47, 49, 55, 123, 164;* of pond, *200;* protects its precincts, *83, 123, 135;* of river, *89, 161, 168, 219;* seen in

temple, *3, 14, 26. See also* divine punishment; Gongting Lake, temple of
Gongting Lake, temple of, *43, 52, 56, 78, 189*
grave goods, *8, 23, 31, 72, 155, 156, 158, 185*
Guanshiyin, bodhisattva, xxviii, xxxii, xliv, *108*
gui (ghost, demon), xxxvii
Guizimu. *See* Mother of Demons
Guo Jichan, 8
Guo Pu, 74

healing, *36;* by capturing demon, *213;* methods and substances for, *69, 70, 134, 182, 186, 221;* in response to piety, *2, 27, 32, 203*
heaven, ascent to, *41, 203*
Hebo (River Earl), *89*
Hou Bo, 3
Huan Wen, 87, 115
Huan Xuan, 116
Huangdi (Yellow Thearch), 94
hun (cloudsoul), xxxviii, *58*

icon, *138, 225;* desecrated, *2*
inn, *87, 98. See also* temple: overnight lodging in
item, defined, xx

Ji Kang, 94, 113
Jia Kui, 88
Jiang, Marquis, *135, 224, 225*
Jiling ji, xiv, 3
Jingyi ji, 3–7
Jiyi ji, 8–9

karmic retribution, *3, 107, 109, 110*
Kong Yue, 9
Kongshi zhiguai, 9–13
Kunlun, Mount, *193*

lamiae. *See* dragons
latrine, *2, 138, 194, 210*
Lei Cizong, 42
Liexian zhuan, xli
Lieyi zhuan, 14–19
life span, 60, *142, 193, 216*